KT-229-820

AUNT LETITIA

DOMINIC LUKE

ISIS
LARGE PRINT
Oxford

Copyright © Dominic Luke, 2012

First published in Great Britain 2012
by
Robert Hale Limited

Published in Large Print 2013 by ISIS Publishing Ltd.,
7 Centremead, Osney Mead, Oxford OX2 0ES
by arrangement with
Robert Hale Limited

All rights reserved

The moral right of the author has been asserted

British Library Cataloguing in Publication Data
Luke, Dominic.
  Aunt Letitia.
  1. Older women - - Psychology - - Fiction.
  2. Large type books.
  I. Title
  823.9'2–dc23

ISBN 978–0–7531–9178–1 (hb)
ISBN 978–0–7531–9179–8 (pb)

Printed and bound in Great Britain by
T. J. International Ltd., Padstow, Cornwall

BROMLEY
PUBLIC
LIBRARIES

AL

CLASS
LPB/F

ACC
0 3084716

INVOICE DATE

UL

CHAPTER
ONE

"I hated my father. Absolutely loathed him."

The policeman listened, watching the steam rising from the old lady's tea. She held the china cup in a gnarled and shaking hand. All around, the teashop buzzed with conversation. Crockery chinked, waitresses hurried back and forth, the door opened and closed as customers came and went.

"I often thought of murdering him. I plotted ways I might do it without being detected. Though I really shouldn't be saying this to you: you could have me arrested."

The policeman could not help wondering if the old dear was right in the head. He knew he ought to get back on duty, but it was cosy in this teashop. Outside it was cold and wet.

A few more minutes wouldn't hurt.

"You could do with a drop of brandy with that tea. For the shock."

"It was brandy which got me into trouble in the first place." The old lady laughed at the policeman's expression. "Oh yes. Drunk and disorderly. You wouldn't expect it at my age, would you! I'm ninety-one."

"You should go easy on the booze. That was a nasty fall."

"It was stupid. A stupid thing to do. Tripping over the kerb. I forget I'm not as sprightly as I used to be. I don't usually drink in the middle of the day, Constable, so you needn't look so disapproving. I had just heard something rather unexpected — unpleasant — and I took a sip or two of brandy to calm my nerves. Best cognac, too. Very expensive on the black market. It was meant for a Christmas present. I'm buying all my presents early. With things the way they are, one never knows what might happen." She paused, an insouciant smile on her lips. "Listen to me! I can assure you, I don't make a habit of talking like this to total strangers. You must excuse me. It's the shock."

"Not the booze, then?" The policeman was professionally cynical.

"It was only a nip, to revive myself. I'm not an old soak — not yet, at any rate. But you mustn't take any notice of me. I'm talking nonsense. All that about wanting to murder my father: it's quite untrue. I haven't got it in me to murder anyone."

"Ah, well, you'd be surprised. I come across some strange goings-on in my line of work." The policeman looked at the old lady through narrowed eyes, thinking: she ain't half as dotty as she makes out.

"My father was a bishop. The most evil man I ever knew."

"And there was I thinking that bishops were Christian fellows. But he can't have been worse than this here Hitler, surely?"

2

"He and dear Adolf would have got on famously." She finished her tea and popped a precious lump of sugar into her mouth. "A pair of bigoted, pompous old bores. But you must be tired of listening to me. I'm keeping you from your duties, whatever it is you policemen do."

The policeman allowed a hint of a smile. "Picking old ladies up off the pavement."

"*Touché!*" She gathered herself together. "The worst of it is, I've got blood on my coat. But it can't be helped. Least said, soonest mended. And now I really must go. I'm meeting my nephew in front of the National Gallery, and I don't want to be late."

The policeman helped the old girl to her feet and handed her, one by one, her hat, gloves, umbrella, handbag, bags and parcels. "I'll hail you a cab."

"It's quite all right, I'll walk."

"I don't think you are in any condition to go walking, madam."

"Oh, tush, of course I am. The day I can't walk the few steps from here to Trafalgar Square is the day you can put me down! Besides, I can pop into the bookshops on Charing Cross Road as I go. Thank you for the tea."

As the policeman held open the door, he felt a pang of regret, wishing they could have lingered over their tea. He had enjoyed listening to the feisty old dear. She showed more spirit than a great many people half her age. If the whole country battled on the way she did, there would be no doubts about winning the war.

As he watched her walk slowly away to be swallowed by the crowds, he suddenly realized that he didn't even know her name. Not that it mattered. He was hardly likely to meet her again. And if he didn't get back on duty soon, his sergeant would take great pleasure in hauling him over the coals.

Letitia Warner used her folded umbrella as a walking stick now that the rain had stopped, making her way — slow but determined — through the crowds on Oxford Street. Red buses passed in procession, but there were fewer motor cars now. Letitia wondered if, with petrol rationing taking hold, horses might make a comeback. It would make her feel young again, to see horse-drawn buses, cabs and carriages on the streets of London; but it would not provide an escape from the war. The signs were everywhere: shattered and boarded-up windows, fallen masonry, walls shorn up by heavy timbers, and notices warning that looters would be prosecuted. This war, even more than the last, was determined to make its presence felt.

Letitia blinked away sudden tears as she walked, rapping her umbrella firmly on the pavement. It was absurd to cry! She was not even sure what had brought it on. Was it the sight of Oxford Street, blitzed and shabby but exhibiting a spirited air of normality? Was it because she had tripped up the kerb and made a spectacle of herself? Was it because she had nearly given herself away in that teashop just now?

It was all of that, perhaps: but most of all it was down to that throwaway remark she had heard in

Selfridges, less than an hour ago. Swiftly and unexpectedly the memories had come crowding back: memories of her father, and of poor Angelica, her sister; memories that stung, that lacerated, that sent her spiralling down into a pit of despair. Everything looked bleak and pointless. The future seemed devoid of hope — which was probably not far from truth. The whole world was in turmoil. Death and destruction rained down from the sky nightly. Things were changing quickly, and for the worse. It was enough to make her wish she had done what she once intended to do, all those years ago, one morning in early spring.

I meant it, too, Letitia said to herself as she laboured along Oxford Street. It had all been planned. No hysterics, no drama: just a calm matter-of-fact decision to take a step into oblivion. If there hadn't been an interruption, if the doorbell hadn't rung . . . But it had, and here she was, ninety-one years old and living through one more day.

However hopeless things seemed, something always came along to lift one up: a gallant policeman; or the sight of London broken but unbowed in this second autumn of the war; or the prospect of meeting one's great-nephew in front of the National Gallery.

Hugh was waiting for her, a static figure amongst the traffic and the people and the pigeons. He was staring at Nelson's Column that reached up into a lowering grey sky. Around the base was a large hoarding, exhorting passers-by to purchase National War Bonds.

"Good grief, Aunt, whatever have you been doing?"

"Having adventures, as usual." Letitia had recovered her poise, was all blasé.

"But there's blood on your coat!"

"Only a speck. It's nothing. A silly accident. No damage done. But I'm afraid, Hugh, I shall have to go back home to change. My stockings are torn, my knees are grazed. I won't be allowed in anywhere looking like this." She took his arm. "Come along. On the way, we can decide where we shall go for dinner."

Washed and changed, Letitia negotiated the stairs in her Chelsea house, taking them one at a time.

"Help yourself to a drink!" she called on ahead. "There's plenty to choose from."

When she reached the old dining-room, Hugh was standing by the sideboard examining an exotic statuette that his father must have sent from India years ago; but Letitia's eyes were drawn to the photograph in a silver frame next to it: Hugh in army uniform looking impossibly young. Taken during the last war, of course: the war to end wars, they had called it. But now here was a sequel, despite everything. How long would this one last? Would anybody be left alive to see its end?

Letitia advanced into the room and Hugh turned. He had a glass in his hand.

Letitia smiled. "I hope you poured one for me."

As they sipped their drinks, sitting on faded chairs, she related with gusto the episode with the policeman.

"He was rather good-looking, too." Her pearls rattled round her neck as she laughed. "What a pity I didn't note down his number."

"Honestly, Aunt, you're incorrigible." Hugh was laughing too.

"I think he deserves some kind of reward, don't you? Not everyone would have been so kind."

"What were you doing drinking brandy in the middle of the day?"

Letitia did not answer, using the prerogative of the old to go conveniently deaf.

"You are being evasive," Hugh accused her.

"No more than you," Letitia parried. "I still don't know what this terribly important work that you do actually is."

"It's all very hush-hush." Hugh took a swig of whisky, before adding, "And naturally very dull."

Letitia laughed. "You haven't changed at all, you know."

"I'm just very much older."

"Oh, tush! Age is nothing. What I mean is that you are still the same in essentials as when I first saw you, a little boy just arrived from India. You have always been very sensible and down-to-earth."

"And boring."

"Not so, dear Hugh. Never boring. Reliable, trustworthy, steadfast."

"In Cynthia's book, reliable, trustworthy and steadfast equal boring." Hugh spoke sharply.

"Cynthia has never known when she is well off. She knows the price of everything and the value of nothing, as Oscar Wilde would have said if he'd ever been unfortunate enough to meet her. Besides, does it really matter any more what she thinks?"

Hugh shook his head, indicating that it did not matter; but at the same time he frowned. Letitia guessed that his wife still had the power to wound him.

He got up and held out his hand. "Another drink? Or ought we to go to dinner?"

"Oh, another, I think," said Letitia firmly. "Let's enjoy ourselves while we can."

Watching Hugh pour the drinks, Letitia was taken back nearly forty years, when she had still lived in the house called The Firs in Warwickshire, and Hugh had been dumped on her by his father without — as Letitia had often afterwards remarked — so much as a by-your-leave. The Firs had been a very pleasant house, not large but nicely situated, isolated from the other houses in the village of Binley. At the back there had been a long, narrow lawn bounded by tall trees. Letitia had thought it a darkly romantic aspect, as if one was standing in the midst of a Russian forest which stretched away endlessly in every direction. It had given one a comforting feeling of loneliness: not the feeling that one was missing out on wonderful times being had by people all around; more the feeling that there was no one around at all, that one was blessedly free of other people and their messy, intrusive lives.

Hugh handed her back her glass. She smiled up at him, and he smiled down, and she said affectionately, "Where shall we go to eat?"

Letitia woke in pitch darkness. She heard the wail of the siren and then, a moment later, a knock on her bedroom door. Hugh was calling her.

Dragging her old bones out of bed, Letitia put on her dressing-gown and opened the door. She could not see Hugh. His voice seemed to come out of the empty dark.

"Oughtn't we to go to the shelter?"

"Fiddlesticks to the shelter. I'm not going outside in this weather. We'll be quite safe in the basement."

She could tell Hugh was not convinced. He obviously thought she was not taking the threat of German bombs seriously. It was, she reminded herself, his first experience of a raid.

Down in the kitchen, Letitia poured herself a large whisky. She laughed at Hugh's expression, remembering the frowning policeman who'd advised her to *go easy on the booze.*

"I find it helps to pass the time."

"I'll stick to cocoa, all the same."

As he warmed some milk, they heard guns firing in the distance and, faintly, the drone of aeroplanes. Before long, the crump of explosions added to the noise.

"We seem very unprotected here." Hugh was nervous, looking up at the ceiling.

Letitia was unconcerned. "My dear boy, it doesn't matter where you are. Even people in shelters or down the tube have been killed when there's a direct hit."

"I can't imagine how you can stay so calm."

"One can get used to anything. This has been going on every night since the beginning of September. It's become a tedious inconvenience more than anything. I never can sleep through it, more's the pity. I've forgotten what it was like to have an uninterrupted night's sleep."

Letitia looked at Hugh, pale and drawn, both hands curled round his mug of cocoa, beads of sweat on his forehead, glistening in the electric light. His dark hair was turning slowly grey; his face was rather gaunt and sallow. She wondered how much the noise of the guns and the explosions reminded him of the years he had spent fighting in the trenches of France and Flanders. He had never spoken much about that part of his life, but at that time he had written her many letters. The early ones had been brutally direct in their descriptions of life at the Front.

"I was having the most peculiar dream," said Letitia, wanting to distract Hugh. "I dreamt of the day when you left The Firs after your first visit. You were off to Hampshire to stay with your mother's family, and poor Arnold was returning to India. Do you remember?"

"No, I don't remember." Hugh was not paying attention. "How far away are those explosions, do you imagine?"

"It was a sunny day," Letitia continued, choosing to ignore the question. "In that respect, it was unlike most of the other days of your visit, when it rained so often. I remember clearly standing on the doorstep to wave goodbye. You looked small and forlorn in your sailor suit as you waited to get into the carriage. It is so clear in my memory — or perhaps it is just the dream that I am thinking of. Such an odd dream. You were in the carriage; I could see your head framed in the window. The horses were stamping and champing at their bits,

10

and the driver was up on his seat holding the reins, trying to calm them. You turned your head and gave me a little wave. Your face was quite expressionless. And then, instead of the carriage starting off, it was The Firs which moved, slipping quietly away as if it was floating on a stream, and I was standing on the doorstep all the while, waving. And everything got brighter and brighter, and it seemed as if I was standing on the stone step in a white void, and in the distance there was a black speck which was you sitting in the carriage. I could hear the horses neighing, but then the neighs turned into the alert, and I woke up."

"How very odd." Hugh looked at Letitia in puzzlement.

"It was so very vivid. I had forgotten about sailor suits. Of course, one trusted absolutely in the navy in those days. Britain was great because of her navy. Back in the days before the naval race with Germany. One had never heard of dreadnoughts then."

Hugh smiled. "You are trying to distract me, Aunt."

Letitia returned the smile. "How well you know me! But from the sound of things, it is the docks and the East End that are getting it tonight. No need for us to worry."

"It is not so much for me that I am afraid. I am, of course, scared by the thought of a German bomb landing on me. But I am mostly thinking of Ian. War is so much worse when you have a child. I find myself thinking about him all the time, wondering if he is safe. I cannot bear that he has to go through all this, when we thought we had put an end to wars forever."

Letitia took his hand in hers. "Ian is probably a lot safer than we are right now."

"For the moment."

Letitia said nothing. Now was just the time, she thought, for a heart-to-heart talk. The scene was perfectly set. They were alone; it was the middle of the night; the threat of death hung over them. There was even whisky to loosen her tongue. Earlier, sitting with the policeman, she had let slip hints and clues, unable to stop herself, shock having disoriented her. The relief, the sense of freedom, had been dangerously exhilarating. How much better it would feel to unburden oneself completely, to confess everything, to be free of it all at last. But that was impossible. To confess to a stranger was absurd in itself. To tell Hugh was out of the question. She would keep her secrets. She would tell no one.

There was a pause and then, in the near distance, the sound of an explosion. It made Hugh jump. Letitia squeezed his hand, holding it tight in her bony fingers. He still needs me, she thought, and this thought gave her strength. It was Hugh who was important now. He had always been the one who mattered, ever since the day when he unexpectedly arrived at The Firs.

Looking down at his hand held in hers, she recalled a tiny boy with wide eyes and dark curls and a little pouting mouth; a boy twisting an antimacassar in his little fists as she told him tragic news in her house in Warwickshire long ago.

CHAPTER
TWO

"When the rain stops," said Letitia in 1902, "we can go into the garden, or perhaps take a walk up Hunter's Hill."

Hugh scowled. His face was pressed up against the french windows and his breath was obscuring his view of the wet outdoors. He did not want to go into the garden or walk up some boring hill. He did not want to be in this strange house with an old woman he had never met before. He did not want to be in this country at all. It was a cold, grey, wet, horrible country.

The house was called The Firs. Hugh knew this because he had seen the name etched in wood on the gatepost. There were a great many tall green trees surrounding it, overshadowing the narrow lawn, rainwater dripping from their sad, drooping branches. An invisible wood-pigeon gave out an occasional *coo-coo coo*. The rising wind stirred in the upper boughs.

Hugh hated the rain. He hated that everywhere was so overwhelmingly green. He was thinking with longing of the heat and dust and dazzling sunlight of India. That was home to Hugh, even though Mummy and

Daddy always referred to England as Home. Why anyone should prefer this beastly country to exotic, colourful India was a mystery. Here everyone had pale skins, not like in India where most of the people had beautiful brown skins, and wonderful deep eyes, and the cooking was rich with different tastes and aromas. Hugh stood by the french windows, wanting not to be in England, wanting his ayah.

The old woman who said her name was Aunt Letitia had something to tell him. She had a piece of paper in her hand, and tears in her eyes. The tears concerned him. He had never seen a grown-up cry. He took refuge behind a chair next to the fire-place. There was a lace cloth draped over the back of it. He twisted it in his fist as the old woman began to speak.

Hugh listened without comment but was much put out. The only reason for coming to this horrid country had been to fetch the new baby. Now he was told there was to be no new baby and, to add insult to injury, his mother had gone off to Heaven all on her own. Not that this unduly surprised him. If Heaven was half as wonderful as everyone made out, then it was just like his mother not to want to share it. He might only be five years old, but even he could see that his mother cared about nobody but herself.

The old woman retreated and Hugh returned to his post by the french windows, watching the rain and listening to the pigeons. In the room behind him, he heard the maid say, "Poor little mite. Whatever will become of him?"

"That is a very good question," said Letitia. "The plain answer is: I don't know."

"Well, it's a good job he came when he did, ma'am, for I was all packed and ready to go."

"I'm sorry about your holiday, Annie. Do you mind awfully?"

"Bless you, Mrs Warner, I don't mind at all. It was good of you to suggest it in the first place — and to offer to pay and all — but I couldn't leave you to cope on your own, not now this has happened. I can go for a week in Great Yarmouth any time. Now, ma'am, I was thinking: perhaps Master Hugh might like some of my walnut cake?"

"An excellent idea! Nobody can resist your walnut cake! You are a treasure, Annie. I don't know what I would do without you."

Later, with several slices of walnut cake in his tummy and his cap jammed on his head, Hugh pushed his way through the trees outside, the water-laden branches soaking his clothes. It was tangled and mysterious; the air damp and cool: all quite unlike India. He was not sure that he liked it, but his interest was aroused.

Beyond the belt of firs was a rickety wooden fence. On the other side of the fence was a meadow and in the distance a big house. Near at hand, a girl was peering at him through the warped slats. She had flaming red hair and was wearing a pinafore dress.

"Hello," she said. "I haven't seen you before. Why are you crying?"

"I'm not crying." Hugh spoke fiercely. "It's raindrops off the trees."

The girl gave him a look as if to say, *I'll believe you, thousands wouldn't*, but all she actually said was, "My name is Megan O'Connor. What's yours?"

"Hugh Benham. My mummy has gone to Heaven."

"Is that why you are crying?" The girl looked at him solemnly. "I would cry too if my mummy went to Heaven."

"It's all right for girls to cry. Boys oughtn't to. It makes them into sissies, my daddy says."

"I don't believe that's true. I don't think there is anything wrong with crying. I cry all the time, if I am sad or hurt, or if I see something very beautiful. Do you like my doll?" She held up a roughly worked rag doll with lopsided features. "She's called Raggety Peg. I've had her for ever so long. I talk to her. She's nice." Suddenly she held out the doll. "You can have her if you like. She will take care of you now that your mummy has gone away."

"Thank you very much." Hugh knew his manners, was gracious in accepting the gift.

"I'm staying at that big house over there." Megan pointed. "There are three boys to play with. You must come and play too."

"I don't know if I will be allowed." As he spoke, Hugh hoped very much that it would be allowed. Megan O'Connor fascinated him. She was unlike anyone he had ever met before. In India, some people talked down to you; most — the servants — talked up to you. Megan talked face-to-face, frank and easy.

"Don't worry," said Megan. "I shall make sure you come." She spoke with utter conviction.

16

She was true to her word. Over the next few days, in her company and that of the three Lambton boys at the Manor, Hugh forgot that he did not want to be in England. He almost forgot that his mother was dead. But he remembered to take Raggety Peg everywhere with him. Strangely, the Lambton boys did not tease him about this. In fact they were rather jealous, because Megan had chosen to give a gift to Hugh and not to them. Like Hugh, all three Lambton boys were fascinated by Megan.

Hugh's daddy, when he finally arrived at The Firs, was not so tolerant of the doll.

"It's an ugly, moth-eaten old thing. I can't imagine why you want to keep it. In any case, you must throw it away. I won't have you playing with it. It will turn you into a sissy. Dolls are for girls."

Hugh's daddy was all pale and cross. He had dark rings around his eyes and was wearing strange black clothes. Hugh had always been in awe of him, but with things being so strange and upsetting, awe now turned to fear. But Hugh had an amount of quiet courage. On the subject of Raggety Peg, he dug in his heels. He would not give the doll up. Megan's giving him Raggety Peg had been the first nice thing to happen to him in England. Her generous-hearted gesture had given him a warm feeling inside. Whenever he looked at the doll, he remembered that feeling. It made him happy to think of it.

"Arnold, don't be so hard on the boy," Letitia said, coming to Hugh's defence. "He is upset, can't you see?"

Arnold muttered darkly but did not press the point. To Hugh's relief, Raggety Peg was saved from immediate extinction.

The subject of the doll was revived after Hugh had gone to bed.

"You are encouraging the boy to be a sissy, Aunt," Arnold complained.

Letitia looked at her nephew darkly. She was not best pleased with Arnold, who had dumped Hugh on her without so much as a by-your-leave, and then expected her to break the news of the poor boy's bereavement. She recalled the offending telegram with irritation. Cecily Benham had *fallen asleep*, as Arnold had put it: a ridiculous expression.

"If you must know, I think Hugh feels a sense of responsibility for the ugly thing. It was given to him by some girl. I expect he thinks it his duty to look after it. Responsibility and a sense of duty are admirable qualities. You should be proud."

"What girl is this?" Arnold was suspicious.

"Some child who is staying with the Lambtons. A pretty Irish girl with bright red hair. Don't worry, Arnold, the Lambtons are frightfully respectable. They would never have anyone to stay who wasn't our sort. In fact, the girl has been rather a hit, from what I hear. The Lambton boys are quite taken with her. I expect Hugh is too. Hence his protectiveness towards the doll. It must be that, because I can't imagine anyone liking that thing for itself. As you said, it is terribly ugly!"

18

Arnold relented, seemed to be reassured by Letitia's words. He was slumped in the chair by the fire, opposite his aunt, staring at the flickering flames. He let out a long sigh. Letitia, unpicking the hem of an old curtain by the light of the hissing gas lamp, looked up.

"Poor Arnold."

Arnold stroked his moustache absently. "Whatever am I to do without her, Aunt?"

Letitia's mood softened. It was not really Arnold's fault. If anyone was to blame, it was his ridiculous wife who had taken it upon herself to travel thousands of miles in her delicate condition, dragging her husband and her son with her, and all because of a sudden whim that her second child must be born in England. Well, now there was to be no second child, and Cecily had travelled all that way merely to *fall asleep* at her parents' house in Hampshire.

"It's hard, I know, Arnold. But you have Hugh still. You must keep a stiff upper lip for his sake."

"For Hugh's sake," murmured Arnold. "Has he been hard hit?"

"It couldn't be otherwise. But he does his best not to show it, the dear little man." Letitia told Arnold how the boy had been uncommunicative when he first arrived, but gradually he had come out of his shell. Annie's walnut cake had played its part, but a lot of the credit had to go to the Irish girl. Through her, he had come to know the Lambton boys, and he had been invited over to the Manor on several occasions.

"I really don't want to kick up a fuss over that doll," said Arnold. "I know nothing about children, that's all.

If Cecily were here, she would know what to do. But she's not here. She's gone, she's left me. I'm expected to cope on my own. I'm not sure that I can. I don't want Hugh to end up hating me. To be hated by one's son as well as one's father would be too much."

"Jocelyn did not hate you." Letitia spoke quietly, snapping the cotton stitches.

"He could not stand the sight of me, Aunt. I was never good enough for him. Nothing I did was good enough. I could never make him love me." Arnold's voice wavered and his moustache trembled.

Letitia heard the bitterness in Arnold's voice. She understood how he must be feeling. Fate had plotted against him; his life was blotted by tragedy. That is how it must seem to him.

She chose her words carefully. She did not want to criticize her brother, who was dead and could not defend himself, but neither did she wish to upset Arnold, who had never understood his father — and small wonder. "It was not that he hated you. It was not *you* at all. Life had been hard on him. It was more than he could cope with."

Arnold was not listening. He sighed again and held his head in his hands, but he did not cry like a sissy. He kept a stiff upper lip, sitting calmly with his aunt whilst the deep wound lately inflicted by fate began imperceptibly to heal over.

Waking in the night, Hugh shifted his position between starched sheets, exploring the cold material with his bare feet. He reached under the pillow to feel the comforting shape of Raggety Peg. Half asleep, he dreamt of Megan O'Connor with her red hair and expressive face, thinking of her smile, how it made him feel good, how he felt angry and hurt when she smiled at one of the Lambton boys instead of him.

"I'll never give you up," he whispered in the doll's ear before sliding back into a deep sleep.

In later years, when the doll was long gone, Hugh still clearly remembered Megan's selfless gesture in giving it to him. It became in his mind a moment of revelation. He had not known anyone be so kind-hearted, so spontaneously generous — and to a stranger at that. Up until that moment, he had believed that one only obtained the things one wanted by guile, like his mother; or by wheedling, like his father; or by shouting and stamping one's feet, which was how he intimidated his ayah. Megan showed him a different way. He realized that being kind to people did not make one weak, anymore than crying made one a sissy.

Raggety Peg had accompanied Hugh when he left The Firs to go to his grandparents' house in Hampshire. The plan had been for Hugh to stay at Overton, whilst his father rejoined his regiment in India and made arrangements for his son to follow later. As it turned out, the call to go east never arrived and Hugh was still in England when the time came for him to start prep school. He was bundled off from Overton to Buckly Priory in Shropshire. *A modern, well-organized establishment in picturesque surroundings*, said the brochure; but to Hugh the place was purgatory. As autumn gave way to winter, the old stone building got daily damper and colder. The relentless routine of tepid baths, inedible food, and frequent beatings seemed to have been going on for all eternity. Hugh did not make friends easily, being naturally quiet and reserved. He felt like an outcast amongst his fellow inmates: wild and savage boys who, for amusement, tormented the weakest and most vulnerable amongst them. They singled out their victims with unfailing instinct. In Hugh's case, what started as mild ragging soon developed into ruthless bullying. The discovery of Raggety Peg made things all that much worse.

Hugh had believed his cupboard was inviolable. He did not realize that, once within the gates of Buckly Priory, all personal property became communal: one of Buckly's so-called *traditions*. Rifling through Hugh's belongings, one of the boys discovered the doll. From that day forward, Hugh's already miserable existence became utterly unbearable. He felt as if he was trapped in a never-ending nightmare. His grandparents' house at Overton seemed like a wonderful nirvana he had once believed in. The Firs and India were blanks in his memory. Indeed, India was blotted out forever during the barbaric era of Buckly Priory. In later years, he could remember nothing of the country where he had been born.

He came to blame Raggety Peg for his plight. If only he had thrown the beastly doll away, as his father had wanted! Possession of it had singled him out, isolated him, made him an object of ridicule. The only solution

22

was to get rid of it. He might then be spared the worst of the tortures.

He took the doll out into that part of the extensive school grounds known as the wilderness, an area strictly out of bounds. He stood on an old, crumbling stone footbridge over the stream which was swollen by rain off the Clee Hills. The swift-moving water was flecked by leaves, pale green, red and faded yellow. Legend had it that an enormous pike haunted this stretch of the stream. There were frequent clandestine expeditions in search of the fearsome fish, but no one had ever established the veracity of the tale. Certainly Hugh could not see even the smallest tiddler as he stood looking down into the brown water, a solemn, lonely boy, cap in one hand, Raggety Peg in the other.

Suddenly, down went the doll, *splash* into the stream. She floated away, her lopsided eyes staring up into the grey sky. Hugh watched as she was trapped momentarily in the rushes before the current caught her, whisking her off around a bend in the stream and out of sight. Hugh did not cry, knowing that would make him a sissy.

Back in the perpetually cold school, he was beaten for missing afternoon class, and again for trespassing in the forbidden area.

Soon after that, the nightmares began. He could never remember what they were about, but they made him call out in the night, waking the other chaps in the dormitory, for which they administered brutal reprisals. To add to his shame and degradation, he also often wet the bed. He earned the sobriquet "Stinky" Benham and Matron made him sleep on a rubber sheet.

He felt that if by some wonderful chance he should ever meet Megan O'Connor again, he would now be too ashamed and degraded to look her in the eye. Despite this, he desperately wanted some report of her, so he wrote to his great-aunt at The Firs. Letitia had no news of Megan, but wrote cheerfully of her life in Binley. The letter gave Hugh renewed hope. There was a world beyond Buckly Priory, a world he might reach if he could just find the strength to survive.

These two letters initiated a correspondence which made life a little more bearable for Hugh at Buckly Priory, a correspondence which was to continue at intervals for over forty years.

"I was at my wits' end," said Letitia, sitting in her basement kitchen with Hugh whilst bombs fell on London. "You would not speak, you would not eat. And then Annie hit on the marvellous idea of her walnut cake. No one could ever resist it."

She reached for the whisky bottle and poured herself another large measure. Hugh goggled. He wondered if pickling was responsible for her longevity. She looked rather thin, he thought, and as worn as a threadbare carpet. Her eyes, though, were the same as ever: bright, sharp, deep.

"You always said Annie was indispensable."

"So she was. But I had to do without her in the end. Do you know, the most terrifying thing I ever embarked on was learning to cook. Girls in my position were never taught such things, back in the days when Victoria was still queen. I became quite a competent cook in the end. But I was never able to make a walnut cake to match Annie's."

"I remember the walnut cake." Hugh was circumspect. Buckly Priory and much that had gone before it was sealed off in a corner of his mind where he tried not to trespass, even now.

"That changed things, the walnut cake. But what really made the difference was that girl. I expect you hardly remember her. An Irish girl with brilliant red hair. Now what was her name . . .?"

"Megan O'Connor."

"Ah, yes. So you do remember."

"Vaguely," said Hugh, not telling his great-aunt of the time Megan had run right into him in Southampton Street.

"I wonder whatever happened to her."

"What indeed," echoed Hugh, picturing Megan at seventeen, feeling a pang: sorrow for his lost youth, desire for Megan.

It had been the spring of 1912 when a young woman in lace-trimmed skirts had come running from the direction of the Strand to collide with Hugh in Southampton Street. Hugh should not have been there. He had used subterfuge to gain time in London. No one knew about his expedition to the metropolis. London was Life, he felt. London was the centre of everything. It offered a panoply of untold delights; it smacked of adventure. And Hugh felt that he was ready for it — ready and willing to taste adventure. But he was not prepared for the adventure that actually befell him.

It had been raining — an April shower — but now the sun was shining again. People were striding along, shaking out their umbrellas, looking doubtfully at the sky. Hugh had no umbrella. He did not mind getting wet. It was the first of the new experiences. London had touched him already.

It was then — with the pavements glistening, and the cart-wheels splashing through rivulets of water, and umbrellas disappearing like mushrooms at dawn — it was then that a young woman came darting round the corner from the Strand. She was not looking where she was going and ran smack into him, leaving them both reeling and gasping.

"Goodness! I *am* sorry!" The woman recovered her poise, laughed.

She did not *look* particularly sorry, whatever she might say. She ought at least to show remorse, Hugh felt. It was all her fault, after all. *He* was not the one who had not been looking where he was going. He was aggrieved, but at the same time rather alarmed. She was a Woman. Hugh did not have much experience with Women.

Then he looked more closely. The woman was in fact little more than a girl, only a couple of years older than him at the most. She appeared excited and nervous and kept looking over her shoulder, for all the world like a naughty child. Hugh drew himself up.

26

The girl was tucking in strands of red hair that kept escaping from under her hat. "I must go."

The red hair stirred something in Hugh's memory. "I say, aren't you . . .?" But the name was lost, and his voice petered out. His eyes were drawn down to her heaving bosom: she was very much out of breath.

"Aren't I what?"

"I . . . I . . ." Hugh stammered. He was quite unable to resist the allure of her breasts, rising and falling as she gulped for air. He felt like a cad; but the girl did not seem to notice.

"I must go," she repeated, already moving away, would soon be swallowed by the crowds.

Hugh did not want her to go. It was not just the red hair or the heaving bosom. There was something about her that gave him a warm feeling inside. Something to do with an act of kindness . . . a benevolent gift . . .

"Raggety Peg!" he suddenly blurted out.

The girl turned and looked at him — looked at him properly for the first time. Her green eyes narrowed. "Hugh Benham," she said slowly, dredging up a deep-sunk name. "It is Hugh Benham, isn't it? Well! Who'd have thought it? This is a coincidence and no mistake!"

Hugh blushed. She remembered his name but he could still not remember hers and he felt at a disadvantage; but at least he knew now who she was. It was the Irish girl, the one who had so selflessly given him her tatty doll, back in the days when he'd been a hopeless little kid at The Firs.

"I'm sorry; I really do have to go." She was backing away again, the distracted look back on her face. "The police . . ."

It was then that Hugh heard the police whistles sounding in the Strand. The girl took to her heels.

"Megan!" At last her name came to him out of his confusion. He shouted it out, startling passers-by so that they turned to look at him with dubious expressions. But the girl ran like the wind, threading through the crowd, skirts flying. She was leaving him.

There was a distant rumble. Crockery rattled on the dresser. The hum of aeroplanes grew louder. None of this could drown out the sound of his own youthful voice echoing inside Hugh's head, shouting out Megan's name like some lonely animal on a windswept tundra calling for its missing mate.

He sipped his cocoa. It had grown cold as he sat there with his aunt, hiding from the German bombs, but he did not notice, lost in his memories. In his dreams over the years, Megan had always been running, running away from him. He could never catch her. She always appeared in those dreams just as she had been that day in Southampton Street: young, breathless, slightly dishevelled — and beautiful. It was a moment charged with significance. He had told himself the story of that day many times and he had come to believe that it had been at that very moment — when Megan collided with him in April 1912 — that he first realized that he loved her.

At the time, it had seemed that he was likely to lose her almost as soon as he'd found her again. She had fled at the sound of the police whistles, and he had stood there wavering. Was it wise to get involved? Why were the police interested in her?

"Come on!" She had flung the words behind her as she ran.

Don't be such a sap! He had lashed himself, ashamed of being so pusillanimous. *You wanted adventure. Here it is. Seize it while you have the chance!*

And so he had run — run at full pelt. He had put on one of those bursts of speed which, two months later, had made him champion over 100 yards at the school sports day; but fast as he was, he had not been able to catch Megan. She had always been a fraction ahead, leading him on as the hare leads the dog.

Hugh looked up as the ack-ack guns in Hyde Park started booming. The noise outside was rising in a crescendo. Letitia turned her glass round and round on the table. The electric light flickered, dimmed, glowed bright again. Despite all this, Hugh found himself drifting back, leaving the basement kitchen to relive the headlong flight with Megan nearly thirty years before. They had left the police flat-footed and crossed Covent Garden, whirling past windows crammed with exotic fruits and vibrant flowers, clipping arms and legs, tripping over umbrellas and walking sticks, stumbling but not falling, dodging glaring faces, outrunning the angry voices.

Hugh smiled, recalling the sense of exhilaration, the boundless energy of youth. Sometimes, during his rare visits to the capital in the long years between then and now, he had tried to retrace their steps, crossing Covent Garden at a more sedate pace, recognizing the brown tiled walls of the tube station in James Street but getting hopelessly lost in the maze of streets and alleys beyond. They had come to rest in a square that might have been Russell Square, or might not (after twenty years and more, it was impossible to say). What Hugh did remember clearly — this at least had not faded with time — was the glow on Megan's cheeks and the glint in her eyes as she leant against the railings, laughing at him and hiccupping; so lovely that even now he felt a catch in his throat and a fierce pang of desire that not even the German bombers could extinguish.

Megan looked up, her eyes dancing. One hand gripped a metal upright, the other was tucking loose hair under her hat. "Fancy meeting you! After all this time! It must be — how long? It was your expression I recognized first. So solemn. So mournful." She laughed, hiccupped, laughed some more. "How old are you now?"

"Fifteen." Hugh begrudged telling her this. Fifteen had seemed very grown-up to him that morning, stepping off the train at Waterloo in search of adventure. But now, suddenly, he felt childish and gawky. It didn't help that he was all hot and sweaty, his cheeks burning. Megan, by contrast, was glowing, looked incredibly alluring.

30

He deflected attention away from himself by asking, "Why are you running away from the police?"

"I've been breaking windows."

Hugh, all proper and high-minded, was shocked. "Breaking windows! Whatever for?"

"To protest at the way women are treated by society and by the government. To draw attention to the fact that we are denied the right to vote. They go on, all these men, about the Home Rule Bill, rights for the Irish, rights for Ulster, but they do nothing about the subjugation of women. We want the Women's Suffrage Bill and we want it now!"

Light dawned. "You're a suffragette."

"A soldier in the battle for equal rights." Megan struck a heroic pose, her eyes dancing.

"But how will breaking windows help? It's criminal damage."

"Criminal poppycock! Nothing will ever change unless we stand up and take action! Men will not willingly give up their long-held positions of privilege. They have to be forced into it. That is what our campaign is about. It's not a spur of the moment thing, you know. Every action is carefully planned. There is a prearranged signal, simultaneous attacks followed by tactical withdrawal (also known as running away). Afterwards we meet up again at headquarters. But I shouldn't be telling you this. You are a man. The enemy."

She laughed; but Hugh scowled. He held a very dim view of breaking the laws of the land, nor did he appreciate being addressed as if he was in a public meeting. Megan had used a pejorative tone when speaking the word *man*. Hugh was affronted, felt that aspersions were being cast. Being a man was a serious business, not something to be laughed at. He was beginning to think he'd made a terrible mistake in following Megan so impulsively.

Megan's bright eyes were fixed on him. "Have you still got her?"

"Got who?"

"Raggety Peg, of course."

"No." Hugh blushed, feeling both silly and guilt-ridden. He had a sudden vision of the doll floating away from him down the stream, eyes to the heavens, apathetically indifferent to her fate. It was a vision that had haunted him for months as he endured the nightmares of Buckly Priory. He hated to think of that place, where he'd forever been known as Stinky Benham, the boy who owned a girl's dolly. *Girl* had been a term of abuse at Buckley Priory. The boys there had casually cast aspersions on the value of femaleness. Hugh only realized that now. It was a new way of looking at things.

The doll was not only a link with the past but also a symbol of kindness and generosity, a symbol which had inspired in him a dogged optimism: the fortitude to endure Buckley Priory and whatever else life had to throw at him (if indeed anything could be worse than that place . . .). He had always felt grateful to Megan for her quixotic gesture in giving him the doll. He tried to recall that gratitude now. He also told himself to stop feeling so inadequate. After all, there was only two years between them, and Megan very obviously came from a lower echelon in society. One had only to compare her clothes with his own expensive suit, made by his grandfather's Savile Row tailor. Her frock had seen better days, the colours faded, the lace *décolletage* torn, the lace itself rather a dirty yellow. Hugh took stock of all this; but he also noticed the whiteness of her skin, and the curve of her breasts.

He blinked and looked away.

"I must go," said Megan.

"Can I come with you?" asked Hugh. The thought of her going off and leaving him was like a sharp pain. He realized he was fascinated by her still. That was why he had run after her. It was more than a sudden whim, it was more than a sense of adventure: it was something else entirely.

"We are not allowed to bring men to headquarters." She looked at him, speculative. Hugh waited with bated breath. "We *could* meet later . . ."

"Yes." Hugh let out his breath.

"I'll be at Piccadilly Circus at half past four."

With that she was gone, and Hugh was left to wait and wonder, standing in the middle of Russell Square just after midday in April 1912.

Four o'clock had seemed an age away. Taking out his pocket watch, Hugh had watched the minute hand creeping round the dial but had been unsure if he wanted it to move faster or slower. He desperately wanted to see Megan again; but nerves were starting to get the better of him. Playing truant in London was all very well, but he had not stopped until now to think about the consequences. His grandparents, should they find out about it, would be very disappointed in him and would make a point of saying so. They would also disapprove of his associating with a girl such as Megan O'Connor. She was *not quite our sort*, they would say.

But that didn't matter. He was fifteen, old enough to make up his own mind. He didn't much care what his grandparents thought. They were jolly enough in their way, but rather old-fashioned and dull. Adventures were kept well away from the fastidious portals of Overton Hall.

None of this helped in solving the problem of what he would say to Megan when they met again. What could they possibly find to talk about? How could they even begin to bridge such a vast gap as ten years: more than half their lives? All he could think about were the things that divided them, not least votes for women and the breaking of windows.

Doubts and fears had assailed him as he made his way through London streets to Piccadilly Circus, but he did not allow himself to be deflected from his purpose. Stronger than all his doubts was his desire to see Megan again. She filled his mind: the unruly red hair, the flashing green eyes, the way she laughed, her carefree manner. She had cast a spell on him. He was caught, and there was no escape.

Hugh had prowled restlessly amongst the crowds, going round and round Piccadilly Circus as he awaited the appointed hour. He hadn't been able to keep his unruly mind in order, had found himself staring up at

Eros poised high above the fountain. What did things look like from up there? Presumably one would notice the hats more than anything, the tops of hats: caps and bowlers, top hats and straw boaters; wide-brimmed hats trimmed with ribbons and feathers and silk flowers; and smaller hats of more recent fashion. There was also the domed helmet of a policeman on point duty. Hugh had watched him conducting the traffic with grave self-importance — and why should he not feel important, wielding such power, motor cars and hansom cabs, bicycles and tricycles, carts and carriages, omnibuses for Clapham or Euston Road all dancing to his tune?

Hugh glanced at his watch. Twenty minutes to go.

He began searching the faces of passing women, looking for Megan and glimpsing her everywhere out of the corner of his eye: amongst the crowds that lingered under shop awnings as solitary drops of rain began to fall, or staring blankly from the top deck of an omnibus, or selling flowers from a vast pannier on the steps below Eros. But none of these girls was the real thing. The real Megan remained elusive.

Worn out by waiting, Hugh sat on the edge of the fountain, trying for an appearance of nonchalance. Above the pediment of the London Pavilion a flag flapped in the rising breeze. The sun shone brightly, then faded. The spots of rain grew more persistent. Years passed.

Megan was ten minutes late. She was more subdued than earlier and there was a dubious look in her eyes, as if she thought she might have made a mistake in coming. Hugh wrenched a smile onto his lips and tried to act the gentleman. He held the door open for her as they took refuge from the rain in a Corner House. He pulled her chair out for her. He deferred to her choices as to which cakes to have. All the time his heart was hammering and the blood throbbing in his cheeks.

They forced out an awkward conversation. Hugh called her "Miss O'Connor" and was scrupulously polite, trying to swallow his tea quietly, doing his best not to choke on his cream bun. He felt sure he was making a frightful ass of himself.

It was only when their talk drifted back to their long-ago meeting at The Firs that they began to lose their reticence. Looking back from the thoroughly adult perspectives of fifteen and seventeen, they laughed at the absurd things they had said and done, amazed at their naivety, and impressed by how wise they had become. Hugh relaxed a little. He began to feel up to the task of asking some questions. He wanted to know about Megan — he wanted to know all about her; but she pre-empted him and he found that he was required to give an account of himself. What, for instance, was he doing in London?

"I'm not really sure why I'm here." He laughed to cover his feelings of foolishness. Nothing on earth would make him admit to such a kiddish purpose as the seeking of adventures. "I am meant to be staying with a school chum. I got on the train at Southampton, but instead of getting off at Winchester, I rode all the way to Waterloo. I have wired my friend, who now thinks I am back at Overton, whilst my grandparents will assume I am with him."

"How completely wicked of you!" said Megan with a gleam in her eye. "But what were you doing in Southampton? Do you live there now?"

"No, I was there with my father and stepmother —"

Megan interrupted. "Your stepmother? But of course, I remember now. When we met at Binley your mother had just died. You had been crying but you would not admit to it. I felt sorry for you — but not sorry enough. I did not know then what it feels like to lose one's mother."

She smiled: a new sort of smile, sympathetic and intimate, bridging the gap across the table. Hugh blushed and despaired. He had done nothing but blush in front of her all day. She must think him such a little boy.

"So your father remarried in the end. I have a vague impression of him, your father. Rather tall and forbidding with a military moustache. He must be a colonel or a general by now, I suppose."

Hugh shook his head. "He resigned his commission in 1902."

"But he was so cut out to be a soldier!"

"So everyone thought; but apparently he always hated the army but never let on until after Mother had died. It was then that he decided to please himself instead of other people and do what he wanted for a change. Of course, his resigning rather upset all the plans. I was staying with my grandparents until such time as Father made arrangements for me to go back to India, but in the end I never did go back."

"What a shame! You talked so much about India. After you'd gone, I used to picture you in those exotic surroundings, just as you'd described them: a million miles from damp old England."

"You thought about me, then?"

Megan laughed, crumbling her cake. "From time to time. I used to wonder if you were taking good care of Raggety Peg. I felt sure that you were."

She was looking up at him, her eyes gently mocking, and Hugh resigned himself to going red as a beetroot. There was nothing he could do to stop it.

"Anyway, carry on with the story. Once your father left the army he came back to England to look after you, I expect."

"No," said Hugh, and he explained how his father had become a drifter, travelling aimlessly from one place to the next: from India to Malaya, then to Australia, New Zealand and South America. Months passed, then years. Hugh stayed on with his grandparents, an arrangement which had started as a temporary expedient and that grew to be permanent. Occasionally, a letter or postcard arrived bearing foreign stamps. Less frequently there would be an address where Hugh could send his reply *poste restante*.

"That's very sad," said Megan.

Hugh felt a frisson of pleasure, his heart leapt. She felt sorry for him! She actually felt sorry for him! But then he had to look away, feeling like a fraud.

38

"I didn't really miss my father," he confessed. "I didn't really know him back then. It's a pity, because I think I rather like him. We have wasted so much time, but now we have an opportunity to put that right. He's going to settle down at last."

"And where on all his travels did your father marry?"

"He has only just got married. He met his bride in the Argentine, or somewhere like that. But she is not Argentinian. She is American. A widow by the name of Mrs Daffodil Mertens. Now the second Mrs Arnold Benham, of course."

"Daffodil Mertens!" Megan giggled, and for the first time Hugh felt a real connection between the young woman sitting opposite him, and the little girl he had known ten years before. She had been prone to giggles, that little girl; and she had been mischievous, instigating all sorts of pranks and naughtiness which had been disapproved of by the grown-ups. Hugh and the Lambton boys had been delighted by it all and had competed to take the blame for all the wrongdoings. They had been knights and she their lady.

Megan was still curious about the wedding, so Hugh told her all about it. The letter had come out of the blue, telling Hugh that his father was coming home. At the end of the term just gone, Arnold Benham and his intended bride had collected Hugh from Harrow and then all three had gone to Aunt Letitia at The Firs.

"Whenever I go back there," said Hugh, by way of an aside, "I always look out for you. I hoped you might have come back to the Manor one day," he ended wistfully.

"I only made one visit to the Lambtons. I was there rather under false pretences as it happened. But go on. You went to The Firs with your father and flowery Daffodil. What next?"

"Father and I had some long talks. It was very strange. Rather like meeting one's housemaster for the first time. Father said he is jolly proud of the way I've turned out. It's odd, because all this time I felt that I didn't much care what his opinion of me might be, but now I feel awfully bucked up that he approves of me."

"I think he is quite right to feel proud." With a sly smile, she added, "That's not to say, of course, there is no room for improvement. Some of that schoolboy priggishness could be rubbed off for a start."

She was looking at him with amusement, her green eyes wide and laughing, freckles across her nose, a faint tinge of colour in her cheeks. Hugh couldn't meet her gaze for long. It made his head whirl. He lowered his eyes, watched as she crumbled the cake on her plate. Her hands, by Hugh's fastidious standards, were decidedly grubby (his own were carefully manicured); but at that moment even her imperfections seemed perfect.

"You're blushing." Megan had laughter in her voice.

"Am I? I mean, yes, I am. It's because you are making fun of me." Honesty was the best policy — the only policy. It was either that, or talk gibberish.

There was a pause in which he knew she was daring him to look at her, but he did not have the courage. Then she spoke up, asked him to complete his tale and he was happy to do so, seizing on the facts of recent events to stop himself being swept away completely. The wedding had taken place on Easter Saturday. Afterwards, he had spent a few days with the happy couple in the New Forest. They had both pressed him to accompany them, which had rather touched him.

"From there, we went to Southampton where Father and my stepmother embarked on the new White Star liner for New York. They are going to Boston to visit my stepmother's family, and afterwards they will come back to England, and we are all to live together like a proper family." He was surprised as he said this to realize just how much he was looking forward to it.

The story brought up to date, Megan got to her feet, and Hugh jumped up too, his heart beating fast, terrified she might be about to leave him again; but she merely said it was time they gave their table to someone else and that she felt like walking. They left the Lyons Corner House, negotiated Piccadilly, entered Green Park. Their pace slowed as they walked beneath the plane trees. It was, thought Hugh hopefully, as if they were both equally reluctant to reach the moment of parting.

Suddenly, Megan skipped a few paces ahead along the path and then turned, blocking his way. She asked where he intended to stay.

"A hotel, I suppose." He had not actually given it any thought until now. His trip to London had been spontaneous, a madcap escapade. "Or there's a chap from school. His people live in Hammersmith."

"You could always stay with me." Megan looked demurely from under the brim of her hat. "I have lodgings near Victoria Station."

"Isn't that . . .? Would that be quite proper?" Hugh stammered as he spoke, trying not to look shocked, trying also to dampen down the anticipation which suddenly flared inside him.

"We could take a cab." Megan's eyes widened, at once innocent and very knowing.

"My luggage is at Waterloo."

"Never mind your luggage. You don't know yet if you'll like my humble abode. It is *very* humble."

"Somehow I'm sure I shall like it." Hugh grinned, daring now to look her in the eye.

She laughed and took his hand and they ran, reliving the exhilaration of their earlier flight from the police.

They took a motor cab to Megan's lodgings. Hugh gave the driver a shilling and afterwards wondered if he had been overly generous. Not that he minded. The mood he was in, he wished the entire world well. What was a shilling? He had others.

Megan put her finger on her lips as they entered the run-down building. "The landlady lives downstairs in the basement. She's a fearsome old dragon. *'I'll thank you not to invite people up to your rooms, and especially not young gentlemen'.*" Megan imitated the landlady in a whisper. "*'I keep a respectable establishment here, I do.'* This way, up the stairs. If you take your boots off you will be much quieter."

As Hugh climbed the stairs in his stockinged feet, he realized that he had never in his wildest dreams imagined just what a whirlwind adventure really was. He was tingling all over; felt as if he was a butterfly crawling out of a chrysalis, stretching its wings, blinking in the new sun. The old Hugh — the Hugh of a few months ago — would never have dared do anything as reckless as this, climbing the boarding house staircase with its peeling wallpaper and bare wooden steps.

Megan's room — for that's all it was, one room — was rather shabby. Hugh sat gingerly on the edge of the bed, too intoxicated by the present moment to wonder what might come next. Megan removed her hat, kicked off her shoes, and arranged her hair, looking in the mirror above the mantelpiece. Finally she turned, looked down at him with bright but guarded eyes, her head cocked at an angle.

In the same fake cockney accent she had used to imitate the landlady, she said, "It ain't much but it's home, sir," and then she laughed.

Hugh remembered every detail of that room, even after twenty-eight years. He recalled the washstand and the iron bedstead; the pile of old newspapers in the fireplace; the paintwork peeling off the chest of drawers, the books scattered on top; the crack in the mirror; the flowery pattern of the dirty wallpaper. The window had looked towards the railway but the view had been obscured by the jutting corner of a neighbouring house. All day and night one heard the noise of the engines and the shrieks of their whistles. It had been a rather unpleasant room, he realized, looking back; but he had not noticed at the time. Megan's presence had brightened it, transformed it. Hugh shivered as, a quarter of a century later, he remembered her voice: alluring yet innocent, full of laughter. "Would you like to kiss me? Because I think I would quite like to kiss you."

Other details of those April days spent in London came back to Hugh as he sat in Letitia's kitchen listening to German bombs falling on the docks. At evening, Megan's room had looked different, the harshness of its squalid reality softened by dancing shadows as the candle flame flickered in the draughts. He remembered Megan's red hair run riot on the white pillow, how it touched his cheek and tickled his nose when she moved her head. He remembered her wide green eyes looking up at him, her lips parted in a smile. He remembered her succulent white breasts and the unexpected red of her nipples.

They had been careful not to attract the attention of the landlady, *the dragon in the basement*. Once, he recalled with a smile, Megan had had to put both her hands across his face to stifle his laughter as he crawled on hands and knees looking for his boots. Why looking for his boots should have been so hilarious he could not now say. It was the laughter he remembered, and the feel of Megan's hand across his mouth, the smell of her skin.

Beyond the confines of the dragon's lair they had laughed out loud and they had laughed a lot: laughed as they tried to light cigarettes in the wind, laughed at the broken windows in the Strand, laughed as they ran to catch buses and hailed cabs. Hugh's money had paid for their meals, their visits to the theatre and the boat trip they had taken along the river; but Megan had refused to let him buy her gifts, however much he pressed her. The only thing she would accept was his new silver lighter engraved with his initials H.A.A.B. It had been a present from his father, but Hugh had been delighted when she accepted it. She had seemed pleased, had promised to treasure it.

He had never talked so much in his life, he remembered. He had never felt the need before. But with Megan hanging on his every word, he had found himself telling her everything. He had told her how he had thrown Raggety Peg into the stream at Buckly Priory, and he had told her of his unhappiness there, the bullying and bed wetting and cold, cold baths. He had found unexpected solace in dragging up every hated detail. In doing so, he had come to realize later, he had expunged those details from his memory.

Megan had stroked his hair and held his hand and said, "How awful to be a boy! How despicable those schools are!" And she had listened, properly listened, and not just from politeness. It was only years later that he had come to understand how rare this was.

When they weren't talking, he was happy just to sit and watch her. He had felt that he could watch her forever, dazzled by her beauty and by the amazing chameleon way she adapted to her surroundings, so that she never seemed out of place wherever she was. And yet, looking back, he found that one of the most vivid memories of all was of a moment when they had briefly parted. She had been off at some meeting or other, plotting ways in which to force Asquith to give women the vote. He had stood on the Embankment, waiting for her, the ground trembling as the trams trundled past behind him, before him the wide brown river slowly rising with the tide, tugs labouring downstream against the oncoming current. He had been supremely content, basking in this brief interregnum, knowing that in an hour he would be with Megan again.

But a real parting had come eventually, as he had known in his heart of hearts that it must. He had just never expected it to come about in the way it did.

In Letitia's kitchen, Hugh stared at the dregs of cocoa in his mug and said, "After Father and my stepmother died, I believed I had killed them. Divine retribution for my sins."

"Tush, my dear boy!" At her age, Letitia could get away with calling a forty-four-year-old man a *boy*. "What terrible sins could you have possibly committed? You were only a child, fifteen. Their deaths were an accident."

Hugh said nothing, for one could not talk of the sins of the flesh to one's great-aunt. Instead, reaching back into his memory, he tried but failed to recall the particular street along which he and Megan had been walking when they saw the terrible headline scrawled on the side of a newsstand: ACCIDENT TO TITANIC.

Megan had been bewildered by his reaction and Hugh, intolerant in his distress, had shouted at her. "Don't you see! That is the name of the White Star liner my father embarked on for America. It has hit an iceberg."

Megan had tried to reassure him. "There's probably nothing to worry about. It is still afloat. Look, it says here in the newspaper that it is practically unsinkable."

Twenty-eight years later, Hugh had come to believe that he had known from the first moment that his father had perished, but at the time there had been a brief moment of uncertainty and hope. This had been shattered forever as the later editions came out, detailing the full horror of the tragedy, the deaths of over 1500 people on a calm night in the Atlantic. Graven on Hugh's mind was the scene outside the White Star offices in Cockspur Street, people gathering, waiting, clinging to straws: desperately wanting news and receiving news they did not want. And amongst the dead had been Arnold Benham and his wife of less than a fortnight. Hugh could not now remember how or when he had learned for certain of their deaths. Nor could he recall at what point during those nightmare days Megan had left his side, vanishing, never to be seen again. There were jumbled images in his mind, a hint that he might have broken down in Megan's room, wept and wailed, beaten his fists against the shabby walls, though he preferred to put that down to imagination, choosing to believe that Megan had not held him in her arms as they lay on her bed, that he had not sobbed into her red hair and felt that the world was ending. In his forties, Hugh was firmly convinced that he was a man incapable of extreme emotion.

"It was such a shock, of course, when *Titanic* went down." Letitia's voice seemed to come from a long way off, summoning Hugh back to the surface from his deep-buried memories. "One had assumed that man had conquered nature irrevocably; but the sea conquered *Titanic*, just as the Antarctic conquered poor Scott. Somehow, those events shook one's belief in progress."

It shook my belief in me, thought Hugh, remembering how he had sat in the library at Overton, trying to make sense of the tragedy, looking for some sort of meaning in book after book until, reading the righteous polemics of his great-grandfather the Bishop of Chanderton, he had come to believe that he had killed his father by earning God's wrath. He had sinned and now he was paying the price. He had even begun to wish that Megan O'Connor had never existed.

"But of course, accidents do happen," Letitia continued, "and that is all they were, the sinking of *Titanic* and the death of Scott, accidents. Recriminating and laying blame gets one nowhere, though it was a favourite ploy of my father's. If anything bad happened, it was always Divine retribution, according to him. I believe he even published some of his awful sermons, explaining his tendentious view that one always gets in life what one deserves, and that everything good is a sin, and that everything bad is retribution for it."

"There were some of his books in the library at Overton," said Hugh.

"Those are books the Nazis could have burned and welcome."

Hugh looked up from his mug, unprepared for the vehemence of Letitia's remark. Her face was set, her eyes sunken, she looked cadaverous in the electric light. Was she in pain, he wondered? Was she ill? Or was it merely the effects of the war, the disturbed nights, the constant fear?

"For us, of course, *Titanic* had personal significance. Not as a spurious act of Divine vengeance, or a symbol of man's frailty, but as a terrible accident, the tragic loss of three lives."

"Two lives," Hugh corrected. Letitia was abnormally vague tonight, he thought: another sign of age. "Father and my stepmother."

Letitia's eyes slowly focusing on him. "Yes, of course. Two lives." She smiled.

"At the point when he sailed for America," said Hugh at length, "I felt I was really getting to know my father for the first time. I was looking forward to us being a family, living in one house together: me, Father and my stepmother. Up until then I had always been under the impression that he was running away from me."

"It was not that. I just think he was never very sure of himself as a parent. He did not have a good relationship with his own father, and he was afraid of making the same mistakes with you."

"Why did he not get on with his father?"

Letitia, going conveniently deaf again, did not answer. Instead, after a moment, she held up her hand. "Listen. The all clear. We can at last retire with impunity."

But when Hugh did get back to bed, he found it difficult to get to sleep. He lay awake, twisting and turning, his mind a jumble of memories. When finally he drifted off, dawn was breaking outside and London was stirring after another night of pounding by the Luftwaffe.

CHAPTER
THREE

Hugh departed after lunch to catch the train from Euston which would take him back to his hush-hush work in Buckinghamshire. Clearing away the lunch dishes, Letitia washed them and left them to drain. It was Mrs Mansell's day off. Since May, when the war had started in earnest, the daily woman had become a four-times-a-week woman. Not that there was much that needed doing in the house now. Most of the rooms were closed off, the furniture covered with sheets, gathering dust and dead flies.

As she pottered around the kitchen — polishing the cutlery and putting it away, wiping the table, sweeping the floor — Letitia gave herself a dressing down. She must learn to be more circumspect. Old age was no excuse for a loose tongue. She had kept her secrets all these years: now was not the time to start letting things slip. It was all very well to tell a complete stranger — that policeman yesterday, for instance — that one had hated one's father, but when it came to one's friends and relatives, one had to be more careful. Careless talk not only cost lives, it also led to awkward questions. Last night, Letitia said to herself, I very nearly told Hugh that his stepmother was carrying Arnold's child when they embarked on *Titanic* that April day long ago. Perhaps Hugh ought to be told; perhaps they ought to have told him at the time, if indeed Arnold himself had known; but it was too late to bring it all up now. It would serve no purpose, merely open old wounds.

Letitia sighed, putting away the broom and lowering herself slowly into a chair, pulling up her legs to prop them on another chair. A real secret, she thought, is one that is never told, one that is taken to the grave. All this deathbed confessing is so much bunkum. It is the coward's way out, offloading one's burdens onto the next generation. And there is always the possibility that, the confessing over and done with, death's door would refuse to open. One would have to go on living, seeing the damage one had done. The very idea was intolerable. Unthinkable.

In the silence of the kitchen, cut off from the world — her only view of the outside was the area, a mere hole in the ground — Letitia drifted back to an evening in early spring twenty-eight years before. In her mind's eye she walked again on the narrow lawn at The Firs with Daffodil beside her. The tall trees had cast deep shadows over the garden, but up above in the sky light had still lingered. It had been a moment for whispered confidences, and Daffodil had not disappointed, revealing her pregnancy and expecting Arnold's respectable aunt to be shocked. But Letitia had taken it in her stride. Arnold had looked happier than Letitia had ever seen him and Daffodil — scatty, excitable, Daffodil — had been congenial company. At the age of thirty-two, she had been unexpectedly naïve, as if life had barely touched her. The prospect of telling Arnold about the baby had, she freely admitted, kept her awake at night with worry.

"I thought I would ask your advice. You are a kind person. I can always tell if a person is kind or not. And Arnold speaks so highly of you. But you see, I am not sure if I should tell Arnold now, or wait until after the wedding. It would seem more proper to wait. We should have waited all round."

Were all Americans as indiscreet as Daffodil? It was Daffodil's openness which Letitia had found disconcerting, rather than the news of the pregnancy. After all, Arnold and Daffodil would not be the first couple whose child was conceived the wrong side of their wedding day. But to confide in a virtual stranger, as Daffodil had done, had seemed to Letitia terribly dangerous. Even then, Letitia noted as she looked back, I had grown used to keeping things close to my chest: but perhaps Daffodil had nothing to hide; perhaps she really was as innocent as she seemed.

"Of course you must tell Arnold as soon as possible," Letitia had said in the garden at The Firs. "He will be delighted."

But had Daffodil taken her advice? There had been, what, four, five days when Daffodil could have done so, before the liner struck the iceberg and foundered in the cold, calm Atlantic. Had Arnold known about the baby? No one now would ever be able to say for certain. Arnold, his new wife and the unborn child had vanished along with the unsinkable ship, their newfound happiness cut cruelly short.

Daffodil had been a good choice for a bride, thought Letitia, listening to her creaking bones as she moved her legs, keeping cramp at bay. She had been just what Arnold needed. Much preferable to the spoilt, caustic Cecily. Letitia had said as much in the spring of 1912, though not so directly.

"Cecily was a mistake," Arnold had said, surprising Letitia as they talked late into the night at The Firs on the eve of his wedding: a happier occasion than the time of their last intimate chat ten years before. "That is not to say I disliked Cecily." Arnold had picked his words carefully. "She had admirable qualities in her way. The other chaps, my fellow officers in India, envied me. She was the perfect military wife. But I found her difficult to love. And perhaps I was not a very good husband. I was certainly not a good soldier."

"Everyone thought you perfectly suited to the army."

"I never really thought about it, not until Cecily died. I just followed the route which had been signposted for me. I joined the army because it was expected of me. It was my duty, Grandpa said."

"Yes, he would have said that." How often had she heard her father say, "*Church, law and army: those are only proper professions for a gentleman.*"

"One had to think always of the good of the family, not what one wanted for oneself. That's what Grandpa taught me. That is why Cecily was such a suitable wife. She was after all from one of the foremost families, rich, well connected, titled."

54

"Hardly good reasons for marriage."

"Marriage should be entered into for the benefits one will accrue."

Letitia had heard those words before, but not from Arnold. Was it then she had first begun to recognize the malign influence of her father still working from beyond the grave? Or had she always known?

It was not the done thing — now or then — for a man to talk openly about his hopes, his dreams, his feelings; but it had been a new Arnold who had come to The Firs in 1912, an Arnold Letitia had never met before. He had been ploughing his own furrow for ten years and had grown comfortable with himself. It had taken time enough. For years, he had confessed that evening, he had considered himself a failure. He had not come up to scratch. Being unhappy with Cecily, being inept as a soldier: he had taken this as proof. He felt he had let everyone down: Hugh for one, his grandpa most of all. The Bishop had had such high hopes of him, had been so very fond of him.

"But I have had time to think whilst I have been travelling, Aunt. I have put all that behind me. This time things will be different. This time I am doing things the right way, for the right reasons. I am awfully lucky to be given a second chance like this."

He had plans. Marriage was just the beginning. There were newfound interests he wanted to pursue. He had designs to become an archaeologist or perhaps an anthropologist. He wanted to be educated.

"Properly educated, Aunt. Not that rot we get taught at school, construing Latin and playing cricket. I want to know about the world, about history and people and places. I want to know where we all come from and where we are going."

Such optimism, Letitia remembered as she sat in her silent kitchen in 1940. Arnold at thirty-eight had had last found his own recipe for happiness. He had a sense of purpose. But then had come the news of the sinking of *Titanic*, and suddenly it was all gone.

Letitia thought of that tragedy not as an act of God or an accident of nature, but as the malevolent power of her father, as potent in death as in life, working to blot out the happiness Arnold had found for himself, just because it did not fit the established template of how things should be. Her father the bishop had thus completed the job he had started long before, ruining poor Arnold by pushing him into the army, uniting him to the inept Cecily. Arnold had wasted twenty years of his life before discovering what he really wanted, and then it proved to be too late.

The tragedy had been Hugh's too. He had just been discovering the father he had never known. A *de facto* orphan for many years, the death of Arnold had made Hugh an orphan *de jure*. Afterwards, Letitia and Hugh had grown closer. He was all she had, the last of her family. It had been important to keep in touch. She felt that he still needed her. Their correspondence had grown in significance as Hugh finished school and looked forward to university until, with the advent of war, all his plans had changed and he joined up instead of going up to Oxford. It was at that point that Hugh's letters, always important, had suddenly become the only thing that mattered.

The letters, thought Letitia: why is it so long since I thought about the letters?

Filled with sudden urgency, Letitia levered herself to her feet, negotiated the stairs, rooted through the old armoire in one of the shut-off rooms, finally unearthing the cardboard box which held the old letters. Here they were, tied into bundles with blue ribbon: yellowing, the ink faded, but still safe and sound. Precious, precious things. Her lifeline through four long dark years.

She picked out one and looked at the envelope. It was stamped "Passed by the Censor" and addressed in Hugh's neat hand:

Mrs L. Waruer
The Firs
Binley
Warwickshire

Holding it, looking at Hugh's handwriting, Letitia was overcome by long-buried emotions: the constant worry, not knowing what was happening across the Channel, the fierce feeling of love for Hugh, as if its very intensity written in between the lines of her replies could deflect the German bullets and shells.

Kneeling on the dusty carpet by the armoire with Hugh's letters in front of her, Letitia felt herself shaking, sobbing, unable to stem the tears which slid across her wrinkled cheeks, the memories biting into her, old emotions rekindled: anxiety, grief, love, burning hatred.

"You're a silly old fool, Letitia Warner," she said, reaching for her handkerchief. "A silly old fool who has outlived her usefulness."

"'Ere," said Mrs Mansell coming into the kitchen next morning as Letitia sat with her eleven o'clock coffee and the newspaper. "I found these on the floor in the sitting-room upstairs. What you been poking around in there for? It's all dusty and 'orrible. Won't do that cough of yours no good at all."

"I've had this cough ever since I got pleurisy and pneumonia at the age of twenty-one." After all these years, she put her illness down to the shock of getting married, handily reversing events and ignoring what it was that had really made her ill. "I don't suppose a little dust will make much difference now."

"Yes, well, you ain't getting any younger, are you? You should watch yourself." Mrs Mansell plonked a cardboard box of letters on the kitchen table. "What shall I do with these? Use 'em for the fire?"

"Good grief no!" Letitia folded her newspaper and put it aside. "These are Hugh's letters from the last war. They have great sentimental value. That is why I have kept them all this time."

"Stone me. Ain't one war enough for you that you want to go remembering the other?" Mrs Mansell sat herself down and began poking through the bundles of letters. "Writing's faded on most of 'em. A bit tatty too,

58

all torn and dirty. And look at the state of this one, all messy, some sort of stain."

"Blood," said Letitia.

Mrs Mansell put the envelope hastily aside. "I don't know what you want to keep *that* one for, I'm sure. Unnerving, I'd call it. Who's blood was it, any road?"

"Hugh's, of course. A piece of shrapnel cut his hand." Letitia picked up the envelope and looked at it, seeing the spot of blood, a dark brown smudge, remembering how the sight of it had shocked her at first, then made her feel somehow closer to Hugh: the flesh and blood Hugh and not Hugh the letter-writer, a detached voice. In his later letters, there had been an impersonal tone which tended to distance her from him; but the early letters had spared her nothing, as if he himself could not believe what he was seeing and needed to write it in words to convince himself it was all real. When he got used to the front, he had tended to gloss over the worst of it, but Letitia had by then become adept at reading between the lines.

Letitia took out the letter and read aloud. Hugh had been in the reserve trenches, writing by candlelight, leaning the paper on his knee. It described the mud, the fleas, the rats, the corpses rotting in no-man's land, the star shells which lit up the night in lurid colours. Mrs Mansell listened with her mouth open, her hands tucked in her apron pocket.

"Well I never. To think such things went on." For once, she was at a loss. "I had a husband, but he never let on about anything like that."

"I think they tried to spare us the full horror of it all." Letitia folded the letter carefully, almost lovingly, and put it back in the box. "You *had* a husband, you said. Were you married before?"

"Yes. He got killed." Mrs Mansell looked unusually thoughtful. "As I said, he never let on what it was like over there, but I think I knew, in my heart of hearts. He changed so much, see. I used to look at him. All different he was, somehow. I used to wonder what had happened to change him and what it was all for. '*King and Country*', he said. '*What's the King ever done for you and me that you want to go fight for him?*' I said. Then again, they said that the Germans wanted to invade us. But what would they want with our country when they've a perfectly good country of their own? And now it's the same all over again. Bombing us to kingdom come. '*Give 'em as good as we get*', they say. That's all very well. But what I say is that Germans are very much like you and me when it comes down to it. At least, the ones down Sandwich Road were that I used to know. And I can't help thinking how there's someone like me, or someone like you, Mrs Warner — ordinary folk over there in Germany — getting bombed by our lot, and sitting in their cellars or down the tube — if they have the tube in Germany. There don't seem no rhyme nor reason to it. I for one don't get no satisfaction thinking of them being bombed and killed. It don't make life any easier for us, now, does it?"

"You are quite right, Mrs Mansell." Letitia thought it ironic that one of the very people her father had so despised — *hoi polloi* he had called them — should speak in terms of tolerance and forgiveness, whereas were the bishop still alive, she felt sure he would have been casting the whole German people into hell-fire and eternal damnation and lauding the work of righteous British bombs in killing and maiming the enemy.

"You ought to sort these out, put them in the right order." Mrs Mansell was still sifting through the box of letters. Her tone was conciliatory and Letitia suddenly felt that she was getting almost fond of the small but belligerent woman, notwithstanding Mrs Mansell's tendency for avoiding the work she was paid to do.

"I often thought of putting them in an album."

"That's what you ought to have done, instead of putting 'em away in a tatty old box. Very descriptive letters, by the sound of it. Not at all like the ones my Ned used to send me. *Dear Maggie, I'm in the Pink, yours, Ned.* 'Cept he weren't in the pink, not when I got his last letter. He was already dead, only I didn't know it."

"I am sorry. It was such a terrible war."

"Ah well. All done and dusted now." Her thick fingers flipped the bundles back and forth, preoccupied. "You've got a soft spot for Mr Hugh, I think."

"Yes, I have. He's the only relative I have left. And he was my saviour too, in a way. He gave me a second chance."

"You don't say." Mrs Mansell held up a letter. "'Ere, this one's got different handwriting from the others. Look."

She passed it across. Letitia looked at it. Not a letter from the front. The postmark was London, early 1915.

"This was not from Hugh," murmured Letitia. "I wonder who . . ." Taking out the letter and unfolding it, she looked at the unfamiliar handwriting, glanced down at the signature: *yours very sincerely, Megan O'Connor.*

Of course, the girl who had stayed at the Manor that long-ago spring, the Irish girl, the one who had been such a hit with Hugh and the Lambton boys. How strange! Her name had cropped up in conversation only the other night. Surprisingly, Hugh had remembered her. A strange expression had come over his face at the mention of her name, a faraway look which Letitia had not recognized. She herself had experienced only guilt, an unexpected emotion which she had not been able to account for. Seeing this letter again after so many years, the feeling of guilt came back, even stronger than before. Other memories began to resurface with it and slowly she realized where the guilt had come from. It was because she had not answered the letter — or, at least, not until it was too late: all because of something Connie Lambton said.

Poor Connie! One barely gave her a thought now from one year to the next.

"But I was a fool to have listened to her!" murmured Letitia. "I played God, deciding who was suitable and who was not when it should have been left up to Hugh. Only he had the right to decide who his friends were. I was no better than my father, riding roughshod, arranging people's lives as I saw fit."

Mrs Mansell was looking at her curiously. "What was that you said? I didn't quite catch . . ."

"Nothing," said Letitia. "I was just thinking how we all like to interfere in other people's lives."

"Like the evacuation."

"The evacuation?" Letitia was at a loss. She did not always follow the logic behind Mrs Mansell's thoughts.

"The evacuation. That was interfering in people's lives if anything was. And what a waste of time it was too. My two youngest, they was evacuated, but they came straight back after a month. Hated every minute. And to tell the truth, I'd rather have them home with me, bombs or no bombs, than off in some stranger's home. They was picked and choosed like animals at a market, our Clive said. All these snooty women were going round saying, '*That one's too ugly, that one looks like it's got fleas, that one's not fit for anything*'. That's just what they said. Our Clive told me. '*Why don't their mothers dress them proper, what can they be thinking*'? All they wanted was cheap servants. Slave labour. There was some government plot at the bottom of it, you can be sure." Mrs Mansell was a great believer in government plots and secret conspiracies. "I mean to say, you wouldn't dream of evacuating any child of yours, now would you, Mrs Warner?"

"We didn't have evacuations in the days when I might have had children."

Mrs Mansell, opening her mouth to pursue the subject, caught the look on Letitia's face and shut it again.

A few days later, when Mrs Mansell came into the kitchen to prepare lunch, she suddenly brought out a faded photograph from her apron pocket.

"This was my Ned."

Letitia peered at the sepia-toned photograph, seeing a curly-haired, square-faced man staring uncertainly into the camera. "He was a handsome fellow."

"Get on with you! He weren't handsome! I said as much to him myself. I said, '*With your ugly mug, I won't have to worry about no other girls chasing after you*'."

"When was he killed?"

"1916. Shot through the head. His captain wrote me a letter, I'll never forget it. Such a nice letter. Said Ned died instantly, which was a blessing. He didn't suffer, that way."

Letitia handed the photograph back without comment. Hugh had once written to her from the front about the letters he had to concoct to send to the families of the men who were killed. "*We always put, 'Death was instantaneous, he did not suffer in any way'. It is better for them not to know the myriad protracted and agonizing ways in which a man can die.*"

"I never see any snaps of your old man about the place." Mrs Mansell's leading question hung in the air as she belatedly set to washing the breakfast dishes.

"I try to forget about him. He was a bully and a coward." Letitia spoke lightly, glossing over the past.

"Oh, I've got one of those. At least, he's more of a useless lump than a bully. I wish he was a few years younger then he could toddle off into the army and I for one wouldn't miss him. But instead it's my Bob who's in the army. It does seem cruel for a young lad like that to be taken up and — Well, heaven knows what'll happen to him. I prefer not to think. I don't know what I've done to deserve such a life, sure I don't. I sometimes wonder what it'd been like if Ned had lived. But there you go. If ifs and ands were pots and pans, there'd be no trade for tinkers." She turned from the sink, her hands covered in soapsuds. "Now, what'd you like for your lunch today, Mrs Warner? Rissoles, is it?"

The letter from Megan O'Connor had arrived completely out of the blue in 1915. It had taken Letitia some time to remember the red-haired girl who had stayed with the Lambtons thirteen years before. When she did remember, she thought it odd that the girl should be asking for news of Hugh all these years later. Rereading the letter more carefully, looking for clues, Letitia had come across the sentence: *We met again by chance in London nearly three years ago* . . . . How odd. Hugh had never mentioned it. That was most unlike Hugh.

There had been no obvious reason why Letitia should not have replied then and there, or at least passed the letter on to Hugh; but something had held her back. She sensed that there was more to the matter than met the eye. So she had gone to see the Lambtons. They ought to know about the girl if anyone did.

"Oh, that girl," said Connie Lambton in the blue drawing room at the Manor. "I'm afraid, Letty, we were

65

most dreadfully deceived in that whole business. It was quite unforgivable. I rather fell out with Lady Mereton afterwards."

Letitia, sipping her tea and nibbling a piece of walnut cake that was not a patch on Annie's, waited for Connie to continue. Connie Lambton was a tall, thin woman with a remorseless grasp on life. A widow, she sat on the *chaise-longue* like a spider at the centre of a web, ruling the Manor with an indefatigable iron will. Her influence extended far beyond her Georgian house and gardens. The village danced to her tune; sometimes it seemed that the whole county was under her sway. Letitia, though favoured enough to be admitted to the inner circle, none-the-less trod carefully where Connie Lambton was concerned.

"What had Lady Mereton to do with it, Connie?" Letitia prompted.

"Well, it wasn't Lady Mereton herself, to speak the truth. It was one of her maids or the housekeeper — I really can't remember. But Lady Mereton really ought to have seen what was going on right under her nose. It was really too bad of her not to put a stop to it right away. I feel awfully aggrieved about it, even now."

Letitia had the patience of a saint, and needed it with Connie Lambton, who had a tendency for going all round the houses. Finally, settled with a second cup of tea and a slice of cake, Connie got to the point.

"Evidently what happened was this, Letty. This particular maid of Lady Mereton's had a daughter. I don't know what happened to the daughter's father, he was never mentioned. We must draw our own conclusions. Unfortunately, that type of thing is only too common amongst people of that sort. Anyway, as I was saying, this woman, the maid, could not manage the child on her own, or else she wanted to defray her expenses or some such thing: I really can't begin to fathom her reasoning. The upshot was, she used to help herself to Lady Mereton's headed notepaper and write letters as if she was Lady Mereton herself. We received one of those letters. It made out that the girl — the maid's daughter — was a niece or a cousin — I can't remember which — of the Irish branch of the Mereton family. Would we, the letter asked, be so kind as to invite the child to stay for a week or so? The company of other children would be beneficial and so on and so forth. One was only too glad to help, with Lady Mereton being unwell for so much of the time. One never *dreamt* it was all a hoax. One had no idea one was being most frightfully used and deceived. Nor were we the only victims of this terrible woman. With Lady Mereton never calling, and hardly ever being at home to visitors, it was only much later when it all came out. I can tell you, we were most *awfully* embarrassed and put out about the *whole* business. I really don't like to talk of it."

You could have fooled me, thought Letitia waiting to get a word in edgeways. She was always uncertain whether Connie used the royal *we*, or whether she spoke for her sons as well as herself — or maybe even the whole household.

"The whole sorry business makes me feel quite ill even now. I wouldn't have mentioned it — one does not

like to advertise the fact that one was made a fool of —
only you so obviously must have heard something,
Letty."

Letitia, who had not suspected anything at the time
of the girl's visit and had hardly thought about her
since, merely smiled. "What happened to the woman,
the housemaid?"

"Given the boot, as my dear Arthur would have said.
Even Lady Mereton was not so foolish as to keep her
on after that sort of scandal. It's the *nerve* of the
woman — the maid — that makes me so cross. Had she
no conscience? Of course, at the time one thought there
was something a little odd about that child. She did not
seem quite to *fit* — I'm sure you noticed it too, Letty;
but one put it down to her being Irish."

"And what became of the Irish girl? Was anything
ever heard of her again?" In her mind's eye, Letitia
could see the letter from Megan lying in her bureau at
home. She decided, then and there, not to mention it to
Connie Lambton. The less Connie knew of one's
business, the better.

"Ah, well, now that is the strangest part of the whole
story, and it only goes to prove that people of that sort
are simply *not* cut out to lead our sort of life. For as
I'm sure you would expect of us, we treated that girl
like one of the family. I believe it was the same in the
other houses she stayed at. And what good did it do
her?"

There was a hiatus in the story at this point whilst
Connie pawed at the bell rope. With her long scrawny
neck, beady eyes and hooked nose, she looked rather

68

like a vulture. But that was unkind, Letitia rebuked herself. After all, her own neck was nothing to write home about these days, sagging and wrinkled. They were all getting old. There was no getting away from it.

A girl came in to clear away the tea things. Letitia turned away, not holding with the idea that servants needed to be watched all the time. Connie Lambton took the opposite view: one had to watch them to make sure they were doing things *properly*.

Looking out past the curtains and the leaves of the giant pot plants, Letitia saw the croquet lawn and recalled a spring afternoon thirteen years before when she had watched Hugh and Megan and the Lambton boys playing on the grass. She had been sitting in this very same chair. The french windows had been open. The sound of childish laughter had carried clearly. It had been such a comfort to see poor little Hugh smile. And now that one came to think of it, the girl had been rather protective of Hugh, shielding him from the boisterous Lambtons.

The servant clattered crockery, knives, spoons on the tray as Connie watched hawk-like. Catching Letitia's eye, she said, "*Elle est un peu retardé.*" The hawk eyes swivelled back to the poor maid. "You are so lucky, having Annie."

"She is indispensable," agreed Letitia, adding silently: *and not available for you to poach*.

When the coast was clear, Connie resumed her tale, speaking of Julian, her eldest son, who had been called to the bar in 1913. "When he was down here on a visit some time ago, he told me that he had seen the blessed girl in court — the very same girl who had stayed here. This was before the war, of course." Connie leaned forward, as if imparting important and confidential information. "I said to him, '*Don't be absurd, Julian, how could you possibly know it was the same girl?*' But he was adamant. He would have known her anywhere, he said."

"The boys were rather taken with her, it is true." *Captivated* would be a more apt word, thought Letitia, remembering how Hugh and the Lambtons had been drawn to Megan like satellites round a planet.

"I can't think why." Connie sniffed, tossing her head. "Red hair, and Irish. Not exactly promising. Anyway, as I was saying, the girl came to no good in the end. When Julian saw her, she was in court. I can't remember the details now. Some tomfoolery to do with those dreadful suffragettes, breaking windows, chaining themselves to railings, invading the House of Commons: dreadful, *unnatural* women."

Letitia had always had a sneaking admiration for the suffragettes. She admired the way they stood up for themselves. Of course, her father would have heartily disapproved of them; but that was one more point in their favour. Letitia was wise enough, however, not to say any of this to Connie Lambton.

"Julian made some enquiries, afterwards. A very meticulous boy, Julian. It seems the girl was involved in all those sorts of nefarious activities. To put no finer point on it, she was no better than she ought to be."

"I thought even Mrs Pankhurst drew a line at girls of that sort."

"Oh, she wasn't one of Mrs Pankhurst's lot. Julian said she belonged to a sort of breakaway group. He looked into it, made quite a study of it, I believe. Meticulous, as I said. Of course, the breakaway group was made up of all manner of undesirables: criminals and so on — socialists too, I shouldn't wonder."

Meticulous did not do justice, Letitia thought, as she waited with infinite patience for Connie to go on with the story. "And the court case? What did that concern?"

"I forget now; Julian was rather vague about that part of the story. I rather think the girl went to prison. Or was it her brother? She ought to have gone to prison, anyway, though how long she would have stayed there is another matter. Cat and Mouse Act my eye! Let them starve to death, I say, and see how they like that!"

Somehow, Letitia could not picture Megan as a suffragette, a criminal or a woman of loose virtue; but then she could not really picture her as anything other than a seven year old girl playing with Hugh and the Lambtons on the croquet lawn. She must be a different person now, thought Letitia: I probably wouldn't even recognize her. Just think how much Hugh has changed: five then, now eighteen and a soldier. The Lambton boys had grown up too, left the village of Binley, headed off into the world. Where were they now? It was only polite to ask, and Connie was never backward in coming forward when it came to her sons.

Julian, a captain in the Guards, was in France, Connie said. Rupert and Justin were both in the Warwickshire Regiment, second lieutenants, in training camps for the moment, safe in England.

"Goodness knows why it takes so long to train them, Letty. Shooting Germans cannot be all that different from shooting partridges. We need our armies at the front, not gallivanting all over England. The sooner we put paid to those frightful Germans the better. Did you hear — I'm sure you must have heard — about those poor Belgian nuns. They are Catholics, I know, but even so . . . And the babies! Those poor innocent babies speared on the gleaming points of the Huns' bayonets."

Connie not only believed atrocity stories, she also embellished them for effect; but this was more than Letitia could bear. The war was ghastly enough without embellishment. Why Connie should be so keen to pack Rupert and Justin off to France was incomprehensible. For her part, Letitia hoped Hugh would remain in England as long as possible. With any luck, the war would be over before he ever got to the front. But just when would the end come? It had already gone on longer than anyone had expected. Christmas had come and gone with no sniff of a victory. But surely it could not be long now?

Walking back to The Firs, passing the church with its square tower of grey stone, crossing the village green, circling the duck pond, Letitia debated what to do about Megan's letter. Connie's information had shed new light on the matter; and whatever reason Megan had for writing, it could not be very important. She and Hugh had met only twice: once, briefly, when they were children; and once in London three years ago. This second meeting troubled Letitia. The fact that Hugh had never mentioned it was unsettling. But was she simply being oversensitive? She hummed and hawed as she passed the post office and the blacksmith's. Turning right into the lane with the tiny farm labourers' cottages, she found that her mind was made up. She would throw the letter away. Hugh need never know.

Walking up her drive, the fitful sunshine making the fir trees glow green, Letitia felt sure she was doing the right thing.

In the end, Letitia had kept the letter but did not send a reply. She never told Hugh about it.

The war had dragged on and on. Christmases came and went. Tidying her bureau one day to distract her thoughts from the latest offensive, she had come across the letter again. It was then that the pangs of guilt had started. The world was a different place in 1917 to what it had been in 1915. Her ideas had changed too. She had told herself that she ought at least to have replied. It was only good manners. And was it not up to Hugh to decide who his friends were? If he was old enough to fight for his country, then he was old enough to know his own mind.

Letitia had written to Megan, sending her Hugh's address. After a few weeks, the letter had come back, the envelope marked ADDRESSEE UNKNOWN. There had seemed no point in telling Hugh anything about the matter after that; but the feelings of guilt remained, buried deep, only to resurface years later as she sheltered from bombs in her kitchen with Hugh himself.

In 1940, remembering that visit to Connie Lambton twenty-five years earlier, Letitia's most vivid recollection was of the girl clearing away the tea tray, small and frightened in her outsized maid's uniform. *Elle est un peu retardé*, Connie had said. Had others once made similar remarks about poor Angelica? Had they spoken in French so she would not understand, forgetting that their eyes betrayed them? Thinking of her sister, Letitia felt sad, angry, impotent. The off-the-cuff remark heard so recently in Selfridge's still haunted her. And she now feared that Angelica's life had been even more tragic than she had ever guessed.

CHAPTER
FOUR

"Oh that dratted siren!"

With an almighty effort, Letitia forced herself out of bed. She checked the blackout, turned on the light, got dressed. Already she could hear the drone of the nightly visitors.

Bombs began falling as she went down to the basement: first the incendiaries, then the high explosives. Tonight's raid was a heavy one, by the sound of it. It would not be over any time soon.

In the kitchen, her sights were set on the whisky bottle on the dresser until she suddenly remembered the expression on Hugh's face as they sheltered here on his last visit. He had gaped at her over his cocoa as if she was an old soak.

Perhaps tea, then. Just this once.

"Goodness, that wasn't far off!"

Waiting for the kettle to boil, Letitia was shaken from her sang-froid by a sudden colossal explosion that sounded far too close for comfort. The noise outside was now intense, rapidly rising in a discordant crescendo. From the recesses of her mind, fear came knocking.

As Letitia warmed the pot and then spooned in tea, she was quite unprepared for what came next.

The noise was deafening, enough to stun her by itself. Several things happened at once. The windows shattered. The air was full of flying shards of glass. It felt as if the building itself had leapt into the air. Knocked off her feet, as she fell she glimpsed the tea pot, kettle, mug, tea caddy and milk bottle being swept off the worktop as if by an invisible hand. A single thought flitted through her mind: *so this is it, the end; ninety-one and out.*

And then even her thoughts were swept away. All she could do was cling on, clawing at the flagstones as if hanging from the face of a cliff. She could feel her clothes being ripped away, her eyeballs being sucked out of their sockets. Glass and scalding water rained down on her.

She was not certain how long this terrible maelstrom lasted. Suddenly it was over. It seemed eerily quiet after the thunderous noise of the explosion. The usual night-time sounds of throbbing aircraft engines, anti-aircraft guns and the crump of falling bombs was like returning to some primeval peace.

Shaking, Letitia raised herself onto her hands and knees behind the heavy kitchen table where she'd fallen. She expected blood and broken bones, but as she took stock she realized she had come through relatively unscathed. Her clothes were torn and she was covered in plaster dust, but the table had protected her from the worst of the flying glass. She paused, gasping for breath, unable for the moment to find the strength to get up.

The electric light flickered. Crouched on the floor, she stared up at the glowing bulb in wonder. The light shade had vanished but the bulb had survived: it seemed remarkable in the midst of the shattered kitchen.

But then she noticed that the blackout had been torn down. She would get into trouble for showing a light.

This apprehension galvanized her. She found from somewhere the energy to clamber to her feet, pulling herself up against the table. She switched off the light and the kitchen was plunged into darkness. A red glow lit the area outside. It glinted on the jagged remains of the windows.

Letitia leant against the table, found that she was shivering violently. Her shoulder was sore, her hip pained her, but it was nothing to what she had expected. It seemed a miracle. Like the light bulb, she too had survived.

Slowly she straightened up. She was not dead. It was pointless skulking here in the basement. Skulking, she told herself firmly, was not in her nature.

She climbed the area steps one by one, staring upwards. A man ran past. He was wearing a helmet. His face was stained red from the light of the fire. From her vantage point halfway up, clinging to the rail, Letitia had the impression she was looking into another world: a world of flames and destruction where impossibly tall men battled hopelessly to stave off

Armageddon. She had an overwhelming urge to see that world for herself. Skulking would not do.

Pushing fear to the back of her mind, she made her way up the last few steps and looked around.

Standing in the road, she looked up at her house. It was undamaged, as if nothing had happened, or so it seemed; but near the far end of the terrace there was a neat hole. Where a house had stood only minutes before, there was now just a pile of bricks and timber. The ruins were lit from behind by a great conflagration in the next street.

She tilted her head, looking into the night sky, half expecting to see German planes swooping low, grinning airmen in goggles hoisting out bombs, but there was nothing, just a milky blackness and the criss-cross pattern of searchlights. She was almost disappointed. She had been ready to shake her fists at the bombers, show her defiance. She was finding her old self. The moment of weakness had passed.

The shocking sight of the ruined house mesmerized her, drew her forward. A crowd had gathered at the scene. ARP wardens, fire-fighters, police were pulling bodies out of the rubble. Voices were raised, hands gesticulating. Onlookers watched, their eyes glassy in the light of the fire. Somewhere a woman was wailing, a thin but piercing sound. It was suddenly cut short as the last piece of wall toppled over, sending up clouds of dust. Flames and billowing smoke were getting nearer, driven by the wind.

Letitia put out her hand, stopped a passing policeman. "Is there anything I can do to help?"

The policeman looked at her unseeingly. "No, madam, nothing. You go on back to the shelter. Take cover."

Letitia turned to go, but at that moment two men passed her carrying a body — or something that once had been a body. Now it was just a mangled parcel of torn flesh and shattered bones. Blood oozed from it, leaving a trail on the pavement.

Letitia turned away. As she limped down the area steps, she began shaking again. It could easily have been her body those men were carrying away: a shapeless corpse. Hugh's words written long before came back to her: *The myriad protracted and agonizing ways in which a man can die* . . . . She had only ever been able to guess at the sights he had seen in France and Flanders, but this time civilians were to experience it all too.

In her wrecked kitchen, Letitia made a show of sweeping up the debris. She blocked up the windows as best she could with whatever came to hand: bits of shredded blackout, tea towels, cardboard. On the dresser, the whisky bottle had also miraculously survived. She took it as a sign. With her torch in one hand and the bottle in her other, she made her way slowly up to bed.

The letter that Letitia had recalled, in which Hugh had talked of the many faces of death, had been written under a tree in Flanders in July 1917. Hugh had been in a camp behind the lines near Poperinghe. The flat dismal countryside lay sodden under a sombre grey sky.

Rain poured down incessantly. Drips slid off leaves and branches, fell onto the paper and smudged his words. But the whole letter was in truth a smudge. He no longer tried to describe his day-to-day life at the front, the horror of it, the squalor. Indeed, horror had become too mundane to be remarked upon. Horror was the normal run of life. Normality, the pre-war life of order and plenty, had become a distant, fading dream.

Some days later, as Letitia far away in peaceful Warwickshire had been reading the rain-stained letter, Hugh's battalion moved up to the front line, relieving a party of Highlanders. Rain continued to fall. The trenches were knee-deep in water. Everywhere was mud. Life was lived in a quagmire. Horses drowned in shell holes, vehicles sank without trace, trench walls collapsed burying men alive. Only the rats prospered.

Hugh sat in his dugout holding a tin cup of tea. A candle guttered on top of an upturned crate beside him. The canvas flap across the entrance wavered in the breeze. In a few hours, with the first hint of dawn, there was to be an attack. The objective was a wood: at least, it had been a wood once-upon-a-time. Now it was nothing more than a few shell-battered stumps sticking up out of the mud. Hugh had looked at it through a periscope. As the light faded, the ghastly scene had sunk thankfully into oblivion, but the image was graven in Hugh's mind as he sat with his tea. He couldn't help but wonder if that blasted, benighted spot was to be his last resting place.

The brief hours of darkness soon came to an end. The guns thundered and roared, the bombardment now at its most intense; but in the trenches there was a hush, an air of anxious expectancy, of tight-lipped fear.

Hugh poured the last dregs of his cold and bitter-tasting tea onto the dugout floor, and put the mug aside. He would not need that in the attack. Amongst the other things he was leaving behind was a letter addressed to Aunt Letitia, to be sent to her in the event of his death. He had written it in 1915. So far, it had never been sent; but his luck was bound to run out one day. After nearly three years, he felt he was living on borrowed time.

There was a stir in the line, whisperings and furtive movement.

The hour had come.

Standing on the fire step, Hugh looked out into the darkness. Far off, all along the line, he could see the flashing of hundreds of German guns, retaliating against the British barrage. As usual, Jerry knew all about the attack. They were ready and waiting.

Hugh's heart beat double time. Today was his twenty-first birthday, he'd all but forgotten. Would he live to see it through?

Only the faintest presage of dawn streaked the eastern sky. Whistles sounded. Hugh scrambled up the ladder. He always led his platoon from the front, felt it was his duty, but today he hardly cared whether they followed him or not. To his right, a fellow subaltern was taking the opposite tack, running up and down the trench with his revolver, driving his men over the parapet at gunpoint.

The trench was left behind. Hugh's feet skidded in the mud as he walked steadily forward across no-man's land. The rain had stopped at long last but the very air seemed saturated. Mist hung in the hollows. And all the time the roar of the guns continued unabated. But now a new and evil sound started up. The German machine-guns had begun their greedy work. Bullets buzzed like swarms of angry hornets. Hugh knew it was only a matter of time before he was hit. Until then, he had to keep going. There was nothing else one could do.

He was dimly aware that his men were with him, strung out on either side. So they had followed him after all. Only there seemed to be fewer of them than he remembered.

So many lost, so soon?

Without warning, a huge column of earth suddenly reared up right in front of him. The sound of an explosion shredded his eardrums. He staggered, dazed, half-blind, as mud and shrapnel rained down on him. A chasm seemed to open up under his feet. He fell into it; and as he fell, his grateful mind took flight, leaving the scene of carnage and ruin far behind.

When he came to, it was eerily quiet. The barrage had moved to another part of the line, the whine of bullets had ceased. It was broad daylight. He was lying face down in mud. The churned up earth stretched away in all directions, brown and sodden. He was sodden too, his clothes sticking to his cold skin.

He knew he must be out in no-man's land; but where exactly? The urge to know was overpowering. It was utter madness, but he couldn't stop himself from trying to stand. Bracing himself, he heaved his body upwards, but there was something wrong. One of his legs was not working. A red stain was spreading through the khaki material of his left trouser leg.

A wound. A Blighty one? It seemed providential, coming on his birthday. So his luck had held once again, and now he'd get away from all this, get back to England. A month's rest, perhaps two: it depended how bad the wound was. It didn't *feel* too bad, just a scratch perhaps. But slowly his euphoria seeped away as he lay there with his cheek pressed against churned-up mud. He was wounded, alone, out in the middle of no-man's land, and with no idea in which direction his own line lay. It was broad daylight; there would be no stretcher parties until the coming of darkness. His leg was leaking blood — it was pouring out: this was no scratch. He was cold to the marrow, felt weak. It was all hopeless. So much for Blighty.

He lay still, listening to the distant guns, the occasional lazy *rat-tat-tat* of a single machine-gun. Somewhere, a man was moaning in pain, the sound rising and falling, guttural and wordless, tailing off after a while into a whimper, then silence.

Hugh stirred. Some deep-seated instinct would not let him rest, was demanding he make an attempt to save himself; so he crawled, pulling himself forward by his hands, dragging his useless leg behind him in the mud. The leg was numb. Why was he not in agony? It bothered him.

After a while he had to stop. He had no energy left and he was getting nowhere. All around the mud stretched on and on. But when he was able to take stock, he found that he had come to a place where many men lay dead: mutilated bodies, detached limbs, gaping mouths, sightless eyes. It made him feel sick. He couldn't stand it, so he turned over on his back, looked up at the grey sky. Such a big sky, vast and empty except for the clouds. He was nothing in comparison, a worm writhing in the mud.

Eventually he felt strong enough to go on. He began crawling again, dragging himself across the pock-marked ground. He was soaked through; his arms ached; he was getting nowhere, but he couldn't stop, he just went on and on, crawling hour after hour — or so it seemed.

Suddenly a shell-hole opened in front of him and he pitched into it, sliding head first down towards a pool of foetid water. He didn't like to think what nameless horrors lurked beneath its slimy surface and he tried desperately to scramble back up the side of the crater, came to rest at last panting with his fingers clinging to the rim.

"Cor! Am I glad to see you, mate!"

The unexpected cockney voice made him jump, as if he'd forgotten about speech, forgotten such a thing existed: forgotten that there was anyone else alive except him. He looked round, disoriented.

On the far side of the crater, curled up near the rim, was a scrawny figure caked from head to foot in mud, as if he was made out of the earth on which he lay. He was hatless, his hair plastered on his skull. White eyes, sharp and alert, blinked out of the grimy face.

"You ain't got a fag, have you, mate? I've got a light, see, but no smokes left."

"Where are we?" Hugh's voice was a barely audible croak.

"I ain't got the foggiest, mate. But I'll tell you something, I ain't shifting from this 'ere hole till its dark, not for nobody I ain't."

Hugh felt a vague sense of unease which he could not pin down. Shouldn't a private address an officer with a bit more respect? But what did rank matter out here? They were not soldiers now. They were barely even men — or, at least, that was what it felt like.

All the same, there had been a purpose to all this once.

"The attack. What happened?" He tried to inject the confidence of a lieutenant into his voice.

The tommy shrugged. "Usual fuck-up, I expect. It was all getting a bit too hot for me, so I ducked down here for a bit until things quietened down; only things never did quieten down until it was too light to move. Fair enough, I says, I'll just lie low till it's dark and then toddle back to our lines, which must be somewhere over that way." He waved his hand in the air. Hugh was uncertain which direction was being indicated. "Now don't get me wrong, I don't mind doing me bit, but it seems to me as the whole thing is one big balls-up.

Those bleeding brass hats, they couldn't organize a piss-up in a brewery. Every bleeding time it's the same. We climb out of the trench; we walk two or three yards, we get cut up. Well, not me. Not this time. I've had enough. I'm not about to get myself done in and all for nothing. So I'm going to sit nice and quiet in this 'ere hole until dark and then head back to the line. But I only had a couple of ciggies on me and I've been gasping. So how about that smoke, mate?"

"I'm not sure if I've still got . . ." Hugh reached into his pocket for his cigarette case. As he did so, he became aware of a dull throbbing pain which had not been there before. His leg had come to life.

The tommy started sliding around the edge of the crater on his buttocks, eager to get his hands on a cigarette. As Hugh watched him, his sense of unease returned. He blinked — or, at least, he thought he'd blinked, but when he opened his eyes, the tommy was right next to him, as if time had skipped a beat. Everything was fuzzy too, as if dusk was coming on, but he could clearly see the whites of the tommy's eyes, and the narrow black pupils.

Hugh offered his cigarette case as if putting a barrier between them.

The tommy helped himself to four cigarettes, holding them by the tips of his fingers. "Iron rations," he said with a grin. He handed the cigarette case back to Hugh and then brought out a cigarette case of his own. It was unexpectedly opulent, gold or gold-plated, looked incongruous in his grubby hands.

86

"Like it?" The tommy had seen Hugh staring. He passed the cigarette case across with a self-satisfied air. "I got it in Blighty one time. There was this tart in the Big Smoke, blond hair, long legs, big . . . you get the picture. She was a right one, no mistake. Said she was an actress. I said, '*If you're an actress then I'm Kaiser Bill*'. Still, she put on a good show for me, if you know what I mean. And after, when she weren't looking, I palmed me money back and took this as extras." He laughed, amused by his own story.

Hugh turned the cigarette case over, squinting at it. It was engraved. *To Dolly, With Much Gratitude, W.R.H.*

"Her name weren't Dolly, neither, so I was only doing what she'd done already. She'd half-inched it from one of her tricks, that's what I reckon." The tommy slipped a cigarette between his lips. "I like to collect souvenirs, to remind me. Places I've been. Girls I've had." He grinned, and fished out a lighter.

Hugh had two cigarettes remaining. He took one out of his case, hoping it might somehow lessen the pain in his leg and help him keep awake. The tommy passed him the lighter in a matey way. It was another of his "souvenirs", by the look of it, probably silver, and also engraved. Hugh peered at it through the fog that was slowly enveloping him, trying to make out the writing. Four capital letters.

Initials.

His own initials.

His own initials!

His hand shook as he turned the lighter over and over, the unlit cigarette hanging from his lips. It couldn't possibly be the same lighter. It couldn't possibly.

But it was.

He stared with blurred vision at the letters, *H.A.A.B.* It was the lighter his father had given him on the dockside at Southampton all those years ago. It was the lighter he had given to Megan O'Connor one April afternoon — an afternoon of golden sunshine and golden smiles which now seemed so remote that he could hardly believe it had ever happened.

Megan. London. Those stolen days in 1912. He'd felt so guilty about it all afterwards, but he'd never regretted it, however wrong it had been.

Hugh gripped the lighter so that it dug into his palm. Rage twisted through him, throbbing in time with the pain in his leg, as he began to piece things together and wonder how the tommy had come by this trophy. *When she wasn't looking, I palmed me money back and took this as extra . . .*

"Let's have it back, then, mate." The tommy, blowing smoke from the corner of his mouth, held out his hand. There was an edge to his words, his eyes watching Hugh narrowly.

Hugh's fist closed even tighter. "Where did you get this?" His cigarette dropped from his mouth as he spoke, lay forgotten in the mud.

"Ah, well, that's got sentimental value, that has."

"I asked you where you got it. You stole it, didn't you?"

"I never did. I got it from me —"

"You stole it. You're a thief. Nothing but a common thief."

"Now listen 'ere, mate, I don't have to take that from you, officer or no."

"You're a thief and a shirker and I shall have you up on a charge. Now get away from me. Get back over there. Go."

"Hold on now. I ain't going nowhere, chum. You're an officer, fair enough. I knew that soon as you opened your mouth. But the way I look at it, out here we're all the same. We're all one step away from snuffing it. So I don't reckon it's right for you to go ordering me about as if we was behind the lines. It ain't right, see?" The tommy smoked as he spoke, manipulating the cigarette with his lips. His voice ended on a menacing note.

But Hugh was not listening, only one idea persisting against the fuzziness in his head and the pain in his leg: he wanted to be rid of the tommy, to get away from him. Only half aware of what he was doing, Hugh found himself yelling at the other man, screaming at him, words tumbling out in a meaningless jumble.

The tommy backed away, eyeing Hugh in alarm.

Suddenly, without preamble, a machine-gun opened up: measured, relentless, deadly. Bullets zinged overhead, thudded into the mud. And then a second gun joined the first in sinister counterpoint.

The tommy spat out the stub of his cigarette, alarmed. "Shut your noise! Do you want Fritz to know we're here?"

Hugh was past caring. If his shouting brought down on them the biggest strafing of the war, so much the better. The tommy would receive his deserts, and Hugh would be saved from this lingering death, his life leaking away out of his leg.

But the tommy had other ideas. He slithered forward, grabbed hold of Hugh. Big muddy hands met around Hugh's neck as if trying to choke the noise off. He hissed fiercely into Hugh's ear. "Are you gonna shut up with that row? Are you?"

As before, when he'd been crawling over no-man's land, instinct now took over. From some deep reserve, Hugh found the strength for one last effort. He grappled with the tommy, tried to wrench the man's hands away. Even as he did so, a stabbing pain shot up his leg and seemed to burst out of him in a savage, guttural scream. They were both slippery with mud. The tommy, losing his footing, slipping from Hugh's grasp, toppled back wards and rolled towards the foetid water. He regained his balance just in time, before the pool could claim him. Immediately he set off back up the side of the crater, crawling on his hands and knees, mud sucking at him, eyes blazing.

The fog was closing in on Hugh. He felt he was about to go under. Without thinking, he reached for his service revolver. He had no idea if it was even there, or if he'd lost it somewhere in the waste of no-man's land. His hand fumbled — grasped the cold butt; but darkness enveloped him at the very same moment. He was blind, helpless, slipping away: at the tommy's mercy.

There was a loud report. His arm jerked back. He heard a splash, followed by the rattling of machine-guns.

Slowly, slowly the sound of the guns faded into the void.

When he next opened his eyes, he could see again. The grey day was just the same as before, if indeed it was the same day — or even the same world. His leg was agony, the pain gnawing away at him: eating him the way rats eat the corpses. But he was still alive, somehow — just. And the tommy?

He raised his head, looked down into the crater. The mud-encrusted body was lying half-in, half-out of the pool. White eyes stared vacantly at the grey sky.

Hugh laid his head back down. His entire life had shrunk now to a scrap of sky, a patch of mud, and the insatiable, devouring pain. His brain ticked over, slowly winding down. It was his birthday. He was twenty-one. He'd killed a man. Or had he? Was it a German bullet or an English one that had snuffed out the tommy's life? What did it matter anyway? Death was death was death. And now death was waiting in the wings for him. Blessed release. Peace.

He closed his eyes and his hand tightened around the lighter which somehow he still had hold of. Walking down blank grey corridors in his mind, turning corner after corner, he searched for his memories and found nothing. The walls were closing in on him. There was nothing left, except for red pain. It filled his head with an inextinguishable fire.

★　★　★

Some time later, he woke. Rain was falling. It fell slowly, halfheartedly, large drops splashing on his face, bouncing on the mud. It seemed to be darker, or else his sight was failing again. He had slid down the side of the crater. His legs were in the noisome water, rotting away. Next to him was the body of the tommy. It seemed fitting they should be side-by-side in death.

The end could not be far off now.

In his Buckinghamshire lodgings, Hugh lay sleepless in November 1940. He flexed his leg. The old wound was giving him gyp. It was always worse in the cold. He shivered, curling up and pulling the bedclothes around him. Whenever his leg ached he was always taken back to the day of the attack. He had been twenty-one and he had expected to die. He ought to have died. The odds had been stacked against him. But instead, men had come out under cover of darkness and borne his unconscious body back to the line and thence to a casualty clearing station. All that was left of that time was his aching leg and the vague idea that he'd killed someone: that, and the lighter. He still had the lighter, buried somewhere at the bottom of his suitcase.

He sighed and turned over and remained sleepless.

CHAPTER
FIVE

News came of the fall of Tobruk. A victory at last, said Mrs Mansell, brandishing the newspaper.

"Only against the Italians." Letitia did not think much of the Italians as fighting men, and she said so. She remembered how, in the last war, the Italians had fought eleven successive battles of the Isonzo against the crumbling Austrians and come out with little to show for it. She was even old enough to remember the humiliation of Italy at Adowa in 1896, four and a half months before the birth of her great-nephew Hugh. Mussolini, it was said, had worked wonders on the country since then, getting the trains to run on time, but Letitia doubted that even he could do anything about the Italian Army. All that talk of a Second Roman Empire was so much baloney, Letitia said.

"A victory is a victory, Italians or no," said Mrs Mansell, not to be denied.

But nothing could raise Letitia's spirits. She was all gloom. The coming of the New Year had failed to bring any cheer. The problem was, she just didn't feel like her old self anymore. There were dizzy spells, occasional breathlessness. She had taken to using a stick when walking, to be on the safe side. It was a depressing reminder of what she called her "increasing frailty".

"There's no need to look so glum," said the doctor on one of his visits. "You've been through a lot just lately, what with the tumble in Oxford Street and then your close encounter with that bomb. It takes time to recover from such things at your age."

"*At my age.* You make me sound like an old crock, which is exactly how I feel. If I was a horse, I'd have been put down by now. I've outlived my usefulness."

"Nonsense." The doctor stuffed his stethoscope into his black bag. "In most respects you are as fit as a fiddle. Give your body time to recover. You can't rush these things. You have to learn to take it easy."

"Take it easy! Don't you realize there's a war on?"

The doctor laughed. He was perched on the edge of the *chaise-longue*, Letitia stretched out along it. They were in what had once been the dining-room, but now served as a sort of reception-room for entertaining visitors. Not that there were many visitors these days. Letitia spent most of her time in her bedroom or in the kitchen.

"The war is impossible to ignore. Even your quiet little square has its bomb damage now. I always think that hole in the terrace looks like a gaping wound, but that's just my medical mind speaking."

Letitia watched as the doctor looked round the room with a keen eye. She tried to imagine how it must appear to him. Undeniably shabby, but it still retained a faded opulence. There were vestiges of the past: a cabinet containing cut crystal glasses; a long mahogany table with a damask cloth; an exotic-looking fruit bowl. No fruit, of course.

"It can't be easy for you, rattling around in this big old place on your own. Why not get out of London altogether? There must be somewhere you could go, friends, relatives?"

"It will take more than a few bombs to drive me out of my home. Besides, all of my friends are dead. I am the only one who went in for longevity in my circle."

"Family then?"

"There's only Hugh. He's off somewhere doing hush-hush war work. There's his son: Ian. But he's in the army of course. I'm not quite sure if Hugh's wife counts as family these days. She has rather drifted away from us. Apart from the two boys (as I call them) there are a few cousins so distant I can't even remember their names. Possibly they may all be dead by now. I forget how time flies."

"It's odd that you should have so few relatives." The doctor was in an unusually chatty mood that morning. "For some reason, I always assumed you came from one of those big Victorian families. I picture you as a girl in the nursery, with a governess and a nanny and a pile of brothers and sisters."

"The nursery and the nanny I'll grant you, but there were only three of us children. Me, my brother Jocelyn, and Angelica. That's Jocelyn scowling over there on the sideboard."

The doctor picked up the photograph. "Yes. I can see the family resemblance. And where is Angelica?"

"There are no pictures of Angelica." Letitia sighed. "Angelica, you see, was not considered normal. She was a rather backward girl. In her later years, I thought of her as a child in a grown-up's body. Father was ashamed of her, of course. Kept her hidden away. The family skeleton. But Angelica never did any harm to anyone. In all my years I've never come across anyone else I could say that about."

"The Victorians had a rather unfortunate attitude in such cases." The doctor replaced Jocelyn on the sideboard, stooped to inspect the Indian statuette. "I'd like to think we'd be more sympathetic in this day and age."

"Are we, though? From what one reads and hears, the Nazis are not disposed to be sympathetic."

"Which is precisely why we are fighting them." The doctor straightened up, turned to face her. "And that reminds me, Mrs Warner. I, too, am going off to do my bit for king and country. But you will be happy to know I am not abandoning my patients without a thought. I have arranged for a locum. Doctor Kramer. She is very good, I am assured."

So that explained his chattiness, thought Letitia. He was in holiday mood, off on adventure, leaving his patients in the care of a woman. Letitia raised her eyebrows at the idea.

The doctor laughed. "Oh come, Mrs Warner, don't tell me you are one of those people who don't hold with women doctors!"

"My generation was brought up to believe women were merely decorative, except when they were bearing children. My father must be turning in his grave, the way things are today: all this war work for women, jobs in factories, on the land, even in the services. Not to mention doctors," she added with a wry smile. "But I am sure I shall learn to get on with this Doctor Kramer."

"I hope so. And now I must be going. I have lingered long enough."

"Still riding around on that bicycle of yours?"

He patted his belly. "It does wonders for my figure, in case you hadn't noticed. I shall say *au revoir*, Mrs Warner, rather than goodbye. For I intend to return once my task is done. And I fully expect you to be here still when I do."

Lying on the *chaise-longue*, Letitia heard the front door close as the doctor left, heard faintly his feet skipping nimbly down the outside steps. The house sank back into silence. There was not even a ticking clock. She had always hated that measured tick-tock, counting away the seconds of one's life.

In the stillness, half dozing, she imagined that she could hear laughter up on the landing: innocent, ingenuous laughter, an echo from the past. Which was ridiculous, because Angelica had never been in this house.

She stirred, banishing the past, concentrating on the present. She swung her legs off the *chaise-longue*, planning the rest of her day, deciding to start with a spot of shopping. As for the doctor's advice, she intended to ignore it.

"Take it easy, my eye! I've never been in the habit of *taking it easy*, and I don't intend to start now!"

"Books have become incredibly popular. The publishers can barely keep up with the demand. Of course, the new editions are not produced to the same standard as before the war. But I always say that it is the words inside the book that are important, not the quality of the paper or the binding."

The shop assistant ended on a note of regret as if, despite her words, a lack of quality was something to be decried.

Letitia listened absently, wondering which of the many books on display it would be best to send out to Ian. "The problem is," she explained, "I have no idea what kind of books he likes." Ian was a bit of a mystery all round.

"The classics are selling well, of course." The assistant spoke with exaggerated patience. "Or perhaps you would prefer something more contemporary. There is always this thing." She pointed to a book called *England's Hour*, an apologetic expression on her face. "It is very topical, though I gather the author is *persona non grata* these days."

"Really? Why is that?"

"She's a pacifist. Need I say more?"

"It's a pity there aren't more of them about. If there were, we might not be in the mess we are in today." Letitia, disliking the officious assistant, decided to take charge of the situation. "Now then, how about a good biography? Where do you keep them?"

"Over here. We have a wide selection, naturally. This particular title is new in this week."

Letitia glanced at the volume indicated, and immediately her heart skipped a beat. The author's name was the same as that of a persistent letter-writer who had pestered her for information and reminiscences about her family. The letters had stopped coming, oh, quite a time ago: before the invasion of Norway last year. Letitia had thought that meant the tiresome man had given up, that she had scuppered his plans to write a biography of her father. But it seemed the odious author must have gone ahead anyway, and here was the finished work. *The Militant Shepherd*, it was called: no doubt because of her father's famously forceful manner. He had been far more opinionated even than this huffy assistant.

The assistant picked up a copy of the book. "This should be right up your street, if you go in for all that Christian charity and forgiveness: love thy neighbour and so on, etcetera."

"Oh, I don't think this particular bishop was a churchman of that type." Letitia gathered herself, was relieved to find she could sound so offhand. "Perhaps you remember — well, no, you wouldn't, you're too young. But you may have heard about the chaplains in the last war who used to bless the guns in the hope that Divine intervention would make them more efficient: more efficient in massacring Germans, that is. I often thought at the time that my father, had he been alive, would have approved. Indeed, I am quite sure he would have been first in the queue when it came to bestowing blessings upon guns, shells, tanks and gas canisters."

"Do you mean to say that the Bishop of Chanderton was your father?" The assistant showed real interest for the first time. "How extraordinary! Then I'm sure you'll want to read *The Militant Shepherd*. It says here on the jacket that the bishop was someone who believed passionately in right and justice and would have approved of our stand against Fascist tyranny. He is compared with Churchill."

"Not a particularly apt comparison," said Letitia. "Even Churchill is not such an egotist as my father. Good day to you."

"But you haven't bought anything!" the assistant called after her. *After all the trouble I've gone to*, was implied but not spoken. Letitia wondered if her abrupt departure would be put down to bad manners or if, given her age, it would be assumed she had taken leave of her senses.

Out on Charing Cross Road, Letitia tried to hurry away from the bookshop but found that she could not. Her hurrying days were over. She leant on her stick, taking small steps, struggled to remain calm, breathing slowly and deeply. Her mind was churning. She very much wondered what the book had to say about her father but knew that she could never bring herself to read it. But the book itself was neither here nor there. It was the unexpected reminder of her father that had really flustered her. He always reappeared when she least expected it, haunting her from beyond the grave: last autumn in Selfridge's, today in a book shop on Charing Cross Road. Would she never be free of him?

The bishop and that shop assistant would have got on famously, Letitia decided as she waited for a bus. The bishop, were he alive today, would speak of pacifists with exactly the same sneer in his voice. No doubt he would demand they be rounded up and put in camps to reflect on the error of their ways. Nobody would be able to convince him that freedom of conscience was one of the things for which Britain was fighting in 1941. It had always been a pointless exercise trying to persuade him that there were two sides to any argument. He had firmly believed that his own point of view was — as it were — gospel.

It was only when she was shuffling onto the bus that Letitia remembered she still hadn't found anything to send to Ian. The failed errand seemed the last straw. Her whole day was in tatters.

Blinking back tears as the bus swung into Shaftesbury Avenue, she just wanted to get home as quickly as possible.

"You really ought to stop doing more than you can manage," said Mrs Mansell as she made hot sweet tea. "And I think you should let me telephone for the doctor."

"There's no need for any fuss. I shall just sit down for a minute or two, and then I shall be right as rain, as you would say."

Mrs Mansell looked at her dubiously. Letitia was sitting in a carver in one corner of the kitchen, surrounded by cushions and draped in an old cashmere shawl. Her stockinged feet were propped up on another chair. She hoped she did not look as frail as she felt just then. The shopping trip had taken it out of her — not that she would ever admit as much.

Mrs Mansell turned her attention back to the tea. "What were you up to, anyway, traipsing all over London?"

"I wasn't 'up to' anything. You make it sound like I was engaged in some nefarious activity."

"So might you have been as far as I know, seeing as I don't have the foggiest what nef — nef — what was it?" Mrs Mansell stirred vigorously, the teaspoon chinking against the mug.

"Nefarious. It means up to no good. But all I was doing was buying some books for Ian."

"And where are they, these books?"

"I couldn't find anything to suit. I'm not sure what Ian's tastes are, in any case."

"Perhaps he don't want books. My Bob now, I know he'd rather I sent him a pack of cigarettes." She handed Letitia a mug of steaming tea. The mugs were Mrs Mansell's innovation. She did not hold with fancy china in the kitchen. "I'd had more than enough of books by the time I left school."

"Books are wonderful things, more precious than treasure. They are powerful too. That is why the Nazis burnt so many." Cradling the mug in her gnarled hand, Letitia wondered if it might be possible to burn that biography of her father. Or perhaps an obliging bomb would fall on the warehouse from which it was distributed. That would scupper the second coming of the Bishop of Chanderton.

102

"Drink your tea," Mrs Mansell ordered, bringing Letitia out of her reverie.

Letitia obeyed, concealing a wry smile. Mrs Mansell would not have lasted five minutes in the old days, when servants were expected to be deferential if not invisible — just how the treasured Annie had been at The Firs. But, having got used to Mrs Mansell, Letitia felt she could no longer do without her. In any case, there was something to be said for Mrs Mansell's way of going about things. One felt more on a level with her. She was a companion as well as a servant. And her advice was often worth listening to. Perhaps cigarettes would be right for Ian after all.

Thoughts of Annie and The Firs, and of Ian who was goodness-knew-where, naturally led Letitia round to Hugh. It was over a month since his last visit. He'd been in a sombre mood back then. Anxious about Ian, obviously; but also feeling neglected: Ian had spent his embarkation leave with his mother in Leicestershire. He was entitled to spend his leave however he wanted, of course; but Letitia, biased in favour of Hugh, felt she would have a bone to pick with Ian when (or if) she saw him again. And perhaps she wouldn't bother with cigarettes, either.

Sipping her tea, she wished there was something she could do to ease Hugh's burden, but she knew there was not. She remembered only too clearly what it was like, waiting for news in the last war. Letters from the front had been a comfort in a way but had never really removed that nagging doubt which one lived with day after day. In the time it had taken Hugh's letters to reach England, he might have been killed a dozen times over for all she knew. Only when he'd been on leave had she been able to breathe, to relax: when he was on leave, and after he'd been wounded. Once it had become clear that he was out of danger, his leg wound had seemed like a beacon of hope. She had wanted him to get well — of course she had — but not too quickly. The longer his convalescence took, the less likelihood there was of his being shipped back to France before the peace came. Although, in the autumn of 1917, one had begun to have one's doubts about peace. The war, it had begun to seem, would go on forever.

Looking back, one was apt to forget that for a while it had been feared that Hugh's leg would have to be amputated. He'd been evacuated to England, spent months in hospital, the wound refusing to heal. She remembered sitting by his bedside holding his hand while doctors held agitated conversations in whispers nearby. And then, out of the blue, remarkable progress had suddenly been made. The leg was saved, Hugh despatched from hospital, a period of rest and recuperation had begun. He had spent most of it with her at The Firs.

She recalled with a sense of cosy nostalgia those days in early 1918 when Hugh was with her, limping along the lane to and from the village, or else sitting and reading by the fire in the parlour. He had not spoken much — not to her, anyway. But then Rupert Lambton had come home on leave and the two of them had spent much time together. Letitia remembered feeling left out. She had wondered what it was they talked about. She had been wise enough not to ask.

It had been Rupert's last leave.

As he sat at his desk in Buckinghamshire preparing digests of intercepted German signals traffic, Hugh was also thinking back to his long months in hospital in 1917. Once his leg had started to heal, he had found himself with time on his hands and nothing to do but lie there and think. One thing had preoccupied him more than anything else: thoughts of Megan.

As the pain in his leg waxed and waned, he had changed his mind about her a dozen times each day. Was she the innocent, generous-hearted girl who had given him Raggety Peg? Was she the daring, vivacious young woman he had met in London in 1912? Was she the lady of the night that the tommy in the shell hole had stolen from? He went over and over the time they had spent together and he couldn't help wondering if he had failed her in some way. Try as he might, he could not recall how things had stood between them when they parted for the last time. It had all been swallowed up in the nightmare of those days following the sinking of *Titanic*. Perhaps if he hadn't lost sight of her, perhaps if they had stayed in touch, then maybe he could have saved her from whatever life of poverty and degradation she had sunk to. He might even have married her, eventually. He had been of an age then, lying in that hospital bed, where he could marry anyone he chose; but no girl he met before or since had ever measured up to Megan.

His drugged mind had raced ahead. He had pictured the scene, Binley Church in high summer, Megan exquisite with her red hair and white dress walking up the aisle towards him. He had laughed, buoyant on painkillers, as he imagined the expression on his aunt's face when she realized who the bride actually was.

But at other times, awake in the dead of night, unable to sleep in the unquiet ward, lost in a maze of pain and dark philosophy, he had wondered if he had ever really known Megan at all. Perhaps she had been walking the streets even back then, in 1912. Perhaps she had counted him amongst her clients. Was the bill still waiting to be settled? Or had he covered it with the meals, the trips, the engraved lighter?

It had nearly driven him mad, the thoughts going round and round in his head, unable to decide where the truth lay, so many different Megans.

After he left hospital, he had found some measure of peace. The Firs had been a place of healing, tranquil and familiar, as if he'd stepped through an enchanted door back into a world he believed had been swept away forever by the deluge of war. But even in the heart of England he had been unable to escape altogether. And as Megan receded slowly into the background of his mind once more, the war had begun to loom larger and larger. His return to the front had grown from a vague possibility to an absolute certainty.

For a time his sense of loneliness had been crippling. He had never found it easy to express himself at the best of times, had found it impossible to talk openly to his aunt: there was nothing approaching the intimacy of their letters. But that was only to be expected. By 1918 an unbridgeable chasm had opened between the men at the front and civilians back home. The divide had always been there: them and us.

Poring over German signals traffic in January 1941, Hugh remembered the relief he had felt when Rupert Lambton came home on leave. There had finally been someone who he could talk to, someone who would understand. Twenty-three years after their last, late-night conversation, Hugh still thought of Rupert as one of the closest friends he had ever made.

"You were gone a long time," said Eleanor Lambton in 1918.

"I was talking to Hugh Benham."

"Not . . . not about us?"

"No, darling. Not about us. I have never told a soul about us."

Rupert had just slipped in through the french window and now kicked off his boots, unwound his scarf, lay down on the sofa in the blue drawing-room at the Manor. His head came to rest on his sister-in-law's lap. He looked up, watching her as she watched the flickering flames of the fire, her face creased with anxiety. There was no other light in the room. Rupert felt safe, warmed by the fire, caressed by the shadows, caressed also by Eleanor, gently stroking his hair and temples.

"Hugh is convinced he will be killed," Rupert said at length. "Whereas I am convinced that I will be spared. Fate's greedy maw has had its fill of us Lambtons."

"Oh darling, don't talk like that. I can't bear to think of such things."

"I know you can't, dearest. And I thank God that you don't have to. For you, all this is what life is." He waved his hand vaguely, encompassing in his gesture the whole shadowy room with its lumpish sideboards and heavy tapestries, bulbous vases bereft of flowers, landscapes on the walls. "You exist in a world of cups and saucers and dressing for dinner. To me it all seems unreal. Hugh says the same. We feel like interlopers."

"But you shan't be glad to go back, surely?"

Rupert thought for a moment before replying. "In a way, I think I will. It is difficult to talk to people in Blighty. It is difficult to talk to anyone who has not experienced it, been at the front. Mother has no idea. You are the only one who even tries to understand." He lapsed into a brooding silence; but Eleanor's distress was transmitted to him through the tips of her caressing fingers and he roused himself. In a lighter tone, he said, "Hugh has rather fallen in love."

Eleanor made the effort too. "Really? With whom? Do we know her?"

"No, I don't believe we do. She was one of the nurses at his hospital in London. Ordinarily a nurse would be beyond the pale, but there are quite a number of our sort who have taken to nursing recently. There was a duke's daughter at the base hospital in France that time I caught one in my arm. Quite hopeless, she was. Fainted at the sight of blood, poor thing. But she felt she was doing her bit. Hugh's nurse wants to go on nursing him even now he's better. She is frightfully keen on him, from what he tells me. But Hugh says he won't get married until the war is over."

"How cruel of him!"

"Cruel? I would have said sensible."

"I don't think it's sensible at all!"

Rupert was shocked at the vehemence in her voice. He hoped she would think it was the cold making him shiver.

Eleanor continued, "If I was in her position, I would want to marry as quickly as possible, because it would be so terrible if he was . . . if he . . ."

"Snatch every moment, you mean?" Rupert reached up and took hold of Eleanor's hand, squeezing it gently. "This is all so wretched for you, dearest. I'm sorry."

"But it's worth it." Eleanor cradled Rupert's head in her free hand. "You are worth it, darling. I could never feel that you weren't."

"Am I?" Rupert frowned. "I wonder. It would finish Mother off if she knew. And there's no hope for us. No hope of us ever marrying, I mean, not unless the law is changed. And sometimes . . . well, sometimes I feel as if I have taken the place of a dead man. Taken advantage of his misfortune, I mean: because he was killed and I am lucky enough to still be alive. Don't you ever feel the tiniest bit guilty?"

Eleanor laid a finger on his lips. "No. Never. I didn't love Julian the way I love you. I was too young and silly. And I don't think Julian had any deep feelings for me." She paused, then said slowly, "Julian was not faithful to me. I found out. I snooped. There was a woman in London. He spent quite a lot of money on her, so I suppose he must have loved her. Of course, he would never have left me. He would never have done anything to cause a scandal. But we both knew it hadn't worked. We weren't suited. He only asked me to marry him because your mother wanted him to, and I only accepted because I was too much of a child to know what it really meant. It was only later that I realized what love really is. It was only when I realized I had married the wrong brother that I understood."

Rupert moved his head so that he could look her full in the face. "Who was she, this woman in London?"

Eleanor shrugged. "I never found out her name. I thought you might have known."

"Lord, no! Julian was a law unto himself." He turned his gaze towards the fire, soothed by the light and the ceaseless movement of the flames. "Another woman, eh. Poor you."

"Oh darling, I didn't mind a jot about all that! I just minded that I was in love with you and couldn't have you."

"Do you think he ever suspected? About us, I mean?"

Eleanor shook her head. "I'm certain he never did."

There was a long silence. At last Eleanor whispered, "Oh Rupert!" and Rupert understood that this was the only way she could express all the longing, fear, and love pent up inside her. He squeezed her hand again, trying to tell her by his grip that there was no point in worrying, that they shouldn't spoil what little time they had left. All too soon, the war would call him back. He thought of Hugh, so certain in the premonition of his own death. Hugh had been in England for months, laid up with his leg, safe from the grinding carnage in the trenches; but Rupert did not envy him. Whilst the war continued, there was only one place to be. However much one longed to be away from it all, there was no real alternative — if one wanted to be a man, that was, and not a shirker or a coward. All one's hopes and dreams for the future had to be put away, mothballed. They would still be there at the war's end. And until then, there were moments like this, moments to be seized with both hands.

He sat up and took hold of her, and hoped for tonight at least everything else could be forgotten and the two of them could lose themselves in each other.

Letitia considered her visit to Connie Lambton in April 1918 as one of the bleakest and bitterest moments of her life.

Hugh had gone back to France. To her despair, he had proved stronger and more resilient than anyone expected. The doctors who in the previous autumn had considered amputating his leg were astounded by his recovery. Letitia had resumed her agonizing wait for news, scanning the censored newspapers for clues, listening anxiously for the sound of the postman's footsteps on the drive, fearing the ring on the doorbell which would herald the arrival of a telegram. At sixty-eight, Letitia had felt ill-equipped to endure the long, weary months ahead; but she had had no choice. There was no alternative but to bear it, for Hugh's sake. Sometimes it seemed incredible to her that the morose child who had arrived at The Firs sixteen years ago, a child she had never seen before and was to see only infrequently in the years that followed, could have come to mean so much to her.

It was not long after Hugh's departure that the dreaded telegram arrived: but not at The Firs: at the Manor.

Poor Connie. Her youngest had been the first to go: Justin, Hugh's contemporary at school, killed aged nineteen at Loos in 1915. Julian, the barrister, had died on the Somme in 1916. And finally came the news of Rupert's death. He had returned to the front just in time for the great German offensive. Thus perished the last of Connie's sons. And it looked at the time as if all their sacrifices might well have been in vain, as the German assault rolled across the Allied lines, advancing further than either side had managed since 1914.

Connie Lambton had been shattered. It was true to say that she never recovered from this final hammer-blow of Fate. Letitia remembered the dreadful, empty silence in the blue drawing room at the Manor. Connie had aged twenty years overnight. She had looked lost as she sat there on the settee, her daughter-in-law beside her. One might have expected the girl to be of some comfort, but she had been utterly silent, gaunt and pale, as if her husband Julian had died that very week instead of years earlier. Two women, Letitia remembered thinking: two women isolated in their misery and desolation, unable to reach out to anyone. The Manor had become a mausoleum.

112

That will be me, Letitia had said to herself as, after a suitable interval, she had made her excuses and left. Walking slowly back to The Firs, she had been convinced she had just had a glimpse of her own future, that sooner or later Hugh would be taken from her and she would have nothing left, her life in tatters.

If that Letitia of April 1918 could really have seen into the future, she would have been astonished. Only a year later, the war was over, already consigned to history; and Hugh, looking fitter and healthier than she had ever seen him, was getting married at Binley Church. The day had been perfect, the sky cloudless and blue. The birds had never sung so loud, as if they were bursting with life. Letitia herself had been rejuvenated. A great weight had been lifted, and in Hugh's smile she found recompense aplenty for all the years of torture.

It had felt like the first spring of a whole new world.

Cynthia Cunningham had been a VAD nurse at the London hospital where Hugh's leg had been so slow to heal. She was a timid creature in those days, very prim and proper, with a gentle manner which Hugh at first had found soothing, and later alluring. For her part, though she was scrupulously fair and tried to treat all patients as equals, Cynthia could not disguise the fact that Hugh was her favourite.

After he had left the hospital, Cynthia had visited him at The Firs. It had been obvious to Letitia the girl was in love with him; but whatever Hugh's feelings — and he'd always been one to keep things close to his

113

chest — he remained, first and foremost, a pragmatic man. He'd been honest with her, telling her that he would not consider marriage until the war had ended. It would not be right to leave a widow so young. Cynthia had accepted this with only a few tears, and had promised to wait for him.

Over the previous years, Letitia had often wished there was someone with whom she could share all her anxieties when Hugh was at the front, someone who was as fond of Hugh as she was. Cynthia should have fitted the bill perfectly, but somehow from the first Letitia had not been able to connect with her. Cynthia remained aloof, a stranger. Letitia had wondered if this was her own fault. Perhaps, she had reasoned, it was jealousy, after so many years when she alone had been Hugh's confidante. She had given herself a talking-to, told herself that her own feelings didn't come into it: all that mattered was that Hugh should be happy. She had refused to admit even to herself the nagging doubts that had been there from the start about Cynthia's suitability as a wife.

Years later, sitting in her kitchen with Mrs Mansell and drinking tea, Letitia remembered the wedding as if it was yesterday, remembered how perfect it had seemed. But Cynthia had turned out to be far from perfect.

Oddly enough, it was that self-important assistant in the bookshop who had brought Cynthia into focus again. They shared the same supercilious manner, the same sneering tone: *the author is* persona non grata, *she's a pacifist . . .*

"What do you think of pacifists, Mrs Mansell?"

"Pacifists? You mean conchies? Well, live and let live is what I say; but where'd we be if everyone took the same attitude? Old Adolf'd be over here quick as a flash, lording it up in Buck House."

"Some Englishmen think that's not too bad an idea. There are people who quite admire Hitler."

"I bet none of them's a Jew, neither."

"No, but one of them is Hugh's wife. At least, she admired him in the Thirties. Perhaps her views have changed now." Sipping her tea, Letitia thought about Cynthia, whom she had not seen for many years. Cynthia then had often spoken in glowing terms of Hitler and Mussolini, admiring the trains that ran on time, the *Autobahnen*, the fact that Communists and Jews had been taken down a peg or two; not to mention those super rallies and marches, and that super boxer Max Schmeling who had proved the superiority of the white races over the Negroes. Had Cynthia changed her mind since? Or did she admire the rape of Czechoslovakia, the anguish of Poland, the fall of France, the bombardment of London? Were these things also "super"? It would be interesting to hear her explain how the so-called "inferior" Jesse Owens had managed to win four gold medals at the Berlin Olympics, and why *Supermensch* Schmeling had been defeated at the hands of Joe Louis.

"A bundle of laughs she must be." Mrs Mansell was perched on the edge of the kitchen table with her mug held in both hands.

"We never got on. I rather think she expected me to depart this mortal coil long before now, leaving my fortune, such as it is, to Hugh, and thus to her."

"A gold digger?"

"Money fills a gap in her life: acquiring it and spending it. I expect at bottom there is something psychologically wrong with her, but I can never fathom what it is." Letitia added, "She could not wait to get her hands on The Firs. She made that obvious."

"This was the country house as you've talked of? You never have told me what happened to it in the end."

"I sold it, not long after the war. It held too many unhappy memories. All those years of waiting for news of Hugh, wondering if I would be receiving the dreaded telegram, or if perhaps he would come back home minus an arm or leg, or blind."

"Plenty did. Sometimes I wondered if the ones that never came back at all got the better deal. Some of the poor old sods you used to see begging on the street, it was a crying shame."

Letitia smiled, admiring Mrs Mansell's forthright approach. It was unfair to compare her with the indefatigable Annie. They came from different eras, different worlds almost. Girls like Annie no longer existed. The war had put paid to them — the first war, that was. That war had changed everything. It had certainly changed Annie. She had given notice, gone to work in an armaments factory where the pay was good and she was doing her patriotic duty. Had young women in Germany done the same? Letitia had sometimes pictured a German equivalent of Annie, making the bombs and bullets which had killed Julian and Rupert and Justin; not to mention Mrs Mansell's husband Ned who had been shot clean through the head so that he did not suffer.

Swallowing the last of her tea, Letitia wondered if she would have felt differently about The Firs if Annie had still been there. In the end it had not been a wrench to sell it. Hugh had married in the spring of 1919. The house was sold in the autumn. That last evening, she had walked through the empty rooms, her feet tap-tapping across the dusty floorboards. She had listened to the faint sound of mice behind the wainscoting, heard in her mind the doorbell tinkling as it had done unexpectedly one day seventeen years before, the day Hugh arrived. Outside in the dusk she had breathed the cool autumnal air which was scented with woodsmoke and the heady smell of those trees which gave the house its name. She had looked back one last time as she got into the motor, then left her old house behind forever.

She had been back to the village of Binley only once since then. That was for Connie Lambton's funeral in 1925. It had been a pitiable affair, sparsely attended. Julian's widow had been there, dour in black, her face impassive. Her eleven year old son Jimmy had appeared bored by the whole procedure. The Manor had passed to him, held in trust until he came of age.

On the village green, the duck pond had been filled in and a war memorial erected. Letitia had looked at the list of names, and traced her finger sadly across those of the three Lambton boys, etched in brown sandstone. None of them had a known grave.

Hugh had bought a house in Northamptonshire, spending money left to him by his maternal grandparents. Letitia had moved gracefully into the background of Hugh's life; or so she had expected. She had decided to live in London, buying for a bargain price the house she now rattled around in; the house where, in January 1941, she was talking in the kitchen with Mrs Mansell.

"Hugh married a woman who was remarkably like his mother."

"They say men do."

"Of course, one knew nothing of Freud in those days."

"I don't know nothing of him now for that matter." Mrs Mansell drained her mug, slipped off her perch on the corner of the table. "What I do know is that this washing-up is not going to do itself no matter how long I sit and stare at it."

CHAPTER
SIX

"Hello! anyone at home?"

Letitia, climbing unsteadily down the stairs to the basement, heard a male voice calling out below. Turning into the kitchen, she saw a young soldier standing in the open doorway, lit from behind by early May sunshine. His kitbag was on the flagstones in front of him. Letitia paused, holding onto the door jamb, at a loss to explain the man's presence, uneasy in her frailty.

"Aunt Letitia! So this is the right house! I did wonder if I'd made a mistake. There is some most peculiar washing hanging out in the area."

"Good grief! Is it Ian?" Letitia realized that the apparent stranger was in fact Hugh's son. It was a little over twelve months since she'd seen him last; but it could have been five years, he looked so different. It was not just the uniform and the cropped hair; he seemed taller, broader, more confident, coarser-grained. He was also very tanned.

"I was rather hoping that you could put me up for a night or two," said Ian, after a pause.

Letitia realized she had been staring rather. The surprise had disoriented her. Gathering her thoughts, she said, "Of course I can put you up. There's plenty of room."

"But what's going on?" Ian lugged his kitbag over to the kitchen table, dropped it with a thud. "I'd swear there are nappies hanging out there on the line! I know you're a miracle worker, Aunt, but at your age that is surely a miracle beyond even your powers."

Letitia laughed, Ian's youth and vitality warming her like the spring sunshine. "Sit down and I'll explain." She put the kettle on and placed bread on the table, adding some butter and cheese as it was a special occasion.

Sitting across from Ian, watching him eat and drink, Letitia told him all the news. The blitz, of course, was uppermost in everyone's minds.

"In February, the weather was so bad that the raids stopped for a while. People were thankful for once for the uncertain English climate."

"Interesting." Ian cut another huge slice of bread and began buttering it. "But what have air raids got to do with nappies?"

"If you will just be patient, I am getting to that part. Once the weather improved, the Luftwaffe returned. A bomb dropped on the Mansells' street, demolishing their house and leaving them homeless. With so many rooms lying empty and shrouded in dust sheets, it was impossible not to offer to take them in."

"Mrs Mansell." Ian wrinkled his nose. "I remember her. Very bossy. Almost rude, in fact."

"But very competent. And in a funny way, we get on."

"Can it be? Is she a 'treasure', like the fabled Annie?"

"Annie was unique. But then so is Mrs Mansell in her own way."

"She is also common."

"Never judge a book by its cover." Letitia spoke rather stiffly, reminded that she was not quite sure about Ian. He had been his mother's boy as a child. That was not to say he hadn't grown out of it, but he had spent most of his last (brief) leave with Cynthia. Hugh worried about him, too. It was hardly Ian's fault if his life was being put at risk because he was doing his duty; but Letitia could not quite shake the irrational feeling that he was in some way to blame.

"Mrs Mansell is a treasure of a different kind, a rough diamond. To call her common is something I'd expect from your mother but not from you."

"And that's me told," said Ian with his mouth full.

Letitia wondered if she'd spoken rather more sharply than was necessary. Watching Ian chewing busily, swigging his tea, wiping his mouth with the back of his hand, she searched for clues to his character. Did he take after Cynthia? Sometimes his grey eyes had a distinctly murky look to them.

"Don't worry, Aunt. I don't subscribe to my mother's opinions, social or political," Ian said, as if reading her mind. "All the same, she is still my mother." He smiled wryly, reached for the cheese again. "With your house full of Mansells, will you have room for me? I had thought of going to Dad, but (a) I don't know where exactly he is out in the wilds of

Buckinghamshire; and (b) I doubt if he'd be able to accommodate me."

"Of course there's room here for you." Letitia was willing to offer an olive branch, but to keep him on his toes, she added, "Your mother is still an admirer of Hitler, I presume?"

"She no longer admits as much." Ian looked away, as if he found the subject unpalatable. In profile, he looked much more like his father. "But she has certain cronies who think the war is a hoot. It's their considered opinion that the British Empire has had it and they scoff at Churchill for carrying on when the situation is, as they say, hopeless. They consider Churchill a drunkard and a *parvenu*."

"One can hardly call him a *parvenu*. He is related to the Duke of Marlborough."

"My mother's friends have an aversion to Churchill because he has put so many of their friends in jail, BUF members and so on. They believe the aristocracy to be decadent and effete, with the exception, perhaps, of the Duke of Windsor. My mother drinks to the duke's health every evening. She also listens faithfully to Lord Haw-Haw and thinks that the BBC is all propaganda."

Ian's face remained expressionless as he bit into another chunk of bread.

Cynthia obviously did not improve with age, thought Letitia. One was rather glad to have washed one's hands of her. Ian, however, did not have that luxury. She was, as he'd put it, still his mother. But he had a father too. That was, Letitia felt, worth pointing out.

"You did not go to see your father on your last leave. You do not write often enough. He worries about you."

"Are you sure?"

"Of course I'm sure; don't be absurd."

"It's not always easy to work out what he's thinking. I find it difficult to get through to him at times."

"You should try harder."

"Should I?"

"You must. There's no excuse. There have been more than enough wasted opportunities in this family."

Ian looked at her speculatively, licking butter off his fingers. "Are you talking about my drowned grandpa? I gather he was never around much when Dad was a kid. I never understood why. But you'll know, Aunt. Come on, spill the beans. Let's have all the family skeletons out of the closet."

"There's no time for all that now." Letitia shut the lid very firmly on that can of worms, pointing up at the clock. "The refugees will shortly start to forgather."

"Talking of which, where are they all? And why the nappies?"

"The nappies belong to Mrs Mansell's granddaughter, who is asleep upstairs with her mother. The others are at work or school, except Mrs Mansell. She has gone shopping, or *foraging* as she calls it."

Ian, having polished off all the bread and cheese and a whole pot of tea, now got to his feet. "Tell me where I can dump my things, and if it is permissible to have a bath. I suppose I must paddle in an inch of water?"

"That is the rule."

Letitia consigned Ian to the attic, not without a shred of satisfaction; but Ian accepted it with good cheer. "I am banished to the servants' quarters, whilst the servants have all the best rooms. Very egalitarian. You'll be joining the Labour Party next, Aunt." He laughed and held up his hands in surrender. "All right, all right. No need to look at me like that. I am only joking. Of course the guests must have priority."

Letitia looked at him closely as he heaved up his kitbag. "You are very brown."

"I've been in the desert." Ian grinned, as if the desert was a picnic; but Letitia sensed that his cheery veneer was suddenly wearing thin. Behind his bright façade was a sense of strain, and his face was grey and pinched beneath the tan. Relenting in the face of this discovery, Letitia decided to make allowances in future. He was only twenty, when all was said and done.

This war was not so very different: not in the way it treated the fighting men.

On the stairs, Ian met Mrs Mansell's daughter Peggy with her crying baby propped on her hip. Peggy looked washed-out, her hair straggly and unkempt, but to Ian, so long bereft of female company, she was like a breath of fresh air.

"Things are looking up!" he said with a grin as he passed.

Peggy looked at him blankly for a moment, then something seemed to stir inside her. Her free hand went up to straighten her hair and her eyes sparked into life; but Ian carried on up the stairs heading for a bath and a sleep. Peggy was left to stand and gape.

People began to arrive in the kitchen. First came Mrs Mansell, bumping her bicycle down the area steps, the basket in front loaded with the results of her foraging. Slim Susie came back from her shop job, fresh-faced Clive from school. Later, Mr Mansell slunk in from work and immediately went upstairs. Mrs Mansell set about preparing dinner for eight, not counting the baby. Letitia leant a hand where she could.

They all squeezed into the kitchen to eat. Mrs Mansell flatly refused to go "traipsing up all them stairs" with plates and plates of food.

"Shouldn't you be evacuated?" Ian, tucking in — his appetite seemed limitless — looked across the table at Clive.

"He didn't like being evacuated, so he came back home," said Mrs Mansell. "He's better off at home, anyway."

"And does he ever speak for himself?"

"He doesn't speak with his mouth full, I know that much. He was brought up decent, not like some as I could mention."

Ian grinned, shovelling food into his mouth. "I'm just a humble private. You can't expect good manners from me."

"W-why are you a private?" stammered Clive. "I thought you'd be a captain or a lieutenant."

"Well, for one thing, I knew that enlisting as a private would be a sure way to irritate my mother, and it's a boy's duty to irritate his mother." Ian winked at Clive, then went on, "It was also a point of principle. Rank should be conferred because of ability, not because of class. The last thing we need is a new generation of Colonel Blimps."

Letitia raised her eyebrows at this. It was not an attitude one expected of Cynthia's son. Perhaps there was more to him than met the eye. He was certainly a hit with young Clive, who questioned him eagerly about his experiences in the desert; but Mrs Mansell looked on with displeasure. She already had one son in the army. It was her fervent hope that the war would be over before Clive's turn came.

Clive was not the only person won over, Letitia noted. Peggy was watching Ian with a rather gooey-eyed expression, and even sensible Susie seemed more animated than usual. Conversation around the table grew quite lively and it was not just Ian with tales to tell. Letitia was reminded of a badge people had worn the previous autumn: *I've Got A Bomb Story Too*. So many different stories. And at the end of the war, who would be left alive to listen to them?

"Oh bloody, bloody hell!"

Ian cried out in exasperation as the wailing of the siren intruded into Peggy's bedroom.

Lying underneath him, Peggy said, "We should go down to the basement. It's safer. I have the baby to think of."

"Damn and blast your baby! I haven't finished yet!"

"I don't want to be bombed with no clothes on." Peggy's shrill voice ended on a rising note, the compliant and co-operative woman of a moment before having metamorphosed into a thin and fretful girl.

Ian swore, swept back the sheets and blankets, and jumped out of bed. He threw on his clothes while Peggy sat huddled with a sheet around her, having suddenly rediscovered her modesty. It had taken him days to get this far — days of wheedling, cajoling, sweet-talking — and now he was to be thwarted at the eleventh hour.

"Aren't you coming? I thought we had to go to the basement. I thought it was bloody urgent."

"Go away. I can't get dressed with you watching."

"You weren't so fussy just now," muttered Ian, stomping towards the door. He had his hand on the handle when he heard the first of Peggy's sobs. Looking back, he saw her sitting on the edge of the bed, tears streaming down her face, shaking. Not exactly the type of damsel in distress one dreamt of, but he couldn't just walk out on her.

He went back, sat next to her, put his arm round her.

"There, there. What's all this? What's wrong?"

Peggy took a deep shuddering breath, opened her mouth — and out it all came in a rush: how life was a nightmare when she just wanted it to be normal, how all she asked for was her own little house, to stand on the doorstep of a morning and talk across the street. What did she get instead? Night after night down the tube with no comfort and no privacy, where it was smelly and cramped and you couldn't even have a wash, where people squabbled and mosquitoes bit and the baby grizzled incessantly whilst catching scabies, impetigo and goodness-only-knew what else. Every day this had gone on, every day for weeks. They had queued for hours and hours to get a half-decent spot on the platform, and queued again for the privilege of using overflowing chemical latrines. And then, to add insult to injury, their house had been bombed flat and they had moved here, to this unknown part of town and this strange big house. Why was everything so horrid? It wasn't fair; she was fed up with it, she wished she was dead!

"There, there, don't cry." Ian felt awkward and inadequate as he patted her on the back. How come this always happened to him? How come he always ended up listening to their life stories when all he wanted was a bit of fun? Did the other lads in the platoon have this trouble? You could bet your life they didn't. His problem was, he was too soft. Too bloody well mannered for his own good.

Peggy dried her eyes on the frayed linen sheet, said that they really should go down now and she'd like to get dressed please. As Ian was going out of the door, she added, "You're mad at me now, I suppose? I've spoiled everything and you won't ever want to look at me again."

Ian said no, he wasn't mad — he was mad, but at himself, which was different. He grinned at her — what else could he do? — and unexpectedly she grinned back.

Going downstairs, he felt somewhat placated. He'd done his good deed — and for once it seemed it might just pay off.

She looked almost pretty when she smiled.

In the kitchen, the clock was striking eleven. Letitia said, "It may be a false alarm."

Clive was holding the kitchen door ajar, looking out into the night. "It's not a false alarm. I can hear aeroplanes already. And there's a full moon. They always come when the moon's bright. Can I go out and look, Mum?"

"No you can't, don't be so daft. Shut that door, Clive, and straighten the blackout. Where's that blooming Peggy, and the baby?"

"On their way down." Ian appeared in the doorway. "I heard them on the stairs behind me."

"Did you now." Mrs Mansell gave Ian a dark look.

Letitia smiled. Mrs Mansell took a dim view of Ian but Ian took no notice. It was like water off a duck's back to him after the Germans and the desert.

Soon everyone was gathered in the kitchen: *the inmates* as Letitia referred to them all, including herself. Susie was sleepy as always but Clive was on tenterhooks, unable to sit still. Peggy, Letitia noted, had been crying. Mrs Mansell noticed it too. She took the baby and set her daughter to make tea, "to keep your mind off things".

Incendiaries were crackling outside now, and before long the high explosives began to fall, making the house shudder. The sound of the anti-aircraft fire rose to a mighty cacophony. As the noise grew, silence fell in the kitchen. They sat as if paralysed, eyes roaming but taking nothing in, all their attention concentrated on what was happening outside. Would the next bomb be theirs? Letitia felt the onset of cramp in her leg but such was the tension she dared not move.

"I hope Mansell is watching out for himself." Mrs Mansell broke the silence at last. Her atypical concern for her spouse, who was out on compulsory fire-watching, seemed to Letitia somehow ominous. Something was going to happen.

Ian was the first to stir. He began to spit and polish his boots, hunched over them, frowning. As Letitia watched him, cramp flared in her leg, gripping it. The pain made her gasp, but such was the din that nobody noticed. She knew she would have to move. Anything to ease the agony.

Putting her hands on the arms of her chair, she prepared to push herself to her feet.

Ian looked up from the shiny black heel of his boot, catching movement from the corner of his eye. Aunt Letitia was getting up but she seemed unsteady, jerky. Even as his eyes focused on her, she swayed then pitched forward. As she fell, she caught her head with a glancing blow on the edge of the table.

"Aunt!" Ian leapt up, scattering boots, brushes and polish. Mrs Mansell hovered over him as he knelt beside Letitia. Feeling for a pulse, he noticed blood congealing on her forehead.

"Is she all right? Are you all right, Mrs Warner?"

Clive was watching saucer-eyed. "Is she . . .?"

"She's not dead," said Ian quickly.

Mrs Mansell straightened, taking charge. "Clive, run and fetch the doctor."

Clive shrank back into his chair, eyes swivelling in fear towards the blackout. "Go outside? I daren't go outside!"

Ian jumped up, galvanized by the emergency but still finding time to give Clive an encouraging wink. "I'll go. Tell me how to get there."

Mrs Mansell gave directions. "You'd best take my bike," she said.

Letitia came to, dimly aware that she was lying down but not sure where. She was able to hear but not, for the moment, to see, which was disorientating. Voices came out of the blackness. One was Ian's. He was out of breath, sucking in air; but it was his tone that caught her attention, made her heart race even before she understood what he was saying.

"It's as if the whole city is on fire. It's lit up bright as day, flames everywhere. I've never seen anything like it. I've never *imagined* anything like it."

"You've put a puncture in my tyre!" Mrs Mansell; aggrieved. The sound of her tetchy voice was oddly comforting as Letitia tried to get her bearings; but then came another voice, a stranger's, a woman's: calm, confident, professional. For some reason it sent a shiver up Letitia's spine as she lay there in the darkness.

"Mrs Warner? Can you hear me, Mrs Warner?"

The blackness began to break up. Dots of light appeared like little stars. The dots grew, multiplied; began to clump together. A picture slowly formed, becoming ever more solid and detailed.

She was in her own kitchen, inexplicably stretched out on the flagstoned floor, swathed in blankets, a pillow under her head. The electric lights were off, flickering candles the only illumination. A woman was kneeling next to her, the woman's face peering down at her, concern showing in her green eyes. It was difficult in the half-light to guess her age: perhaps late forties.

"I'm Doctor Kramer. How do you feel now, Mrs Warner?"

So this was the locum, the female doctor who was reputed to be very good. *But if I can remember that,* thought Letitia, *then there can't be much wrong with me.*

"I'm . . ." Letitia cleared her throat, summoned her reserves. Now was not the time to be feeble and helpless, not with all the inmates watching. "I'm quite all right. Just a bit of a headache."

"That's not surprising, the way you bumped your head when you fell." Mrs Mansell still sounded aggrieved. "You gave us a quite a turn, falling down like that."

"I just got up too quickly, that's all. A dizzy turn. It happens. There's no need for all this fuss."

"I'll be the judge of that," said Doctor Kramer. "If you'll just let me examine you . . ."

Letitia felt it best to acquiesce. She didn't, in any case, have the strength to argue.

Doctor Kramer was competent and reassuring: no bones broken and the head wound just a graze. All the same, she said, she felt it would be best if she returned tomorrow — or later today, as it was — simply as a precaution. Letitia was about to say that there was really no need and that she already felt much better, but as Doctor Kramer turned to pack her instruments back into her bag, candlelight glowed on her red hair and Letitia had a sudden and overpowering feeling of *déjà-vu*. She frowned as her mind, muddled after her fall, groped to make a connection . . .

The sound of an explosion came pounding and crunching into the kitchen, making the crockery rattle. Letitia's eyes widened as she remembered the raid. How could she have forgotten it when there was so much noise, bombs falling, guns booming, aeroplane engines throbbing high above?

"I must go," said Doctor Kramer. "I will be needed."

Letitia's train of thought had snapped, she was firmly back in the present moment. The doctor seemed entirely a stranger now as she picked up her bag and headed for the door. She hesitated a moment, looking back as if she was about to say something, but Letitia barely noticed, her attention given to the raid.

Doctor Kramer let herself out. As the blackout fell back into place, Letitia caught sight of a pulsating glow outside and was reminded of Ian's words: *it's as if the whole city is on fire . . .*

The house shuddered as another bomb exploded nearby and suddenly Peggy leapt to her feet, shouting wildly, waving her arms. "I can't stand any more of this! I can't stand it!"

"Be quiet, Peggy! Don't be so silly!" Mrs Mansell spoke sharply, shoving her daughter into a chair, but Letitia felt that Peggy had spoken for all of them as they crouched in the basement like rats in a sewer. The young at least had resilience, energy, belief in their own immortality. But what reserves were left at her age? And it seemed she could not even stand up without coming over all dizzy.

She closed her eyes but did not sleep. The aeroplanes kept coming. The night wore slowly away.

She woke late in her own bed, feeling cold and shivery. Her head ached.

There was a knock on the door and Mrs Mansell entered, bearing tea in a cup and saucer — it was in order to use the best china upstairs. Letitia sat up and sipped the hot tea whilst Mrs Mansell fussed around, taking down the blackout and opening the curtains, plumping up the pillows, tut-tutting at the state of the dressing on Letitia's forehead.

"I feel quite my old self this morning," Letitia lied. "I may even get up later."

"I'd wait until the doctor's been if I was you, Mrs Warner."

Letitia changed the subject. "Is Mr Mansell all right?"

"All right? Well, I suppose you could call it all right. Black as the ace of spades, he was, when he finally got home. And he says Parliament got hit, and the Tower,

134

and Westminster Abbey, and hundreds was killed, and the fires was so hot you couldn't get near 'em. They just burned and burned and nobody could do nothing about it." She gave a heartfelt sigh. "Ah well, it's all over now. Till tonight, any road. You just lie there and rest. I'll come and check on you later. Oh, and that Mr Ian said he will come and sit with you, but you just send him away if he gets to be a nuisance."

Doctor Kramer did not come until the afternoon. Letitia, who had been snoozing, woke to the sound of voices, Ian and the doctor talking by the foot of the bed.

"She was talking in her sleep," Ian was saying. "Something about a baby. Peggy's baby, I presume. There is nothing the matter with Peggy's baby, but Aunt Letitia seemed worried about it."

"Ian thinks I'm deranged." Letitia struggled to sit up, was irked to find this was more difficult than she'd expected. "He thinks I damaged my brain when I hit my head on the table."

Ian had said nothing of the sort, but Letitia was annoyed with him — annoyed with herself, too. Had she really been talking in her sleep? She wished now that she'd sent Ian away, out of the room; but she'd not had the heart. He'd looked so anxious, like a puppy seeking approval.

"I don't think we need worry on that score," said Doctor Kramer. "It can only have been a glancing blow. There's a little scratch, hardly any bruising."

Then why, Letitia asked herself, *do I feel so frail today?*

Doctor Kramer ushered Ian out of the room, commenced her examination. Her diagnosis was something of a relief.

"As I thought, no lasting damage from the fall. The wooziness you are experiencing is probably just a touch of flu. Nothing to worry about."

"I will not pass out every time I stand up?"

"The fainting fit was a symptom of the flu, I would say, rather than vice versa." Doctor Kramer pulled on her coat, smiled. There was something very reassuring about her. "I should stay in bed for a couple of days, if I were you. Let your friends make a fuss of you."

"I hate fuss."

"Humour them. They just want to feel useful. I must go now, I am rushed off my feet today, but I shall call back tomorrow or the day after — if you don't think it too much of a fuss, that is!"

It was impossible not to respond to Doctor Kramer's warm smile, and her voice had a soothing lilt to it. Letitia was reminded of the feeling of *déjà-vu* she had experienced last night, but Doctor Kramer departed and the feeling faded again.

The fuss began. It was not, however, as bad as she had expected, and the subject of her health was soon eclipsed by the momentous events of last night's raid. London was still reeling, by all accounts. There had been nothing to match it throughout the blitz. Was it a taste of things to come?

That evening, there was an alert just before ten. Letitia struggled down to the basement, leaning on Ian's arm.

"Now we're really for it," whispered Clive. After the inferno of last night, he no longer thought of air raids as a big adventure.

They sat waiting, faces pinched and drawn, ears straining for the sound of approaching aircraft. But it turned out to be a false alarm. The all clear sounded, and Letitia returned thankfully to bed.

Flu and the effects of the fall kept her bedridden for a week. There were no more raids, but people lived in a state of fear, expecting the worst. The next raid, they said, would be heavier than the last — might even be the knockout blow which would end the war. But the days passed and the knockout blow did not come. The night skies remained empty.

Ian departed, heading back to North Africa via Buckinghamshire and a brief meeting with his father: making the effort, as Letitia had asked. Doctor Kramer called regularly, seemed pleased with Letitia's progress. She had a friendly, no-nonsense manner which Letitia warmed to. Mrs Mansell, on the other hand, regarded the red-haired locum with suspicion.

"I don't hold with women doctors, and that's the truth."

"There is no reason why women shouldn't be just as good doctors as men."

"If you say so."

"I for one like Doctor Kramer. She is . . ." Letitia searched for the right words, surprised herself by saying, ". . . like an old friend: it's as if she were an old friend."

Mrs Mansell pursed her lips. "Well, that can't be right, for a start. *Over-familiar*, I call it. Don't go letting yourself be put upon, Mrs Warner."

Letitia stifled a smile, sensing that Mrs Mansell was marking her territory. "I'll come to no harm with you to look out for me, Mrs Mansell."

"Yes, well . . ." Plumping the pillows, Mrs Mansell seemed to pound them rather vigorously to Letitia's mind, before replacing them. "I'm only doing my job, Mrs Warner."

Doctor Kramer, too, was only doing her job, but she had a way about her that made it seem so much more. One felt that one had known her for years. It was, as Letitia had said to Mrs Mansell, as if she was an old friend.

An illusion, Letitia told herself: simply a well-rehearsed bedside manner. Perhaps Mrs Mansell was right; perhaps one should not allow oneself to get taken in.

"You don't seem yourself today, Mrs Warner." It was the doctor's fourth or fifth visit. "Anything I should know about? Any aches or pains?"

"I feel fit as a fiddle," said Letitia; but that wasn't entirely true.

Doctor Kramer looked at her thoughtfully. "You had a close encounter with a bomb last autumn, I believe. Your regular doctor told me about it."

"You talked about me?"

"We talked about all his patients — now my patients for the duration, of course."

Doctor Kramer was brisk, professional, reassuring. It was ridiculous to be wary of her. One shouldn't be influenced by Mrs Mansell's suspicious mind. If one didn't feel quite right, then it was a medical matter. It was quite in order to discuss a medical matter with one's doctor.

She tried to explain.

"Being caught in a bomb blast," said Doctor Kramer, "is enough to knock the stuffing out of anybody, young or old."

But in Letitia's mind it had not started with the bomb; it had started with her fall on Oxford Street. At the time she had not taken much notice. There had been other things on her mind, and there'd been Hugh to think of: one had to put on a brave face for Hugh. In retrospect, it seemed very lucky to have escaped without breaking anything, though it had been bad enough even without that, grazing her hands and knees and jolting every bone in her body, leaving her shocked and shaken.

It had started off wet that day, she told Doctor Kramer, but she had not let that put her off, and the ordinary act of shopping had become exciting and patriotic in bomb-blasted Oxford Street where defiant signs declared *Business As Usual* and *Hitler Won't Beat Us*. She had felt buoyant — almost youthful — until, browsing in Selfridge's, an overheard remark had worked as a catalyst, bringing back memories of Angelica.

Letitia paused. She had rather strayed from the point, thinking aloud. She was supposed to be talking about the effects of the fall, asking for Doctor Kramer's medical opinion, but the fall did not make sense without mentioning Angelica. Letitia wanted to make it clear that she had not tripped because she was a doddery old woman but because she had been too upset to see where she was going.

And yet, perhaps that in itself was a symptom of old age, memories crowding in on her and — she glanced at Doctor Kramer — her mind playing tricks.

The doctor was sitting on the edge of the bed, neat in her grey skirt and jacket, her eyes a brilliant green. Looking at her, it was as if she had stepped out of a dream, or from the pages of a long-forgotten novel: one felt that one had met her before. It was this which led one to let one's guard down — to talk about things that were best left hidden.

But why shouldn't I think of Angelica if I want to, Letitia said to herself with a surge of anger; *why shouldn't I speak about her, too?* Unlike their father, Letitia had never been ashamed of her younger sister, or so she had told herself; but keeping quiet, avoiding the issue, wasn't she treating Angelica as a skeleton in the family closet? Was she not, in effect, colluding with her father to erase Angelica from history?

Some secrets, Letitia realized with sudden clarity, become shameful by the very act of keeping them. It had taken a knock on the head the other night for her to grasp this. The terrible air raid had not been without its uses. One might even say that it was Hitler who had paved the way for her.

"I had a brother," Letitia said, her voice sounding in her own ears surprisingly firm and composed, "who, as a boy, was the apple of my father's eye. But my father was nothing if not prudent. He wanted another son — a spare, as he put it — in case anything should happen to Jocelyn. But he was thwarted in his aim when Angelica was born, a girl. He came to regard her as a miscalculation. But that was not the end of it."

Letitia reached back in her memory, dredging up her shock and confusion at seeing her father's reaction as Angelica's shortcomings slowly became apparent. Shame, humiliation, disgust: she now recognized these for what they were. Yet for a time she had thought her father merely looked down on Angelica because she was a girl. Letitia had known, even at her tender age, that girls were inferior: her father had made it clear. She had accepted it, as children do, and it had not lessened her love for her big brother, the chosen one. It seemed entirely natural that he should be put on a pedestal. But she had loved Angelica too: Angelica who had laughed a lot, who had been unfailingly happy and open-hearted and, at times, touchingly helpless. Father had said that Angelica was *different*; but if she'd been any other way, she wouldn't have been Angelica. It was only gradually that Letitia had come to realize her father saw Angelica's strong points as her weakness, that her naivety was something to regret and feel ashamed of.

It was much, much later when a change had come over Angelica. She had become silent, withdrawn, weepy; she no longer looked people in the eye. Perhaps,

Letitia had thought, she had finally realized that she was flawed; perhaps she was lamenting her inadequacy.

"I never thought to question it," said Letitia. "I never thought to wonder what had happened to her."

She paused, gazing round the room, seeing it as if from a great distance, the window small and remote, the sunshine outside like a glimpse of another world. There was a web of memories like a mist around her — or was it tears in her eyes? Doctor Kramer had moved closer, was holding her hand, and it felt entirely natural, as if she was a little girl walking with her nurse in the garden at Chanderton long ago.

"You haven't told me what you overheard," Doctor Kramer prompted gently. "In Selfridge's that day."

Selfridge's, thought Letitia. And yet, having come so far, why not finish telling Angelica's story? She was not ashamed of her sister. It was the others who should be ashamed, for what they had done to Angelica.

Letitia took a breath. "I was in Selfridge's, last autumn, listening to someone else's conversation: a bad habit of mine."

"We all do it from time to time."

"I wish I hadn't that day. It was when the scales fell from my eyes. I understood at last what had happened to Angelica."

There had been a pushy, brassy-faced girl, the type one saw more and more of these days. She had been wearing a WAAF uniform, talking to a hopeful-looking Guards captain. Letitia, looking through a rack of skirts, had felt rather sorry for the soldier who was, she'd surmised, doomed to disappointment if he

142

expected any change from the fast and ambitious WAAF girl. Her sights were no doubt set on higher ranks. Rubbing material between her fingers, Letitia had suddenly frozen as the girl was speaking.

"Of course, in the old days, in the big houses, rather than lock their retarded daughters in an asylum, they often used to keep them up in the attic. They came in useful," she'd added, *sotto voce*, just the other side of the skirts, "if there were male guests who wanted certain . . . comforts."

She hadn't given a knowing wink, thought Letitia: that was just imagination, embellishing after the fact; but the effect had been the same, the WAAF girl indicating that she was a woman of the world, a modern girl, and nothing could shock her.

Letitia remembered feeling dizzy, stumbling into the rack, dropping her umbrella, grabbing hold of the skirts to keep her balance. An assistant had come bustling up. Was madam unwell? Would madam like to sit down for a moment? It had been just what Letitia would have liked: to sit down, to catch her breath, to put her thoughts in order. But the WAAF girl had been watching by then — quite a crowd had gathered, in fact — and it had seemed essential not to appear weak and fragile in front of such a slip of a girl. Declining any help, waving the assistant aside, Letitia had swept out into the noise and bustle of the street where, leaning against a wall, she had opened her bottle of black market cognac and taken a surreptitious swig or two to settle her nerves. But her nerves hadn't settled and she had wanted to escape: get away from Selfridge's, get away from the terrible realization taking shape in her mind. It had been then that, hurrying to cross the road in a state of agitation, she had tripped up the far kerb and gone sprawling over the pavement, to be rescued by that very gallant if somewhat lugubrious policeman.

"Gallant and rather handsome," said Letitia lightly, glossing over the turmoil of the event. "I never did thank him properly."

"But Mrs Warner ..." — Doctor Kramer was gripping her hand still, earnest green eyes searching her face — "surely you can't believe that ...?"

"I think there can be little doubt that something of the sort went on." What other explanation could there be? Angelica as an adult had been a pale shadow of her laughing, happy childhood self: a thin and desolate waif who flinched at the sound of a voice, recoiled if anyone tried to touch her; who was particularly terrified of men. Letitia had seen little of her in those years, married as she'd been and preoccupied with her own problems. She had hardly been aware as Angelica slowly faded away into an early grave.

"I can't believe that such awful things really happened," said Doctor Kramer.

"That is how they got away with it. Nobody believed it was possible. Nobody suspected. Suspicions of that nature were brushed under the carpet."

"But your father was a bishop, a man of God, beyond reproach. I have been reading about him, there's a new book. He did good works, helped the poor, was a missionary in his youth."

144

That book again, thought Letitia: coming back to haunt her. She looked at Doctor Kramer with sudden suspicion. Why had she been reading it? Coincidence?

But even without the book, no one would believe her father capable of cruelty — of evil. *I would not believe it myself*, thought Letitia, *if I did not know: know what he did to Jocelyn, what he did to me . . .*

"In his public life he appeared a great man," said Letitia warily, watching the doctor closely. "Possibly he was. Possibly he did do good works. But I only ever knew him as a father; and as a father he failed us."

"Us?"

"His children. And our mother, too. He failed her." *Killed her . . . .* "He was warned that another confinement would weaken her, perhaps fatally; but he took the chance because he wanted a second son: the spare."

"That was a typical attitude of the time!" cried Doctor Kramer, getting up and pacing the room. "A son meant everything, was given every advantage, whereas a girl was merely decorative, a possession, something to bargain over, to sell in marriage to the highest bidder. And once they were married, women lost everything: their name, their belongings, their freedom — even their lives, as your mother's story shows!"

The room — which had seemed tranquil, moiled in the past, weighed down with memories — was suddenly swirling with emotion, Doctor Kramer's passion whipping up like a sudden squall. And in the midst of it Letitia suddenly heard a voice from long ago, clipped,

145

crabbed, precise: ... *those suffragettes ... dreadful unnatural women* ... Connie Lambton, in the blue drawing-room at the Manor, talking about her duplicitous guest. *We were most dreadfully deceived in that whole business ... it was quite unforgivable ...*

"Megan O'Connor," said Letitia.

Doctor Kramer stopped her pacing, turned, her expression circumspect, eyes veiled, the passionate depths that for a moment had broken through now hidden again.

"Megan Kramer, now, of course," she said slowly, "but, yes, that's me. How clever of you to remember. It must be nearly forty years. I recognized you at once, of course. You haven't changed at all. But I didn't think you'd know me."

Megan O'Connor, Letitia repeated to herself. The girl who had so fascinated Hugh and the Lambton boys — bewitched them; Connie, too, for that matter: because it was only in hindsight that she had taken against the red-haired Irish girl.

And now, all these years later, I too have been bewitched, thought Letitia. *She has put me at my ease, wormed it out of me, things I have never told anyone.* But at least she knew she was still sharp. She had felt there was something familiar about Doctor Kramer: she had been right.

". . . and I will pop in again in a day or two . . ." Doctor Kramer was getting ready to leave, seemed in a hurry suddenly, gathering her bag and coat. "You are well on the way to recovery now, Mrs Warner, fall or no fall. It takes time at your age, that is all." She paused at the door. "Try not to dwell too much on the past. It doesn't do any good, I find. We can't change what happened."

She was gone, and Letitia lay back, closed her eyes, feeling suddenly drained. Why had she let her tongue run away with her like that? Yes, it had come as a relief to be able to talk about Angelica at last; but talking to a stranger — an anonymous professional — was one thing; it was quite another when that stranger turned out to be someone one knew.

Yet what did she actually know about Megan O'Connor? Letitia searched her memory for a picture of Megan as she'd been in 1902 when staying at the Manor, but all she could come up with was the lopsided face of that dreadful doll. Hugh had been quite taken with the ugly thing. What had become of it in the end?

Megan O'Connor . . . . There was a twinge of guilt associated with the name. It came back to her. The letter, of course. The letter from 1915 which she had never answered, never passed on to Hugh; which she had still, bundled up with Hugh's letters from the front: a disturbing reminder of how easy it was to fall into the trap of interfering, of playing God, something she had always promised herself never to do.

Would she have to confess all to Hugh now? Why oh why hadn't she just passed the letter on at the time, like she should have done? Connie Lambton was to blame. It had been something Connie had said that had raised doubts, led one to question whether Megan O'Connor was a suitable acquaintance for Hugh.

Letitia's eyes roved behind paper-thin lids as she tried to recall what it was that Connie had said; some hint or information that the Irish girl was no better than she should be. Something to do with Julian. But surely Connie had got her wires crossed — if she hadn't simply made the whole thing up. One was reminded of those atrocity stories she had repeated so avidly in the war: it was only later that one realized they were compete bunkum. One had begun then to wonder if one could believe even half of what Connie said. Not that one would have said as much to her face: not then, after the war, when the poor thing had been at death's door. It was the war that had killed her in the end: less directly but just as surely as it had killed her three sons, Julian, Justin and . . . and the other one . . .

What had the other one been called? The things one forgot in old age, the simplest things, a name one had known for forty years.

Trying to recall the name of Connie's middle son, Letitia's head slowly tilted on one side and she drifted into sleep.

"I can't leave you alone for a moment, Aunt, without you getting into a scrape of one kind or another."

"Hugh!" Letitia surfaced from her afternoon nap to find the room bright with sunshine and her great-nephew standing by the bed with his hat in his hand. "I didn't know you were coming!"

"I wasn't so sure myself, and as it is I can only manage one night. I have to be back tomorrow."

"All the same, it is good to see you." She reached for his hand — those long, pale fingers; smiled up at him. His old grey suit looked decidedly shabby hanging off his wiry frame; in fact, he looked shabby all round, flecks of grey in his hair and lines under his eyes and a hint of that hangdog expression which took her back nearly forty years, to a boy fresh from India staring moodily out at the rain. Since that day, she reflected, she had been ever-present in Hugh's life, sometimes stepping forward, often retreating into the background. Getting the balance right was like walking a tightrope. By luck or judgement, she had not often put a foot wrong; but now she had another decision to make, another tricky passage to negotiate. Should she tell Hugh about Doctor Kramer? About the letter in 1915? Why rake over the past? Was it not best to let sleeping dogs lie? Yet in a way she felt she had no choice. Confession was inevitable. She had interfered in something she did not fully understand, and now she had to pay the price.

Hugh had been anxious about Letitia since hearing of her dizzy spell and fall. He had made a dash to London at the earliest opportunity. Arriving at the house, he had been accosted by Mrs Mansell: he was not to tire the old lady with too much talk, he was not to get her over-excited, she needed peace and quiet and plenty of rest. The doctor said it was a touch of flu, but doctors didn't know everything, women doctors least of all. Hugh had been irritated by Mrs Mansell's peremptory manner, bossing him about like she owned the place:

why did Aunt Letitia put up with her? But he'd also been alarmed, wondering if things were more serious than he'd realized. *A touch of flu* might mean anything, could be significant at Letitia's age. He'd half expected to come up and find her at death's door. His heart had been in his mouth as he entered the room and saw her lying there apparently unconscious. But she'd been asleep, not unconscious and, waking, she'd greeted him in her usual indomitable style.

He nodded and smiled, felt her hand squeezing his, watching her all the time from behind his façade. She was not at death's door, that much was obvious, but didn't she seem a little frailer than normal? And she was rambling, rather, something about a letter: he was not really listening, his mind still a jumble of codes and ciphers and train times.

He made an effort to concentrate. Somebody had sent a letter, Letitia had not replied, she seemed to think it remiss of her. It had happened, it seemed, during the last war — years ago: one would have thought she'd have forgotten about it by now. But wasn't it typical of Aunt Letitia, the embodiment of rectitude? No doubt it was all down to her Victorian upbringing, doing one's duty and so on and so forth . . .

It took some time for Letitia's meaning to penetrate the miasma in Hugh's head, and even then he couldn't piece it all together: the letter, Megan O'Connor, something about a doctor . . . He was still struggling with it when the doctor herself walked in. Then, suddenly, he understood.

150

He recognized her instantly — would have known her anywhere; but he couldn't work out if she recognized him. His senses were reeling and he could hear a voice in his head, a Cockney voice: the long dead tommy in no-man's land. *I like to collect souvenirs, to remind me of the places I've been, the girls I've had . . .*

Girls such as Megan O'Connor?

Except she was Megan Kramer, now. Married.

Married.

"Hello, Hugh." She was greeted him coolly, guarded.

"Megan."

He was as tongue-tied as that boy in Southampton Street twenty-one years ago, sweat running down his back, mouth dry, hand trembling. He took a deep breath.

"Broken any windows lately?"

It was an absurd thing to say — absolutely ridiculous. He could see out of the corner of his eye Aunt Letitia looking at him in amazement. But he had not known what he was going to say until it was too late to stop himself.

There was a pause then Megan — Doctor Kramer — said, "I've rather gone off breaking windows. I was in Soho last June, when the Italians declared war. It was not an edifying sight, all those restaurants wrecked."

That puts me in my place, thought Hugh, watching as Megan turned away, busied herself with her patient.

He retreated to the window, feeling like a flunky dancing attendance, ignored, unwanted. Megan was brisk and efficient, took Letitia's temperature, felt her pulse, asked pertinent questions. Was this really her —

151

really Megan O'Connor — or was it just another dream? There had been a time when he couldn't sleep without dreaming of her. She had appeared anywhere and everywhere, in all manner of guises; for her to turn up now as a doctor seemed at once incredible and yet strangely inevitable.

He stole glances at her, convincing himself that she was real, that there was no mistake. There were lines around her mouth and eyes, her cheeks seemed slightly sunken, she was thinner; but her hair was still a fiery red, her eyes still bright with possibility just as they'd been when she ran into him in Southampton Street all those years ago. A judicious and sparing use of make-up gave to her face a mature and incisive beauty. Next to her he felt rather old, rather worn, the years having taken their toll.

She was already getting ready to leave, snapping her bag shut, exchanging a few last words with Letitia. Hugh was both relieved and disappointed. He had imagined this moment so many times, meeting her again; but it had turned out to be a damp squib. The years had driven them apart; they were strangers to each other.

In the doorway Megan paused, looked back at him. "We must catch up sometime."

"Yes," said Hugh. "Yes."

He struggled for something else to say but it was too late, she had gone. He turned to the window, looked out, but saw nothing except a golden haze, tears blurring his vision.

Well, he said to himself, *so that's over.*

152

Later he helped Letitia downstairs. She insisted on getting up for dinner.

"I'm quite all right, just a little shaky on my legs still. It will pass, Doctor Kramer assures me." She looked at him, her arm threaded through his. "Why the long face?"

Hugh sighed. "I feel old."

"Oh, Hugh!" Letitia laughed. "Next to me you are a spring chicken!"

"Why must we go all the way down to the kitchen? What is wrong with the dining-room?"

"We eat in the kitchen in case there is an alert — although, saying that, there have been no raids for over a week now."

"Ominous, I call it," said Mrs Mansell, appearing at the foot of the stairs, wiping her hands on her apron.

"Yes, that's just what it is: ominous," said Letitia. "I feel that they are saving something really big for us."

"Perhaps," said Hugh shortly.

Mrs Mansell looked at him, pursed her lips; but all she said was, "Dinner is ready."

Next morning, sitting on a crowded train making unsteady progress out of bomb-damaged London, Hugh recalled Aunt Letitia's sense of foreboding. She was not the only one. The question was on everyone's lips: when will the Luftwaffe be back? But there were other questions crowding Hugh's mind: questions about Megan Kramer. Married now — well, so was he, technically — a doctor, a changed woman. For all he

153

knew she might not even remember those April days in 1912. He'd sometimes wondered since if that time had been a mirage, his feelings unreal. But now he knew beyond doubt that he'd loved her back then — because he loved her still. It had all come flooding back the moment she walked into the room. All the same, a part of him wished he could have gone on as he'd been, not knowing. If their situation in April 1912 had been hopeless, then now it was beyond recovery. He was losing her all over again, but this time it was final.

The train jerked to a halt once more. They had finally left London behind. Hugh looked out at a field of green wheat. A blue sky arched overhead, smudged with grey cloud. The branches of an elm swayed in the breeze. There was so much inside his head, and so little of it that he could let out. Megan would not be interested in his love. And as for the Germans, he knew but could not tell anyone that for now London was reprieved. Decoded Enigma messages had revealed the Luftwaffe had gone East: Hitler's next target was the Soviet Union.

CHAPTER
SEVEN

When Hugh returned to London that summer on a flying visit, he found Aunt Letitia back on her feet, getting out and about again. She used a walking stick now, he noted, but in essentials she seemed to be back to her old self.

Megan Kramer was still around. As far as Hugh could tell, she called now as a friend rather than in a professional capacity. That his aunt and Megan should be friends seemed incongruous to Hugh at first: they were separated by age, by class, by everything. Yet in other ways they were similar: vigorous, independent, not afraid to voice their opinions. Aunt Letitia, as Hugh had long known, was kind, compassionate, generous: even that old trout Mrs Mansell had been won over. It came as no surprise that Megan should like her too. As for Megan, there was something beguiling about her, something out of the ordinary: Hugh had never been able to put his finger on it.

He remembered how, at the age of five, he had been captivated by her, had never met anyone like her. The Lambton boys, too, had fallen under her spell. Hugh had competed with them, trying to please her, to serve her in any way he could. The jealousy he had felt back then was still vivid in his mind — so powerful even after all this time that he wondered how his five-year-old self had been able to contain it. He had lain awake at The Firs, clutching Raggety Peg to his chest and telling her in a whisper all the ways he had devised to rid himself of his rivals: pushing them down the well at the Manor, locking them in the attic at The Firs, or sending them away to be killed by the wicked Boers.

He could not say any of this to Megan. What, then, could he say? Did she want him to say anything? But he could not let his visit pass without making some sort of effort, futile though it might prove.

His imagination ran ahead. He conjured up an intimate restaurant, candlelight, a gentle piano in the background and the two of them picking up where they had left off. But it did not turn out like that at all. She was busy, could spare only a half-hour, suggested a walk. Thus they came to be strolling in the summer sunshine as the war raged on unabated, the Wehrmacht advancing hundreds of miles at a time in the Soviet Union, capturing Lvov, Minsk and Smolensk, taking millions of prisoners, bombing Moscow from the air; while in the desert a lull in the fighting did not mean that Ian was out of danger.

Those battlefields seemed impossibly remote in the somnolent heat of Hyde Park, with the smell of grass invoking pre-war memories of picnics and languid games of tennis; yet all round were reminders of war: broken buildings, people in uniform, barrage balloons in the sky. Megan seemed at ease with the silence between them, walked with assurance, her heels

156

clicking rhythmically on the path. She wore her hat at an angle and her hair, once straight, was now done in a permanent wave. Hugh would have liked to examine her from top to toe, to catalogue everything that was different and everything that was the same, but he was too shy to take more than an occasional glance, as diffident and unsure of himself as he'd been at fifteen — the only saving grace being that he no longer blushed so readily.

When they began to talk at last, they talked about Aunt Letitia: a safe subject.

"It seems a strange quirk of fate," said Megan, "that has led me to become acquainted with Mrs Warner after such a long time. You can't imagine how I envied you when I was seven. There was I up at the Manor where everything was oh-so-proper and Mrs Lambton only had eyes for her boys; and there were you at the homely Firs with a lovely old aunt who made time for everyone and lavished affection on you. I didn't think it at all fair!" She laughed, stirring in Hugh memories of London in 1912; but then she said, "All that is ancient history. Let us bring ourselves up to date."

That was easier said than done. Hugh could not tell her much about his hush-hush job in Buckinghamshire, and Megan spoke only in general terms about her own work. He wanted very much to ask about her husband, the mysterious Mr Kramer who was never mentioned, but he hadn't plucked up courage before Megan suddenly said, "Tell me about your wife. I heard somewhere that you'd married. *The Times*, perhaps."

There was nothing hush-hush about his marriage, but when it came to it he found it as difficult a subject as his job. What could he say about Cynthia?

Once upon a time he had been besotted with Cynthia: by her gentleness and innocence and school-girl charm; and he'd been touched by the tears she shed when he told her he would not marry anyone until after the war. In those days — the spring of 1918 — *after the war* signified a vague and distant point far in the future: perhaps years away, perhaps never. People had already been talking about *the 1919 offensive*. No one had predicted that the terrible slaughter would end so suddenly that very November.

The Armistice, demobilization, marriage: these events had pointed to a fresh start. Hugh had felt as if he'd aged ten years in the trenches, but when the nightmare had come to an end he had woken up and found that he was still only twenty-two. The world was full of peace and promise. He was set fair to live happily ever after.

Looking back more than twenty years later, he was cynically amused by that younger Hugh's gullibility. He felt there must have been clues that he missed, indications he ignored, pointers that might have warned him of what was to come. Disillusionment had been quick to set in. Cynthia had been unhappy in the house he had bought in Northamptonshire which was, she had said over and over again, too small, with too few servants, and too far away from her friends. Those friends, Hugh soon discovered, were a ghastly set: snobs, profiteers, incipient Fascists. None of them had been closer to the front than the comfortable chateaux which had served as staff headquarters. They were malcontents, too, outraged that the war's end did not signify a return to Edwardian opulence and rigid class distinctions. When the Labour Party formed a government in 1924, they spoke of it as the thin end of the wedge and warned of an impending Bolshevik revolution. The Zinoviev letter only served to prove their point.

Hugh had been appalled by those people. He could find no common ground with them. That had not helped things between him and Cynthia. But what had really undermined the marriage was Cynthia's antipathy to what she termed Hugh's *pestering* her. It had come as a shock to Hugh that a woman who had nursed soldiers for two years could still be so sexually ignorant. She found Hugh's advances repellent. She had tolerated them to start with, accepted that it was a wife's duty, but Ian's birth had changed all that. She would never ever, she'd announced, put herself through such an ordeal again. Hugh was banished to the spare room. Cynthia's bedroom door remained resolutely shut. Two years into his marriage, Hugh began to suspect he had made the biggest mistake of his life, but there had been nothing to do but carry on, make the best of a bad job, for Ian's sake if nothing else. And so the marriage, fatally wounded, died a long slow death.

To explain any of this to Megan seemed out of the question. It was all too close to the bone. And no doubt Megan had made a success of her own marriage which would make him feel even worse. But he had to say something, offer some account of himself.

"My wife and I are . . . separated."

"I'm sorry."

"It was for the best."

She sounded like she meant it, that she really was sorry; but he didn't want her sympathy and he didn't want to dwell on the subject of Cynthia. He searched for something else.

"It's . . . strange . . . that you're a doctor."

"Does it really seem so incredible?"

"It's not what I would have . . . well, predicted."

"And what would you have *predicted*?"

They were up another blind alley. Every opening led to fresh difficulties, embarrassment, confusion. All the questions he wanted to ask seemed impossible. How had she found the money to study, to qualify? How had she contrived to get by all these years? He remembered her threadbare clothes, her single room. He remembered, too, the tommy in no-man's land: *she put on a good performance, if you know what I mean; and afterwards I palmed me money back . . . .* That suggested one way at least in which she might have earned her keep. In 1912, Hugh had not thought to wonder how Megan survived. Her poverty had been part of the charm, part of the adventure: like Marie Antoinette playing at peasants. It was years before he realized — before it actually struck home — that an unearned income was the exception rather than the rule. And then, in 1917, the tommy had unwittingly provided an explanation which Hugh had not wanted to hear — which he had thrust to the back of his mind — but which had festered there, tainting all his memories of Megan, yet never destroying them entirely.

"I suppose you think the medical profession should not be for the likes of me," said Megan, breaking a silence of which Hugh had barely been aware.

"No, of course I don't think that, it's just . . ."

"Just what?"

"I never expected —"

"Never expected to see me again?"

"I wanted to see you. I never stopped thinking about you."

"But you just disappeared without a word."

"I was . . . confused. My father had just died and I couldn't . . . couldn't . . ."

"And then not so much as a letter or postcard, nothing. What was I meant to think?"

"I . . . I felt guilty if you must know."

"Guilty?"

"Guilty about what we'd done. It was . . . sinful."

"And that's all it was to you, something sinful, something to run away from? And I suppose you thought I was to blame, I was the siren who had lured you from the path of righteousness. It's always the woman who's at fault."

Hugh was appalled by the direction the conversation had taken, cringed under the amused glance of a passing Wren who obviously thought she was witnessing a lovers' tiff. He had given Megan the wrong impression. She did not realize how he had cherished those few heady days in 1912, how they meant more to

161

him than almost anything. And yet he *had* felt guilty in the aftermath, struggling to come to terms with all that had happened: his adventure with Megan, his father's death. In the turmoil of his mind, the two events had somehow become linked as he sought for explanations of the tragedy of *Titanic*. He remembered sitting in the library at Overton, wanting to be alone, wrestling with his thoughts. He had by chance come across a book by his great-grandfather the Bishop that described the evil temptations of women, their lack of moral fibre, their propensity for leading men astray, the punishment of God on those who transgressed. It had seemed to fit at the time, it had seemed to offer a solution.

Another silence had fallen between them; their steps had slowed; they seemed now to be walking aimlessly. They passed an elderly couple sitting on a bench, reading from the same newspaper, leaning in to one another. Hugh looked at them, then looked away. Sunlight glinted on the Serpentine. It was hot, breathless. Hugh's clothes hung heavy, stifling him, his shirt clinging, damp with sweat.

It was all going wrong. Instead of getting reacquainted with Megan he was finding out just how little he knew about her — about the real Megan, not the one who had haunted his dreams for thirty years. They were getting further apart with every step.

They drifted to a halt, standing hesitant on the path, looking ahead, looking back, looking up at the blue of the sky: looking anywhere but at each other. But after a while he found his eyes drawn to her, watched her

162

would recommend him to Megan. "Your . . . husband. A refugee, you said. A Jew?"

"A communist. At least, he used to be a communist. I rather think he changed his mind about that around about the time of the Nazi-Soviet Pact. He couldn't stomach what he was being told by Comintern. He knows at firsthand what the Nazis are like whereas we, for all our propaganda, do not."

Hugh squirmed, another pitfall opening before him as he remembered his time in Germany in the twenties. He'd felt a certain distaste for the Nazis back then, but he'd been blind to what they were really like. No doubt Heinrich — that paragon Heinrich — no doubt even back then he —

Megan was still talking. ". . . and now that Hitler has invaded Russia, I expect Moscow has changed its tune — not that Heinrich will be inclined to swallow Comintern's line so easily in future."

All this talk of marriages of convenience, communism, the Comintern: it was as if another illusion was being peeled away and Hugh was seeing another Megan, cold, calculating, strongly political. Yet perhaps she'd always been like that, perhaps her beauty had blinded him. Had she not smashed windows in the name of female emancipation in 1912? One could not get much more militant than that.

"You're a Communist, then?" said Hugh dully.

"Good grief, no!" Megan looked startled at the suggestion. "I'm a paid-up member of the Labour Party, if you must know — though that is seen as tantamount to communism in certain circles." She glanced at him sidelong, wary. "What about you? I seem to remember hearing or reading — I may have got this wrong — that your wife was mixed up with Mosley's lot?"

"Cynthia and I have gone our separate ways in politics as in everything else." The hope which had leapt in Hugh's heart just minutes before was now extinguished as he remembered how mistaken he'd been about Cynthia — how mistaken he was about everything. "I can't imagine how we ever found enough in common to want to get married."

Megan said nothing and they walked on for a time before coming to a halt, avoiding each other's eyes as before, standing in silence. Except that this silence had a different quality, there was a background hum and bustle. Looking round, Hugh realized they had left the park, were standing in Knightsbridge. The moment of parting loomed suddenly near.

"Well . . ." said Hugh, tongue-tied.

Megan smiled, a little sadly it seemed. "This has not been a success, has it?"

"It's been . . . I've enjoyed . . . we should . . . try again. Try again."

"But everything is so uncertain. We are no longer in control of our own destinies. In a month or so, Russia will fall and then Hitler will turn his attention back to us. Who knows what will happen then? It's not a time for beginnings."

"This is not a beginning. It began long ago, in Warwickshire, when we were children."

"Oh Hugh." That smile again: valedictory was the word. She was slipping from his grasp just as she had always done in his dreams, carried away like Raggety Peg on a rain-swollen stream.

He watched her walk off in the direction of Hyde Park Corner, dwindling into the crowds. He had not told her how he felt — how did he feel? — he had learned virtually nothing, did not even know where she lived. It had not been a success, as she had said. He had wild ideas of running after her, taking her in his arms, saying, "I love you!", or simply kissing her, but it was not the way he was made. Sensible, cautious, boring: that was him, always had been.

He began walking, turned into the Brompton Road. London basked in sunshine, the terror of the air raids fading, the war remote; but Hugh merely felt miserable as he made his way slowly back to Letitia's.

Preoccupied as he was when he got back, even he could not fail to notice that there was an atmosphere in the house. Mrs Mansell's expression, grim at the best of times, was this afternoon positively splenetic. What was wrong now? Hugh hesitated to ask.

"It's Peggy," said Letitia, *sotto voce*. "She is *with child* as they say in polite society."

"But I thought her husband was a POW?"

"So he is."

"Then . . . ah, I see."

Hugh sighed. Letitia's house, once a refuge, a haven of peace, was anything but now that the Mansells had taken root. He decided that, all things considered, he

167

would be glad when the time came for him to return to Buckinghamshire.

Peggy's baby caused a great deal of trouble one way or another. Stubborn and sulking, Peggy said that she had "done nothing wrong" and "couldn't say" how she came to be pregnant. "In which case," Mrs Mansell remarked sourly, "it must be the second Immaculate Conception." The name of Ian was not mentioned but with hints and dark looks Mrs Mansell made it clear that she thought him not entirely blameless in the matter. After careful consideration, Letitia felt that Mrs Mansell might have a point. But Peggy had told her story and she stuck to it.

The child, Peggy's second, was born in February 1942, Ian still entirely in the dark. As it happened, whilst his daughter was making her debut in the world, he was arriving in Alexandria on leave, the front having stabilized for the moment after Rommel's rapid advance to Gazala. Alexandria was teeming. A fierce sun beat down from a bleached sky. A forest of masts and funnels marked the docks. In the dusty streets, the crowds ebbed and flowed in the face of packed trams and army trucks and all manner of horse-drawn vehicles. Beggars and salesmen accosted passers-by.

Ian took refuge in the cool and shade of a shop, pushing his way past piles of rugs, and bales of silk and cotton. The shelves on either side were stacked with jewellery and perfume in bottles.

"Something for your wife, sir?" said the shopkeeper. "For your fiancée?"

"No wife," said Ian. "No fiancée."

"Then this, sir. Ambergris. Very good, very potent. Will make you a powerful lover, sir."

Ian laughed. "After all those months in the desert, I've no need of help in that department, trust me."

"But, sir! You are not going, sir? You have bought nothing, sir!"

Outside the shop, Ian mopped the sweat off his brow as Egyptian boys came running, grabbed his hands, tugged on his arms.

"Soldier! Hey, soldier! You want a bint? Then you see my sister! She very nice, very clean."

And Ian allowed himself to be led through the crowds, resolved to make the most of his leave, to forget the war — forget everything — until he had to return to the front for another instalment of the Benghazi Handicap.

It was just over a month later when Hugh, snatching a weekend away from Buckinghamshire, travelled to London, reading his newspaper from front to back as the train inched its way towards Euston. The war news was all bad. Singapore had fallen, Rangoon was occupied, the Japanese march on India looked unstoppable. But the printed words blurred and shifted as he turned page after page, thinking of the letter burning a hole in his pocket.

It should not have come as a surprise. By rights, they should have divorced years ago. He accepted that his marriage was over, but divorce marked The End, ruled a line under that chapter of his life, forced him to take stock. And why now: why had Cynthia chosen this moment to act, after all this time? Could it be that she'd found someone else, wanted to marry again?

She had never been short of admirers. Some of them she had singled out for special attention even before their marriage had disintegrated. *Your lovers*, Hugh had once called them in a fit of pique — said it to her face; and lovers they had remained in Hugh's mind. But Cynthia at the time had laughed, as if the idea was absurd: which it was, for Hugh knew that it was not just him who was forever barred from her bed. Sex she found repellent, but men she loved. She craved attention, longed to be admired. Yet the men she took up with! There was one Hugh particularly remembered from their time in Germany, a superior specimen of Aryan manhood called Ulf, who had been a staunch anti-communist and later, so Hugh had heard, a captain in the SS. But many of Cynthia's other "lovers" had been equally unpalatable. Hugh had felt humiliated by them, though he'd never been able to decide if this was because of the way she flirted with them openly in front of him, or because her choice seemed in some way to reflect badly on him.

Hugh sighed, folded his newspaper, put it aside, looked out at the heavy grey sky pressing down on the grey London suburbs. He wondered if he should tell Aunt Letitia about his impending divorce. Perhaps not. Going over and over it would be like rubbing salt in the wound. And his aunt would not be able to enlighten him as to Cynthia's plans. It would be better to question Ian surreptitiously next time he came on leave

— if he ever did come on leave again. There'd been no word from him in months. There seemed to be a lull in the desert just now, but no news did not necessarily mean good news. Anything might be happening out there.

Letitia's house was bedlam. Hugh, craving peace and quiet, wondered how she put up with it, yet she seemed to be thriving. There was a new addition to the inhabitants, a fractious baby whose shrieking reduced Hugh's overtaxed nerves to shreds. He couldn't understand, either, why Mrs Mansell kept casting black looks in his direction. She had never exactly taken to him — the feeling was mutual — but had hitherto contented herself with largely ignoring him. What had changed?

It was Megan, of all people, who appraised him of the situation. She had called round to see Letitia — in a non-professional capacity — and sat with the old lady over a pot of tea, talking about — Well, Hugh didn't know what they talked about, couldn't begin to guess, took himself out of the way, feeling surplus to requirements. But he was driven out of one room after another by the Mansell hoards until in desperation he stepped out into the area to get away from it all. There he bumped into Megan smoking a cigarette.

They eyed one another warily.

"This is the only place where one can find any peace," said Hugh at length, feeling for some reason that he needed to justify his presence.

"The soothing lullaby of London." Megan blew out smoke, smiled, the hum of the city all round them, a constant background noise one scarcely noticed.

171

It was her smile that did it, sabotaging all the careful months when he'd gradually weaned himself away from thoughts of her. His heart skipped a beat, the hum of London not so much a lullaby as a soaring symphony, celebrating his love for her. Love. At his age. It was ridiculous, he told himself. But he couldn't help it.

Even out here, however, that was no escape from the pandemonium. The shrill sound of the baby's wailing seemed to follow one — as did Mrs Mansell's dark disapproval.

"It's as if she suspected me of wanting to bash its brains out," said Hugh, aggrieved.

"It's not that," said Megan. "It has more to do with the child's putative father." She stubbed out her cigarette, explaining about the Immaculate Conception and the part Ian was suspected of having played.

Hugh was aghast. "Why did nobody tell me? Why was I kept in the dark?"

Megan shrugged. "It's one of those things that everybody knows but no one admits to knowing."

"What can Ian have been thinking of? The girl is married, for pity's sake. What is that husband of hers — this POW — what is he going to make of it all? Is he likely to want retribution? Should Ian be warned?"

"We are all likely to be dead long before then, the way the war is going."

"All the more reason," said Hugh, "to make the most of every moment. But this house is impossible. I can't hear myself think, let alone have a quiet word with you. Could we not go to your house?"

172

"My place is just as busy and a lot smaller. Four of us are sharing."

"Then there's nowhere."

Megan looked at him speculatively, as if weighing him up. "There might be somewhere," she said slowly. "A house in Paddington. It's often empty."

"A house? What house?"

"Eleanor Lambton's house. She's doesn't use it much. I have some spare keys."

"You have spare keys? To Eleanor Lambton's house? Surely you don't mean Julian Lambton's widow? I haven't heard of her in years! How on earth did you get to know Eleanor Lambton?"

"You sound surprised. Do you think she is above my level?"

"Of course I don't think that! You are putting words into my mouth. Well, if we are going, let's go now and put this madhouse behind us!"

Hugh had surprised himself, being so pushy, taking charge, giving orders. It was not his usual manner, had been born out of weariness, irritation, frustration, with news of Ian's trespass the last straw. Throwing his weight around might have ended in disaster but instead — improbably — it had worked wonders. Megan had acquiesced, which must prove something; and so here they were, alone together, in Eleanor Lambton's Paddington house.

Being alone with her was a lot more awkward than he had bargained for. He was suddenly tongue-tied again. Megan seemed inhibited too. They avoided looking at each other and Hugh, unable to sit still, drifted around the room, scrutinizing Eleanor Lambton's possessions as if they were of the utmost importance. There was something impersonal about the place, he decided. It was spic and span, spacious, comfortable; but he got the impression that it was not much used. He wondered how often Eleanor came here and where she lived the rest of the time. Did the family still own the Manor at Binley as in the old days? He could remember very little about Eleanor. He had met her perhaps half a dozen times; but that had been years ago.

He formed questions in his mind, they were on the tip of his tongue, but he thought better of it, recalling his *faux pas* earlier and Megan's angry response: *Do you think she is above my level?* He had not meant to imply that by his question; but it was certainly an odd association, one had to admit. How had Megan and Eleanor ever come to meet?

It was just one more reminder of how little he knew about Megan.

"We need a drink." She had been sitting in the window seat, looking through the glass, but she now got to her feet, businesslike. "A proper drink, I mean." She made it sound like a prescription.

"Is there any to be had?"

"Eleanor hides it in vases."

"In *vases*?" Hugh gaped at her.

"And other places." Megan laughed at Hugh's expression: they were looking at each other now. "Jimmy, Eleanor's son, sometimes uses this place," she explained. "He eats all her food and drinks all her drink

174

and never replaces anything. He sounds rather self-centred, I often think; but of course one can't say that to his mother. However, Eleanor has found a solution. She secretes emergency supplies in unlikely places. We have only to look."

After a short search, Hugh unearthed a bottle of gin and found glasses to go with it.

"But there are no mixers, not even any ice," he said, handing Megan her drink. She was back in the window seat, framed there against a background of grey daylight.

He sat down in an easy chair, cradling his glass, watched Megan as she took a sip of her drink, grimaced, put it aside.

"I'm sorry. I can't stomach gin."

"I didn't know. Perhaps I can find something else?"

Megan shook her head. "It doesn't matter. It's broken the ice, anyway. At least we are talking now."

Talking, but getting nowhere. Hugh took a convulsive gulp of his drink, said, "It's hopeless. I know nothing about you, not even what you like to drink. And you know nothing about me."

"That's not entirely true. And it could be fun finding out about each other."

"Fun?"

"We will have plenty to talk about."

"But it doesn't seem right, starting with the basics at our age."

"Oh, Hugh, we are not that old!"

She smiled and then turned to look out of the window. It had grown brighter outside and her hair shone red in the sunlight. Hugh felt an intense desire to touch it, to stroke it, to let it run through his fingers as he'd done before — years ago.

He tore his eyes away, looked down at his drink, was surprised to find his glass empty. Surely the gin would take effect soon, loosen his tongue?

When he looked up, he found Megan's eyes on him.

"Tell me something. Anything. Something about you that I don't know. Something about your life, your past."

His life. What was his life but a catalogue of failure and missed opportunities? Even now there was a letter in his pocket reminding him of the débâcle of his marriage. He couldn't tell Megan about that. He didn't want to whine and complain. He didn't want her to feel *sorry* for him.

Then he rallied. Thoughts of Cynthia and her "lovers" put him in mind of the time he'd spent in Germany in the 1920s. He could tell Megan about that.

"We'd been fighting Germans all those years. Now that peace had come, I wanted to find out more about them."

"That makes sense. Go on."

"You see, at times during the war I felt that we soldiers in the trenches had more in common with our supposed enemy on the other side of no-man's land than we did with the generals living in the comfortable chateaux behind the lines — let alone the Hun-hating civilians back home, obsessed with the shortage of sugar."

176

"I have never thought of it like that before. One felt that the country had come together, that we were all on the same side for once, rich and poor, high and low. But I can see that the war also drove people apart."

"It was not the war which drove us apart!" Hugh blurted out. The gin was having an effect now: making him hasty.

"Then what did? God's punishment for our sins?"

High felt himself blushing, recalling how he'd blundered last summer in Hyde Park, talking about sin and feeling guilty. Megan had not forgotten either, but her voice was amused now rather than accusatory. Her eyes gently mocked him. It had been the same all those years ago, talking dismissively about men, an ardent suffragette. His heart skipped a beat, remembering her breathless and glowing in Russell Square.

"God," he said firmly, "did not come into it. It did not take me much time to work out that I was far too insignificant for God to have taken an interest."

"You were never insignificant to me," said Megan, and smiled.

Later, in the master bedroom, Megan let out a world-weary sigh and moved away from him, terminating their inconclusive fumbling.

"You were right. About us being old. I am too old for this. Forty-seven is too old."

"You are not old." Hugh gently stroked her arm, looking down at her. "You are beautiful."

"I do not feel beautiful. I feel as if I am all frayed round the edges. Desiccated. I am sorry, Hugh."

She reached for her cigarettes and Hugh lay back, disappointed, helpless. However hard he tried, the gap between them never seemed to grow any less. Maybe after all this time it was unbridgeable.

They had closed the curtains, shutting themselves in, but they could not keep out the world entirely. The sound of traffic, the cooing of a pigeon percolated into the room. *In 1912*, thought Hugh, *I did not notice those things; there was nothing else, just us.*

"It's not you," said Megan, breathing out smoke as she spoke. "Please don't think it's you."

"Is there any hope at all, do you think?"

"For us?" Megan regarded the cigarette between her fingers as if the answer lay there, as if it was an oracle. "Maybe we have left it too long," she said at last. "Maybe we missed our chance."

Flecks of ash dropped from the cigarette, scattered across the counterpane. They lay there, silent.

In the train heading back to Buckinghamshire, Hugh tried to remember the laughing, vivacious girl he had known in London so long ago, but all he could summon into his mind was an image of Megan's unhappy face on Eleanor Lambton's pillow. All his old dreams were disappearing, the Megan who had haunted him for so long slowly fading from view. Would he be left with nothing?

Looking out of the window, seeing his own tired reflection in the glass, he wondered if it might have been better had they never met again.

CHAPTER
EIGHT

The war was never-ending, thought Letitia, leaning heavily on her stick as she shuffled along the pavement. Here they were, yet another spring passing into yet another summer and still no sign of the finishing post. *I am likely to come to my end before the war ever does,* she said to herself as she struggled to reach the corner of her square. Gone were the days when she meandered at leisure along Oxford Street and browsed in the bookshops of Charing Cross Road before sitting to a lunchtime concert in the National Gallery. Those early days of the war seemed like a lifetime ago now. She remembered on the day of her tumble — nearly four years ago — she had said to that gallant policeman, *The day I can't walk from here to Trafalgar Square is the day you can put me down.* Well, that day had come; but she was not ready to give up on life just yet: not with things so unsettled, not with the war still raging.

The sun was shining. The warmth of it on her wrinkled face revived her. Her daily dose of fresh air breathed new life into her. She hobbled forward, her stick tap-tapping, and she smiled, thinking what an old crock she must look, wondering if anyone was watching from the many windows that glinted in the white-fronted terrace. She had rather lost track of her neighbours. People came and went so quickly these days. Perhaps there were still some who knew her, peering out and saying to one another, "There's old Mrs Warner from number twelve. Getting vague, she is. Didn't recognize me yesterday when I passed her in the square. The old are so forgetful."

But it was not forgetfulness that was her problem: just the opposite.

Towards the end of the terrace was the gap where the bomb had fallen in 1941. That had been the worst moment of all, the closest she had come to death. She remembered clearly the horrible sensation of the suction and compression of the blast, and the way the windows had shattered. Scalding water from the kettle had burnt her. There was still a mark on her arm, but it had faded almost to nothing now. The ugly wound in the terrace had also been transformed. It had become over time a little wilderness. Grass grew there, and clover. To this green was added the red, white, yellow and purple of fireweed and plantain and Oxford ragwort. There was also a more exotic plant, name unknown, said to be an escapee from Kew. On a broken beam up-thrust from the rubble, a blackbird sat trilling, watching her with a glassy eye.

If she closed her eyes, breathed in the scent of the grass and the flowers, let the song of the blackbird wash over her, she could almost imagine herself back in the days of her youth, walking in a summer meadow, a place she had often visited once upon a time. The sun had been hot there too, and she had waded through the long grass, her hat dangling, pollen tickling her nose. She had lain on her back looking up at the sky, bees buzzing, the grass rustling in the gentle breeze, the long chirping song of a skylark cascading out of the blue.

Letitia opened her eyes, smiling at the memory, and began walking back towards her house. She cast a shadow before her now and, watching it move slowly along the pavement, she remembered how a similar shadow had fallen over her as she lay in the long grass. She had sat up abruptly, momentarily afraid, shielding her eyes against the sun. A young man had been standing over her, etched against the sky, his shirt tatty, his waistcoat frayed, string tied round his trouser legs below the knees, a scythe in his hand. To Letitia, dreamy-eyed, contemplating the beauty of the world, this sudden apparition had seemed the most beautiful thing of all — the essence of everything she had been thinking and feeling just moments before.

Wicked! Immoral! Unregenerate sinner!

The vision in her mind abruptly changed. Darkness engulfed her. The summer meadow had gone. She was kneeling in a black void, small and frail, looking up not at a young man with the sun in his hair but at a monstrous figure, a terrible demonic spirit wearing the robes and symbols of a bishop. There was no face beneath the mitre, just a fiery glow, like London aflame in the blitz. One twisted claw held a staff; the other gripped his pectoral cross. The image was so real, so terrifying, that it set her heart racing. She shivered, stumbled, jerked her stick out to stop herself falling, breathing heavily.

It troubled her that she could not remember what her father looked like — as if being able to picture him as an ordinary man would diminish him, lessen the fear. Had there been any family resemblance, any facial hint of the bishop in Jocelyn or Arnold? Impossible to say. She had only the vaguest memories, had spent a lifetime trying to blot him out, was not sure now if he had been tall or short, thin or stocky, whether his nose had been aquiline like Jocelyn's, or snub like Hugh's, if he had had Arnold's black hair, or Hugh's mousy colour, now turning grey. The bishop had become a presence rather than a person, her father no longer.

There was still a portrait of him in the chapter house at Chanderton, or so she believed, but she had not been back to Chanderton since the night she'd been being bundled into a furtive carriage and driven away, over seventy years ago.

At last she was back by her own front door. She took the area steps one by one, clutching the rail. The house was quiet, most of the Mansells out. Peggy was somewhere about. The two girls aged four and two were no doubt in the old drawing-room which was now a play-room, where they made stains on the carpet and scratched the armoire and spread their toys all over the floor. Peggy rarely admonished her children, and never cleaned up after them. A lazy girl, Peggy. *A slattern*, Mrs Mansell had been known to call her, losing patience: *young people today* . . . she added bitterly, leaving the sentence hanging. Letitia sometimes felt nostalgia for the days when her house had been her own, but she knew that she would no longer be able to cope alone. She needed looking after in her decrepitude. Having the Mansells here made a virtue of necessity.

Sitting in the kitchen, laying her stick aside, Letitia closed her eyes for her afternoon snooze, trying to recapture that feeling of walking through the long ago meadow as a girl who had known nothing of gout or arthritis or varicose veins.

Letitia was in bed but not yet asleep when the alert sounded. It must be around midnight, she thought, staring round at the dark. It always set one on edge, the siren, bringing back memories of 1940 and 1941, cowering in the basement night after night as the Luftwaffe roamed the skies at will. More recently there had been the little blitz which had made everyone so jittery. Since then, nothing. Surely this must be a false alarm? But it drove sleep just that much further away.

Sitting up in bed, Letitia switched on her bedside lamp and reached for her book.

Mrs Mansell tapped on the door and popped her head round. "I'll just check the blackout for you, shall I, Mrs Warner?"

Letitia gave a wry smile: *check up on me, is what she means*.

Mrs Mansell busied herself at the window. She looked, thought Letitia, rather tired and run-down.

"Why don't you come down to the kitchen, Mrs Warner?"

"I don't think so. I shall just sit here quietly and read. It will only be a false alarm."

"As you like." Mrs Mansell stopped fiddling with the blackout, came over to hover by the bed. "Feeling all right are you? Didn't eat much of your tea."

"Somehow I can't get used to sausages made from whale meat."

"No. I suppose not."

The screaming of a child interrupted them.

"The Immaculate Conception." Mrs Mansell sighed. "No rest for the wicked." She departed.

The Immaculate Conception: it was an old joke which to Letitia's mind had worn thin long ago. She thought of it as Mrs Mansell's way of reminding her of Ian's culpability in the matter of Peggy's daughter. Mrs Mansell could, at times, be somewhat acerbic, not to mention repetitive. On the other hand, she cooked, cleaned and foraged voraciously, and on top of all that she had taken a job in a munitions factory "to make ends meet". Fractious grandchildren were the last thing she needed and this evening Peggy's two had been particularly bothersome. "We don't like these sausages, Granny," they had grizzled. "They don't taste nice; we won't eat them." One could hardly blame them. One might have blamed Peggy, who could do more to help; but to the young the war must seem to have been going on half their life. No wonder they got despondent at times.

Letitia opened her book. Her eyes followed the words down the page but her restless mind was elsewhere. Where was Ian now, whose child would not eat whale meat sausages? Was he still in England, or was he over in Normandy in the thick of the fighting? It was a nasty business, over in Normandy: at least, that was the impression one got, reading between the lines in the newspaper.

She looked up from her book, distracted from her thoughts by distant gunfire, the faint sound of explosions — yet no hum of aeroplane engines. It was unsettling. There had been nothing like this since April. One had assumed, with the advent of D Day, that the Germans would have too much else on their plate to think of mounting raids. One tended to forget what an ingenious and resourceful race they were. *Tenacious,* thought Letitia: *like me.*

The book slipped off her bed as Letitia nodded in fitful sleep. The distant noises of war merged with her dreams. She was wading in her nightdress along a flooded First War trench just as Hugh had described them in his letters, guns booming all along the line. There were piles of corpses at all the traverses. Letitia picked amongst them with arthritic fingers, searching for Hugh, whom she believed was dead; but nowhere could she find his body . . .

Next morning the alert was still in force. This was unusual and disquieting. Clive was of the opinion that it was a mistake: someone had forgotten to sound the all clear. His father muttered darkly about the foolhardiness of venturing out of doors when there was a raid on, but to Mrs Mansell this was simply an excuse not to go to work. She gave him short shrift. Peggy was still in bed.

The house emptied. The all clear sounded at last, only to be followed almost immediately by another alert. Nothing seemed to happen: no aeroplanes, no bombs; but hearing the siren in broad daylight was odd, giving a touch of the surreal to things, as if she was still dreaming.

Alert or no alert, Letitia was not to be denied her daily constitutional. She struggled up the area steps with her stick after lunch to meet a grey, oppressive afternoon, the sound of the city muffled and distant. The very air seemed stale and heavy. Even the bomb-site wilderness failed to charm.

Back in the kitchen, she sat listening to the raucous sounds of the children upstairs. The Immaculate Conception was exercising her young lungs vigorously. Peggy was no doubt lolling on the sofa taking no notice. Letitia turned on the wireless to drown out the noise. The news was on. There was no change in Normandy. Did this mean Ian was alive, dead, missing an arm or a leg? Or still safe in England? The BBC newsreader, sounding calm and disinterested, announced that reports were coming in of pilotless planes being used against southern England. Was this, then, the reason for the unexpected alerts: some new devilry on the part of the inexhaustible Germans? *Have we not suffered enough?* thought Letitia feeling suddenly very weary. Air raids, the blackout, rationing — and now this. It was interminable.

She reached across, switched off the wireless, not wanting to hear about death in Italy, death in the Pacific, death in Russia; but there was no escape from it, even in the silence of her kitchen. The war seemed to permeate everything — even the air one breathed.

By the time Megan called round on Sunday, the mysterious pilotless planes had become ominously familiar. After three days' bombardment, Letitia had grown to recognize the sound of their buzzing engines and once, stepping out for a breath of evening air, she had seen a little flickering flame pass by overhead.

Megan knew more. Pilotless planes, she said, had dropped on a hospital in Kensington and a convent in the Bayswater Road; that very morning one had hit the Guards' chapel killing many of those attending matins.

"There is no respite," said Letitia as they talked in her bedroom, away from the multitude of Mansells. "These things come indiscriminately, day or night."

"Why not leave London for the time being? It's worth considering."

"Oh, tush. I've got by thus far in my own house. Do you think I'm going to be driven out now that the war is nearly over?"

Megan smiled. "You are stubborn."

"It has been said."

"At the very least, you should spend more time in the basement, not up here, exposed on the second floor."

"If there is a direct hit —"

"You would still stand more of a chance downstairs."

Letitia sighed, rubbing the arm of her chair. "The problem is, I can't bear to be in the kitchen nowadays, listening to that girl going on and on, and her children caterwauling. I know that I sound like an old grouch. I don't begrudge the Mansells finding shelter here, I really don't; but my ears are more sensitive than they used to be. And there was I thinking that one went deaf in old age."

Since the advent of the buzzing bombs, Peggy had taken up residency in the kitchen and refused to budge for anybody. It was a very big kitchen, she said, with plenty of room for everyone. But it did not seem so big with the children running round shrieking and bumping into one's legs. The kitchen had been a place of refuge since the early days of the blitz in 1940, but now there was no peace morning, noon or night. Letitia had been driven out.

"If these pilotless planes keep coming," said Megan, "there may be a new evacuation scheme. That would get Peggy out of your hair. I shall keep my ear to the ground."

"That would be one solution. I really don't want to fall out with Mrs Mansell because of her wretched daughter." Letitia sighed. "I joke about being crotchety, but I am not usually like that. I don't know what's come over me lately."

"The deprivations of war. Everyone is the same. And with this new menace . . ." Megan shrugged. "It will get worse before it gets better."

"It's the shortage of whisky I take exception to," said Letitia. "There's none to be had for love or money, unless one is prepared to pay in gold. I had quite a good supply at the start of the war, but it has dwindled to nothing — dwindled, I might add, with the

188

considerable help of Mr Mansell. I have never known such a nose for spirits. He sniffed out all my hiding places."

"I may be able to help there too," said Megan, getting up. "I have my contacts." She tapped the side of her nose as she departed.

Letitia hauled herself out of her chair, went to stand by the window, watched as Megan bumped her bicycle up from the area, got on, pedalled away. The square looked decidedly dilapidated, railings missing, house fronts peeling, potatoes growing amongst the plane trees. But it was a wonder she could see anything, the window was so grimy.

Letitia stretched out on her bed, thinking of Megan. Like Mrs Mansell, Megan was always on the go, but one knew so little about her. She kept her life compartmentalized. Who, for instance, were these "contacts" she had mentioned? Who were her friends? One had not known her parents; she did not have a pedigree stretching back half a thousand years. She did not quite seem to fit anywhere. She was unique, a one-off.

She is no better than she ought to be, Connie Lambton had said all those years ago. But Connie had judged by class, had used derogatory labels indiscriminately, *woman of ill-repute* and *criminal* being interchangeable with *socialist* and *suffragette*. But even Connie had been captivated by the girl Megan, before it was discovered she was *not one of us*.

Megan had been married, one knew that much. A marriage of convenience, Hugh had said. Had she been much upset when, recently, her German husband had passed away in the internment camp on the Isle of Man? It was impossible to say. She kept things close to her chest. But then so did Hugh. One did not really know what was going on between them, Hugh and Megan. Anything or nothing? At times, Letitia had felt there was something tangible: friendship assuredly, affection most probably — and something more? Yet it seemed to lead nowhere. After three long years there ought to have been some progress made, if progress was ever to be made at all. One hesitated to interfere. One did not want to go blundering in only to find that one had trampled all the delicate shoots into the mud. With Hugh one was on slightly safer ground. One knew him as well as anybody. But Megan . . . who was she? Where had she come from? How had she come to be staying at the Manor all those years ago?

One day, thought Letitia, picking up her book and searching for the right page, *one day I shall pluck up courage and ask her*.

But one had to admit, whatever Megan's origins, she contrived to look elegant as she cycled about a London drab in utility. Even Connie Lambton would have admitted that much.

The pilotless planes, soon renamed buzz-bombs or doodlebugs, continued to rattle and roar their way over London as the summer of 1944 wore on. Peggy and her children were evacuated to the country, Mrs Mansell seeing them off at Paddington.

"A nightmare," she told Letitia. "The place was in chaos, the trains full, people crushed like sardines in a can. I had to pass the Immaculate Conception through the window."

Letitia found some comfort in being able to reclaim her kitchen, but Mrs Mansell was sunk in gloom. A week's holiday from the munitions factory had given her time to brood. However much she railed against Peggy, she hated to be parted from her — hated to be parted from any of her children. She was anxious about Clive, too. He had left school and found a job on the tube, but the day when he would be called up was getting nearer and nearer. Only the end of the war could save him. Hope had sprouted in the heady days after the Normandy landings, but then withered away when the doodlebugs began to arrive and the fighting continued unabated in France.

"I couldn't bear to lose them both — both my boys. This whole business should have been cleared up months ago. What are they playing at, these cabinet ministers and generals? If they think that bombing Germany will win the war, they've got another think coming. It's a waste of time. We never surrendered during the blitz, and the Jerries aren't going to now. Stands to reason. Not that I've any sympathy for them, those bastard Germans. I wish our bombers could flatten their whole blooming country. I hope they all burn. But our planes would be better off used to bomb them places where they launch the doodlebugs, so why don't they do it? Tell me that!"

"I expect they have tried," said Letitia circumspectly. She wished to see an end to the war as much as anyone, but she felt no hatred for the Germans as such. They were as much victims in this as anyone, to her mind. They weren't all evil, they couldn't all be tarred with the Nazi brush. And how many of the atrocity stories were actually true? Connie had repeated such stories in the first war; they had all turned out to be fabrications.

Mrs Mansell herself had seen things differently once upon a time. Letitia recalled her saying — years ago, it seemed, now — *I for one don't get no satisfaction in thinking of the Germans being bombed*. But that had been in the days before her elder son Bob had been killed aged twenty.

"They've tried, you say. Well, they should try harder. I don't know how they expect us to carry on as normal when there's sirens going off all hours of the day and night, and the fighting in France going on and on. They'll have our Clive in the end, you mark my words. And Mansell's no help. *What will be will be*, he says. Huh! I wish a bloody doodlebug'd land on him and see how he likes it. *What will be will be*, my eye."

Mrs Mansell got to her feet and began to wash the dishes, clattering and banging and muttering under her breath. The kitchen was a gloomy place now. Clive had put boards over most of the windows because of the danger of flying glass. A safety-conscious lad, Clive. Too safety-conscious, in Letitia's opinion. *He'll worry himself silly if he's not careful*, as Mrs Mansell put it.

Sitting in her old carver, Letitia tilted her head back and closed her eyes, taking a quick catnap before she went out for her daily dose of fresh air. One had to work up to it. Even a short walk didn't come easy these days. But, as she snoozed, she found herself back in the days when she didn't need a stick, when she could grab her coat and her hat and dash out of the house in the blink of an eye. And look! Here she was passing through Green Park already, turning right into Piccadilly — except that in her dream there were no trenches and no moorings for barrage balloons in Green Park, and there was not a uniform in sight on the pavements of Piccadilly. On she walked, through the straggling suburbs and out to places where the buses were green instead of red and fields receded endlessly. How quick and easy it was to reach the countryside on foot! Why had she never thought of doing it before? It would not take her long to reach Chanderton (she was going to Chanderton, she remembered that now); indeed, she was almost there, the spire of the cathedral unmistakable, sharp as a needle against the sky. And here was the meadow she'd known as a girl. It looked exactly the same, even after seventy years: the tireless bees dusted with pollen, buzzing from flower to flower; the butterflies dancing in the sunlight, mounting higher and higher before fading into the overarching blue; and was that the sound of a skylark? But her eyes were drawn to the far corner of the meadow where a man was busy with his scythe, making hay. It couldn't be, after all this time; but it looked very much like —

193

"Tom! Tom!"

"What was that?"

Letitia's eyes jerked open. The gloom in the kitchen seemed thicker than ever after the bright sun of the meadow. Ah, but of course, she'd been dreaming . . .

Mrs Mansell was standing by the table, a dishcloth in her hand. "Did you say something just then, Mrs Warner?"

"No. Nothing. I was just . . . just . . . I was miles away."

The dishcloth hovered, dripping, over the table. Mrs Mansell knitted her brows. "I thought I heard you say a name. I thought I heard you say *Tom*. Now that wouldn't be your husband's name, would it, Mrs Warner? He was a lot older than you, wasn't he?"

"Yes. He was. A lot older." Letitia buttoned her lips, keeping her husband locked away.

Mrs Mansell waited, as if hoping for more. One had to take care at times: her curiosity could be cunning. But Letitia was experienced enough now not to be taken in.

Mrs Mansell sighed — sensing, perhaps, that she had been thwarted. As she began to scrub the table, she returned to the well-worn theme of her own husband.

"Mansell, now: Mansell is nothing but a nuisance. Ned would have been different. He was not handsome in looks, my Ned, but he was handsome enough in his deeds." She straightened up, unusually thoughtful. The dishcloth, dangling in her hand, now dripped onto the flagstones. "Doctor Kramer says that women are put

194

upon, and I can't argue with her there. She says we ought to stand up for ourselves."

"Does she indeed?" Letitia looked with interest at this new version of Mrs Mansell. The old one would not have given Megan the time of day. "I expect she is right; but it will take a long time for things to change."

"Ah, but everything is different now, Mrs Warner. Where I work, for a start. That's nearly all women. And nowadays you see women posties and clickers, women in uniform, even women bus drivers."

"It was the same in the last war. Afterwards — when the men came back — women had to return meekly to their allotted place in the home."

"Maybe so. But this time things will be different, you mark my words. Folk ain't going to go back to how things was before. We ain't fought this bleeding war just to keep Winnie in brandy and cigars."

Letitia wondered if Mrs Mansell might have a point. She had her doubts, but one had to admit that things *did* change — albeit slowly. Women had the vote now, for one thing. Her father must have turned in his grave when that happened.

She closed her eyes again, but the meadow was gone, Tom no longer there: Mrs Mansell's talk had driven it all away. In the back of her mind now a shadow lurked, barely discernible but disconcertingly real: not her father, but that carbon copy whose name had been William Warner.

Megan popped in and produced from her bag a gift: a bottle of whisky.

"It's the real thing, too," she said. "Proper Scotch. I thought you'd prefer it to the cheaper alternative of tinted methylated spirits."

"You are a marvel!" exclaimed Letitia, fetching glasses from a cupboard. The bottle of whisky seemed to glow in the gloom of the kitchen. "You must stay and sample it, and afterwards help me find a hiding place that even Mr Mansell will fail to discover."

Megan's eyes were on her as she poured, but for once her hand did not betray her, was steady as a rock. The smell of the whisky seemed invigorating in itself.

Megan protested. "Enough, enough! I shall fall off my bicycle if I drink all that!"

"Oh, tush. It's no more than an eyeful. Drink it down. It will do you good."

As Letitia savoured the half-forgotten taste, Megan said, "There's more. I may be able to get my hands on an old bath chair. It's rather ramshackle but still serviceable."

"I should feel like an old crock, wheeled around in a contraption like that. And who will have the time to push me?"

"I don't think you will be short of volunteers, if you can bear the indignity."

"Anything to get me out of the house." The whisky coursed through Letitia's veins and she had visions of Oxford Street, Hyde Park, the River. The whole of London awaited her. She would no longer be confined to her little square. "Bless you, my dear. I don't know what I should do without you — though I don't know why you should take so much trouble over an aged specimen like me."

"There are many reasons. You are Hugh's aunt, for one thing." But at the mention of Hugh, Megan's smile seemed to falter. She took a sip of whisky, pulled a face as she swallowed, so that her expression of a moment before was erased and Letitia began to wonder if she'd read too much into it.

I hate loose ends, that is the problem, said Letitia to herself, raising her glass to sniff again the smell she had missed for so long. The war was a loose end that was beyond her power to do anything about; but when it came to Hugh and Megan, the temptation to interfere was becoming overwhelming. She had to remind herself of the harm she had already caused by her meddling, not forwarding Megan's letter in 1915. This situation might have been resolved years ago but for that. There might have been no Cynthia, Letitia might have had a great-niece of whom she could be truly fond.

But was she getting ahead of herself?

"I feel that so much time has been wasted," she ventured to say: not interfering, merely seeing how the land lay. "We ought to have been friends for years."

"I was not always quite as respectable as I am now — if I am respectable even now. You might not have approved of me back then."

"Fiddlesticks! I am not some dyed-in-the-wool snob like Connie Lambton."

Megan looked at her curiously. "What was Mrs Lambton's real opinion of me? I've often wondered."

"Connie thought that suffragettes were the handmaidens of the devil."

Megan laughed. "I can well believe it."

But Letitia was annoyed with herself. Mentioning Connie Lambton had been a slip of the tongue brought about by thoughts of that letter. To compound that mistake by mentioning suffragettes was unforgivable. It might suggest to Megan that she was being talked about in Binley long after her one and only visit. It might raise awkward questions. It might smack of prying and meddling.

Whatever happened, Letitia was determined to draw a veil over her conversation with Connie Lambton in the blue drawing room twenty-nine years ago.

On her way out, Megan bumped into Mrs Mansell at the top of the area steps. Mrs Mansell, dour in her headscarf and threadbare cardigan, nodded curtly, which Megan had come to recognize as a munificent gesture of camaraderie.

"Those bags look heavy, Mrs Mansell."

"Huh. Not heavy enough. And how is Mrs Warner today, Doctor Kramer?"

"In fine fettle."

"I have noted," said Mrs Mansell, picking over her words as Megan imagined she would pick over produce at market, "that she seems at times to be preoccupied with the past."

"It is hardly surprising. One must have so many memories at ninety-five."

"Ah, but it's as if something is troubling her. I have heard her mentioning someone called Tom." Mrs Mansell pursed her lips, brows jutting. "You might think as it is none of my business —"

I wouldn't dare say anything of the kind, thought Megan, wondering if perhaps there was a part of Mrs Mansell who still resented her — who saw her as trespassing on the territory of others.

"— but I'm only looking out for her," Mrs Mansell continued. "I have her best interests at heart. I owe her a lot, when all is said and done."

Megan — who liked Mrs Mansell, who rather admired her, who saw her as a soldier on the front line of a different war — made an attempt to allay suspicions and curry favour, without making it too obvious. "Who was Tom? Was he Mrs Warner's husband? You would know, Mrs Mansell; she will have spoken to you about her husband."

"She has. But now I come to think on it, I don't believe as she's ever mentioned him by name. I do recall as she once said he was something of a bully; yet when she spoke this Tom's name she had a smile on her lips." Mrs Mansell sniffed. "I suppose you think I'm being nosy."

"Not at all. As you said, we have her best interest at heart, you and me."

"That we do."

"And I know I can rely on you to take care of her."

"You can."

Mrs Mansell trudged down the area steps with her shopping bags. Watching her go, Megan felt that some rapprochement had been achieved.

She climbed onto her bicycle — a man's bicycle, inherited from Letitia's regular doctor along with his patients — and pedalled off, winging her way through streets where destruction wrought in the far-off days of the blitz had been added to of late by the deadly doodlebugs. Swooping through the summer sunshine, Megan went over her conversation with Letitia and began to wonder just how much the old lady knew about her. How much had Hugh told his great-aunt? What had Connie Lambton said in Binley long ago? Letitia had dropped the word *suffragette* into their talk, a hint perhaps that she knew more than she let on. Letitia might have learned from Hugh of Megan's suffrage activities, but Megan had got the impression that he had never gone into details about their meeting in London in 1912. Perhaps, then, the information had come from Connie Lambton. Perhaps that was why Letitia had become suddenly vague. Perhaps she did not want to go into details of what Mrs Lambton might or might not have said.

Not that it matters, Megan said to herself, pushing down hard on the pedals, flowing with the traffic, whizzing past pedestrians: people who, like the streets, looked worn and threadbare in this fifth year of the war. Not that it mattered, but what else had Connie Lambton said? What had Hugh heard? There had been a moment in Hyde Park in 1941 when she had headed him off, changed the direction of the conversation, because it had been so painful to see the doubt in his eyes. *It's so strange that you're a doctor . . . .* What, then, had he expected? That she'd been no better than she ought to be, that she'd earned a living by nefarious means?

As it happens, Megan said, speeding along with the breeze behind her, *as it happens, I dodged all that, never sank so low.*

But it had been touch and go, she admitted. In the latter stages of the first war she had been alone and penniless, had struggled to stay afloat, had been desperate enough to try anything. And then, out of the blue, entirely unlooked-for, luck had smiled on her — luck had come to her rescue even as she was sliding slowly into the mire.

Luck was all it was, too, said Megan, wondering if, without it, she would ever have found the strength to haul herself back to respectability when it was so much easier to sink still lower. There were others who had never had her good fortune. She did not presume to judge them. She was not one to throw the first stone — unlike Mrs Lambton, whose stones, deserved or not, had always hit their mark.

Joining the dots in her mind, Megan wondered if Mrs Lambton had gained knowledge of her suffragette activities through her eldest son, Julian.

He called me a suffragette on many an occasion, he called me a lot worse, too. He insulted me to my face, flung those words at me, as I flung words at him: snob, hypocrite, pompous pig. She smiled, remembering the words they had used, words which had become terms

201

of endearment as they tried — and failed — to fight against the mutual attraction that bound them.

Megan rang her bell to alert some careless pedestrians as she swept along Kings Road towards Sloane Square, her joyous smile tinged with sadness as she thought with fond remembrance of her long-dead lover, Julian Lambton.

CHAPTER
NINE

"Look at those trees," said Letitia. "The leaves have fallen already. Autumn has come early this year."

Sitting in her ramshackle bath chair with a rug over her knees, being pushed through the streets of Chelsea, Letitia was at leisure to look around and see things properly, not having to worry about her unsteady legs, uneven pavements, unexpected kerbs. Clive Mansell was puffing and panting behind her. The chair was quite a weight, and he was not exactly a brawny lad.

"It's the doodlebugs what do that, Mrs Warner," he said. "The leaves are blown off the trees when they explode."

"How extraordinary!" said Letitia, looking up as they passed beneath the stark, bare branches.

The doodlebugs had become commonplace, falling on London in an endless swarm; but one never quite got used to them. Just the opposite, in fact. Their sheer number magnified their awe and terror. People got more and more jumpy, were always on the alert, listening out for the stuttering, buzzing sound of their engines. It gave everyone a distracted mien, as if they were only ever half-listening when one talked to them. And so the fifth summer of the war wore away and victory — which had seemed within touching distance in June — receded into the future.

Down by the river, Clive took a breather, taking off his hand-me-down jacket with the elbow patches and mopping his brow as Letitia looked out towards Battersea Park, the wind in her face, the rippling grey water flowing unabated, the sky a patch-work of cloud. Being by the timeless Thames gave her a sense of perspective. The river, she thought, had been here long before Chelsea Embankment had come into being. It had been here when London was just a few huts within a wooden palisade on the terraces of a wide flood plain; and it would still be here when all this was forgotten. It would be flowing serene through a city of the future when doodlebugs would be a thing of the past, if remembered at all. Everyone now living — all the people fighting and dying, sheltering from bombs, scratching out an existence in the ruins: they would be nothing but dust by then. It was somehow comforting to think of time marching implacably onwards — to realize the insignificance of a human life. Nothing endured forever. Even the war would end one day.

Letitia closed her eyes, enjoying a moment of calm, the breeze caressing her face, the hum of the city faint and soothing.

And then the siren sounded.

Letitia listened, eyes shut, as the wailing of the alert rose and fell and rose again, its effect undiminished even now: one felt suddenly queasy, as if the ground beneath one's feet had begun to pitch and toss like the deck of a ship.

She opened her eyes as the sound tailed away to find Clive leaning over her wringing his hands, his pasty face creased with anxiety. "It's the alert, Mrs Warner. The alert. We didn't ought to have come so far from home. We didn't ought to have come so far."

His fear bolstered her, reminding her, oddly enough, of Hugh sitting in her basement in 1940, experiencing his first raid. He, too, had needed reassurance.

She reached out a steadying hand, laid it on Clive's arm. "It will be all right, Clive. There's no sign of danger yet."

But even as she spoke the faint sound of a flying bomb was carried on a gust of wind from across the river. Clive ran round and tried to move the chair — but it seemed to be stuck.

"It won't budge, Mrs Warner! It won't budge!"

"Steady, my dear. Steady. No need to panic."

A wheel had jammed. Clive knelt to try and free it. His knuckles were white as he wrestled with it, beads of sweat on his face, his breathing rapid and uneven.

The sound of the doodlebug became more and more distinct — then suddenly cut out. There was an ominous silence. Letitia heard Clive counting under his breath. "One . . . two . . . three . . ."

The explosion came after ten. It was a long way away: to the south and east on the other side of the river. After a moment, a distant plume of dust rose above the rooftops and slowly mingled with the grey of the sky. Someone had *caught it hot*, as Mrs Mansell would say.

Clive let out a shuddering breath. A little calmer now, he was able to free the wheel and face the journey home. He pushed the ponderous chair as fast as his scrawny frame would allow. He was all flesh and bone, his mother often said disapprovingly. Like Hugh, thought Letitia: Hugh as a boy, coming to her on brief visits during holidays from school.

They had not gone far when the unmistakable buzzing noise started up again, growing rapidly louder. It was not unexpected. The infernal things seemed to travel in flocks: where one led, others followed. As Clive struggled with the chair, bumping her up and down pavements, dashing along the straights, Letitia watched people all round her, some diving for shelter, others braving it out, all with glazed expressions: their ears were attuned to the noise in the sky.

"This one's chasing us!" Clive burst out, as if he couldn't stay quiet a moment longer. There was fear in his voice. He would have liked, Letitia felt, to run for cover as fast as his legs would carry him; but he went on pushing the chair with a dogged persistence that came from experience — from the neurotic's dour battle with the daily grind.

He reminds me of Jocelyn, thought Letitia suddenly. It seemed obvious, hearing his voice but not being able to see him as he pushed her. They were alike: not so much in looks or build, but Jocelyn, like Clive, had been a dogged character, quiet and sensitive underneath a veneer of boyish enthusiasm. Jocelyn had gritted his teeth and got on with life — until the day when it finally got too much for him.

206

It seemed incongruous to be thinking of Jocelyn with the flying bomb droning and stuttering towards them, but she couldn't blot out the growing feeling of dread. She was aware, though, that her fear was of a different timbre to Clive's. The doodlebug would land where it landed; it would be pure chance whether it landed on her or not. But Clive had said, *this one's chasing us*, as if he was being singled out, persecuted. Jocelyn had felt the same: that he'd been singled out; which in a sense he had. He'd been the son and heir, the chosen one: entrusted with the family name, the family honour, and all of their father's hopes for the future. It had been a heavy burden for such slender shoulders; and in the end Jocelyn had proved as big a disappointment to the bishop as Angelica.

They were close to home at last, just turning into the square. Looking up, Letitia caught a glimpse between rows of chimneys of the sinister winged tube passing them by: pure chance speeding it on its way to north-west London.

"I've heard all about your adventure the other day," said Megan when she called round.

"Clive told you, I suppose. He has told everyone. To me the risk was worth it, being outside, but he has been traumatized by the whole experience."

Letitia spoke lightly as she heaved herself out of her chair to put the kettle on, but in truth it was not just Clive who'd been affected. She had been given pause for thought. The blitz was a distant memory, the war in its last chapter, but death still lurked round every corner. She might have less time left than she imagined. And yet still this shilly-shallying went on between Hugh and Megan.

"There is something particularly terrifying about the doodlebugs," said Megan. "Lots of people feel it. They are impersonal, inanimate, yet also somehow alive."

Letitia, making tea, was only giving half her attention to the conversation. She had prided herself on not interfering, she had always taken a step back when Hugh seemed settled, content. She had been at pains not to make a nuisance of herself, but there seemed to be a barrier between Hugh and Megan that they were incapable of surmounting themselves. Perhaps only a third party could remove it. One would need to tread carefully, however. One did not want to turn into a second Connie Lambton. Connie had never shied away from interfering: on the contrary, she had thought it her duty. Indefatigable, condescending, she had been something of a Victorian relic. There were no women like her now. Her species was extinct.

They went into the area to drink their tea where they could get some fresh air and proper daylight. As she lowered herself onto the steps, Letitia was still thinking of Connie Lambton, remembering the particular inflexion in Connie's voice when she said of Megan, *Oh, that girl. I'm afraid, Letty, we were most dreadfully deceived in that whole business* . . . . Poor Connie! How she had hated being bamboozled in that way! Little had she known that the villagers, resenting her high-handed and meddle-some ways — they had called her Lady Muck amongst themselves — had gone out of

208

their way to thwart, block and scupper her plans at every opportunity whilst, to her face, curtsying and doffing their hats.

"Why are you smiling?" Megan, holding her mug in both hands, was standing looking at Letitia curiously.

"I was thinking of Connie Lambton and how the village liked to hoodwink her. Your mother, of course, was eminently successful in that sphere." It was such a roundabout way of approaching the subject of Hugh, that no one would ever suspect her of meddling, thought Letitia.

"You are referring to my visit to the Manor in 1902, I presume."

"I never knew your mother, of course, but I always admired her for pulling that off. She must have been a very resourceful woman."

"She was. She had learned to be."

"Tell me about her, my dear."

One had never known much about Megan. Perhaps she preferred it that way. She came from humble origins: that much was clear. One might have suspected her of being ashamed of that fact — deliberately obscuring it — but somehow one could not see her as the type of person who was embarrassed by poverty. At any rate, she seemed perfectly willing today to talk about her past — or some parts of her past, at least.

Perhaps I have passed some sort of test, said Letitia to herself: *perhaps after all these years she finally trusts me.*

Sitting on the steps whilst people passed on the pavement above, Letitia listened as Megan spoke about her mother. The early details of her mother's life were unclear. She had come to England from County Mayo as a child or young woman with her parents, but was soon orphaned. She had married — it must have seemed the only option, said Megan — but the marriage had been unhappy and childless. Before long Bridget O'Connor had found herself abandoned and alone. She had lived on her wits. She had taught herself to be bold and enterprising. She had hustled, she had beguiled, she had foisted herself on prospective employers; she had inveigled them into promoting her and raising her wages; she had forged signatures where necessary and invented impeccable references; she had helped herself to whatever was going.

"She was obviously a formidable woman," said Letitia.

"Few dared pick a fight with her," said Megan. "Fewer picked a fight and won. But she avoided confrontation where possible. *Never approach a problem head on*, she always said. She was clever. She used people's fear of emotion to manipulate them, and at the same time she made herself indispensable. It was all in the cause of bettering herself and providing for her children. Don't get me wrong. She was very good at her job. She would not have been half as successful otherwise. But she always made sure that people knew just how good she was."

"And did she ever remarry?" asked Letitia, thinking of Connie Lambton's words nearly thirty years before: *This maid had a daughter. What happened to the*

210

father I don't know. He was never mentioned, so we must draw our own conclusions.

"No, she never married again. I was in fact born on the wrong side of the blanket, if that makes any difference."

"No, of course not, my dear. In any case, even if one takes the view that illegitimacy is wrong, I could never understand why the sins of the parents should be visited on their children. My father . . ." She trailed off, remembering the bishop's polemics. What a hypocrite he had been, concerned only with appearances, the superficial. In his eyes, it did not matter what crimes one concealed, as long as one observed the proprieties; as long as one maintained a righteous and respectable façade.

Letitia stirred, found that Megan was watching her closely.

"Your father, you were saying?"

Letitia thrust the bishop aside. "It is your father we are talking of."

"Just who my father was remains a mystery. I never knew for certain, although I had some suspicions. There was an old gentleman in Wiltshire whom my mother worked for in the 1890s. She always spoke fondly of him. I got the impression she would never have left that situation, had she not fallen pregnant. Pregnant housemaids were frowned upon, swept under the carpet. My mother handed in her notice before she could be sacked. But afterwards the old gentleman kept in touch. He used to send money, which is how I first came to know about him. I used to see the envelopes arrive, the address written in the same neat hand. My mother was a proud woman and although never one to look a gift horse in the mouth, she was adamant about not accepting charity. That is what made me wonder if the old gentleman was in debt to her in some way. Mother would never discuss it. She would not say if he was my father or not. She always told me, *I am your mother and that is all you need to know.* We rowed about it — which I came to regret later."

"You never thought of going to see the old gentleman yourself, confronting him?"

"By the time I was old enough to be suspicious, he was dead. It was only when I was fifteen, sixteen that I finally put two and two together." Megan looked at her watch. "How time flies. I must go, I'm afraid."

She helped Letitia to her feet, lent her an arm as they went back into the kitchen with their mugs.

"You are a wicked woman, Letitia! I have spent all this time talking about myself, and have learned nothing about you!"

"My life has been terribly dull. I have nothing to confess." Letitia was barely conscious of lying as she settled in her old carver. "Before you go, you must tell me one last thing. How did you come to be staying at the Lambtons'? I heard Connie's explanation many years ago, but Connie tended to embellish the truth."

Megan sat down at the table, her coat draped over her lap. She looked unseeingly at Letitia as her mind reached back into the past. At the time in question, she said, her mother had been working for Lady Mereton, the latest in a long line of jobs. Put bluntly, Bridget

O'Connor had been poached: Lady Mereton had been notorious for it, appropriating other people's cooks and housekeepers and lady's-maids. Bridget had built up quite a reputation by then, and Lady Mereton had been determined to acquire her services. The salary on offer was generous, but there had been one drawback: Lady Mereton detested children.

"Lady Mereton," said Letitia looking back. "I had very little to do with her. She was an invalid, or imagined she was. I suppose that would account for her dislike of children and the noise they make. All I remember is that she used to lie on her *chaise-longue* wrapped in carriage rugs and send for patent medicines through the post."

Megan laughed. "Ghastly potions, they were! I saw them once, all lined up in a cupboard. That was on one of the occasions when I stayed a night in between visits elsewhere. Lady Mereton swore by her medicines. And sal volatile! I hated the smell of it ever after!"

"But carry on, my dear. You mother was working for Lady Mereton . . ."

"And we went with her, my brother and I — to start with, anyway. Mother impressed on us that we had to be on our best behaviour, quiet as mice. But of course, being children, we carried on as children do. We were excited about our new home; there was so much to see and do, so many rooms to explore. We ran hither and thither, chased down the corridors, made a nuisance of ourselves."

Lady Mereton had objected, Megan went on: she had objected strongly and at great length. Bridget

O'Connor, loath to give up such a highly remunerative situation, had had no choice but to send her children away. Her children, she reasoned, would benefit far more from the money she made, than they would from a mother sinking in poverty.

"So we were sent to Aunty Eileen in London. Aunty Eileen was none too pleased. She had a houseful already, eight kids of her own and just two rooms. Jack she could just about cope with — he was a placid child, quite unlike the tearaway he later became. But I was a handful already, and Aunty Eileen was at the end of her tether. So she packed me back to Warwickshire and I became Mother's problem again. And that is when the duplicitous visits began. It was the only solution Mother could come up with, and typically ingenious. Thus it was that I came to be staying with the Lambtons in 1902." Megan stood up and put on her coat. "And this time I really must go."

"But you have not tied up all the loose ends. For instance, what happened to your brother?"

"That," said Megan firmly, "is quite another story. Goodbye, Letitia." She kissed Letitia on the cheek.

"Goodbye, my dear." Letitia gripped Megan's hand then released it.

With Megan gone, the kitchen lapsed into silence. Letitia settled in her chair, closed her eyes, snoozing as she waited for the Mansells to foregather.

Hugh was miserable. Walking along a leafy lane in Buckinghamshire, he coughed and sneezed, his nose ran and his head ached. It was typical, he thought, that he should get a cold at the height of the summer. It might even be flu. It certainly felt bad enough for it to be flu. He usually enjoyed his solitary walks. Not today.

Sunshine was slanting down through the foliage in isolated beams. The branches of the trees entirely overhung the narrow lane. The hedges were tangled with flowers: wild roses, black bryony, blackberry blossom. In a few weeks the blackberries themselves would appear, heralding the approach of autumn. Once upon a time, he had enjoyed blackberry picking in the fields near The Firs, although it had been an activity tinged with sadness, for it marked the end of the holidays, the imminent start of a new school term. Hugh felt nostalgia for those holidays long ago, before the wars, and for those wonderful apple and blackberry pies made by the indispensable Annie. Illness and nostalgia together made him lachrymose, but he shook his head and would not cry, for he had been told long ago that crying made one a sissy.

His mind reached further back, to the days of Raggety Peg, the unlucky doll. He had been able to tell her all his secrets: his homesickness for India, his resentment towards his deceased mother, his alienation from his father. Raggety Peg had listened and never let on. And how had he repaid her? Treacherously, that's how, dropping her into a swollen stream in Shropshire. The image of her cloth face with its lopsided eyes floating off into oblivion still had the power to move him in the way such seemingly unimportant memories often do.

Throwing away Raggety Peg had been his first betrayal of Megan. He was betraying her still. Try as he might to block out the picture of Megan as a prostitute, it kept reappearing and reappearing. What business was it of his how she had lived her life? Who was he to judge? And what did it matter now? But it did matter, and it was an insurmountable barrier. It kept him apart from Megan and made him angry and frustrated.

Later that day, Hugh's superior called on him at his lodgings.

"You're doing no good to anyone sitting here and festering. Take the week off. Get away from it all. Have a complete break."

"It would be nice . . ." Hugh admitted.

"I think we can manage without you for one week. After all, we can hardly lose the war now, can we?"

Hugh packed and got on a train for London. People looked at him oddly as he sat in a corner wrapped in coat and scarf and woolly hat as if it was the middle of winter rather than a hot August afternoon. Hugh was oblivious to their stares and was soon asleep, not to wake until hours later when a guard roused him at Euston.

"How is Hugh?" asked Letitia, as Mrs Mansell came into the kitchen.

"I have told him to stay in bed. He will feel a lot better tomorrow after a good rest and some of my cabbage soup."

Letitia wrinkled her nose at the thought of Mrs Mansell's infamous cabbage soup. She had a sneaking

216

suspicion that Mrs Mansell was enjoying bossing Hugh around.

"I think it is the war more than anything," said Letitia. "Hugh is suffering from the war. It chips away at you, wears you out."

"I expect you are right." Mrs Mansell was peeling potatoes, didn't look round.

"You are the exception. You do not seem ever to get worn out."

"I'm as tough as old boots." Mrs Mansell was concentrating on making the potato peelings as thin as possible. Watching her, Letitia experienced a pang of jealousy. Was it not enough that Mrs Mansell had taken over her kitchen, without taking over Hugh as well?

Mrs Mansell glanced at the clock on the wall. "How long does it take to fetch a pint of milk?" she said; and Letitia immediately felt guilty about her unreasonable jealousy. She recognized the anxiety behind Mrs Mansell's tetchy manner. Clive had been despatched to the shops three-quarters of an hour ago and since then an alert had come into force. There was no tell-tale buzzing in the sky, no sound of explosions; but Letitia suspected that Clive would be lying low somewhere, in a shelter or down the tube. He had developed an all-consuming fear of the flying bombs — or so she guessed. He would never have said as much. He gave very little away, did Clive.

Hugh was the same. There was obviously something weighing on his mind. She knew the signs by now, had become adept over the years at reading his little mannerisms, just as she'd learned to read between the lines of his letters, so that she had known without having it spelled out that he was unhappy at his prep school, or afraid in the trenches, or disillusioned with Cynthia. But knowing something was wrong was one thing; getting him to talk was quite another. A certain amount of ingenuity would be required. In the meantime, let Mrs Mansell do her worst. It was not, Letitia admitted, as if she was in any position to nurse Hugh herself.

Letitia laid her plans as Mrs Mansell prepared the dinner.

Luxuriating in a tepid puddle of a bath in Eleanor Lambton's Paddington house, Megan found herself lamenting her rash revisiting of the past during her recent visit to Letitia. A multitude of other memories and half-buried emotions had been stirred up which she felt ill-equipped to deal with after a day run ragged at work, on top of the stress of five years of war.

She relived that last argument she'd had with her mother in 1910, standing on the back stairs of Lady Mereton's house, her mother on the way to the drawing-room with a tray in her hand. (Afternoon tea, had it been? Lady Mereton had been partial to egg-and-cress sandwiches, no crusts.) Her mother had been sending her away again, another of those visits under false pretences.

"I won't go this time. I've had enough. I want to stay here with you."

"Don't be an idiot, Megan. You know you can't stay here. I shall lose my job, and then what will become of us?"

"You care more about your job than you do about me! I'm sure my father wouldn't be as cruel as you are. Who is he? Tell me!"

"For the last time, no."

"I shall go. I shall leave. But not where *you're* sending me."

"Go, then, and see how far you get!"

But she had got all the way to London, her heart in her mouth the whole journey long: for she'd had barely sixpence to her name and had been kept on her toes, evading the guards and the ticket inspectors. She had made her way to Aunty Eileen's in the East End where her brother Jack was still living.

She had never seen her mother again. Bridget O'Connor had died unexpectedly less than six months later.

"Such an *inconvenience*," Lady Mereton had bewailed; but to give her her due, she had arranged and paid for the funeral, one last perk for the most efficient housekeeper she had ever had.

Aunty Eileen, with eight growing children of her own and now receiving nothing by way of Jack's keep, had shown them both the door. They had been homeless, penniless, on their own.

"Now don't you cry, Meggie. I'll look after you, you'll see." But Jack had been little more than a boy.

They had found somewhere to live eventually, had taken what jobs they could find, did their best to survive. Jack had grown up quickly. He had taken after their mother, with an eye to the main chance; but not having Bridget O'Connor's charm and feminine wiles — being a rough-and-ready sort of lad — he had chosen a different path to the one taken by their resourceful mother. A little pick-pocketing and burglary, he'd discovered, was much more remunerative and far less monotonous than slaving all hours for a pittance.

"Oh, Jack, you mustn't! Say you won't steal again! You'll get caught and put away and I'll be left on my own!"

"I promise, Meggie. This will be the last time. I'll never do it again after today." But he always did. "Don't be so hard on me, Meggie. I'm doing it for us. And I only ever nick stuff off of toffs. They don't miss it. They've got plenty: more than enough, if you ask me."

She had been exasperated by him, had despaired of him — but she had loved him, the only family she had left. If she was honest, looking back, something of his rumbustious nature had rubbed off on her so that, in due course, she had found herself ready to take up the mantle of a suffragette. Smashing windows on the Strand had been just as illegal as any of Jack's nefarious activities; but she had never got caught, unlike Jack.

Jack had been fourteen when he spent his first brief spell in prison. It had seemed like the end of the world at the time; but later she had come to think of it as the work of providence, for it meant that Jack was not around when, in April 1912, she had met Hugh again. Jack would not have approved of Hugh, one of those toffs whose possessions were fair game. Nor, she felt, would Hugh have taken to Jack. It would have been a clash of opposites. She had been glad in retrospect that the two of them had never met.

It was when Jack had been caught for a second time and hauled up in court that her path had crossed that of Julian Lambton once more. Julian that day had been doing his level best to have Jack locked up and the key thrown away; but as the case progressed, his eyes had begun to stray more and more towards the gallery where Megan, glaring at him, had been calling him all the worst names she could think of under her breath.

I was naive, idealistic, and I saw things in terms of black or white, thought Megan looking back in 1944: *and of course, I had no idea then how thin the line that separates hate from love.*

The bath water had grown entirely cold. Megan got out of the tub, pulled the plug, dried herself, began to get dressed, thankful for the peace and privacy that Eleanor's house afforded. What would Eleanor's son make of the arrangement, she wondered, whereby his father's mistress availed herself of the comforts of the Paddington house with the connivance of his own mother? One thing was sure, said Megan to herself, laughing as she pulled on her stockings: Jack would have heartily approved of her taking advantage of the toffs in this way.

Hugh ventured down to the kitchen next morning once the Mansells had vacated the house for the day. He was wrapped in a blanket.

Letitia laughed. "Now we are two old crocks together."

"I am sorry, Aunt. I should be taking you out and about in that ridiculous chair instead of sitting here shivering and sneezing."

"Nonsense. Rest is what you require. Rest, and a little something to perk you up."

Hugh looked apprehensive. "Not cabbage soup?"

Letitia laughed as she put the kettle on. "No, not cabbage soup. Hot toddies are called for, I think. For medicinal purposes, naturally."

"Isn't a bit early in that day for that sort of thing?"

"In my experience it is never too early for a good thing. And never too late, either."

"I don't know what you mean, Aunt."

"I am talking about Megan."

"Oh, that." Hunched over the table, disconsolate, Hugh said, "I sometimes think it would have been better had we never met again."

"Oh, tush!" Letitia brought the hot toddies across to the table, eased herself into her chair. "You were meant to meet again. You are meant to be together."

She took a sharp breath, hearing her own words, knowing that she was going to break her own cardinal rule. *Now*, she thought: *now I have shot my bolt. Either my meddling will produce results, or it will blow up in my face. Either way, I am too old to be treading on eggshells.*

"There is something holding you back, Hugh."

"Oh? Do you think so?"

"I may be physically decrepit, but my mind has not entirely ceased to function."

Hugh was silent for a time, playing with the spoon in his glass of whisky and water; but the alcohol, working on his empty stomach, began to have the effect that Letitia had hoped for: it began to loosen his tongue.

It was Megan's past he was worried about, he admitted. He was vague on details, but Letitia didn't need to be told. She had heard those rumours before.

"I don't believe a word of it. Connie Lambton told me a similar story once upon a time. It was only later that one began to realize how Connie embellished her stories, exaggerating the truth, inventing where she felt it was necessary."

Hugh looked up. "What on earth did Mrs Lambton know about Megan?"

"Megan stayed at the Manor once, if you remember."

"But that was years ago, when we were kids."

"And it was under false pretences, too. Connie was most put out when, a long time later, she found out she'd been duped. Naturally she did not have a good word to say about Megan after that. Possibly it was with Connie that those absurd rumours you seem to have heard started."

"Possibly," said Hugh, not sounding convinced, fingering something in his pocket.

"Well? Does that lay to rest any lingering doubts?"

"Not . . . not quite. You see, Aunt, there's this."

He took from his pocket whatever it was he'd been fiddling with and handed it across to her. She took it in her gnarled hand and looked at it curiously. It was a lighter, a cigarette lighter, and —

Her heart lurched, for there engraved in the metal were Hugh's initials, just as she remembered.

It's a going-away present for Hugh. There was a voice from the past in her head, clear as day. *You know him better than I, Aunt. Do you think he will like it?*

Arnold, in the garden at The Firs, long ago.

Letitia remembered gripping Arnold's arm, reassuring him, telling him that of course Hugh would like the gift, it was perfect. But she had never known in the end if Arnold had passed it on or not — if he had balked at the last moment, reticent of any display of emotion. She had not liked to ask Hugh about it, given the circumstances, and had never seen him use it. She had come to believe that Arnold had taken it with him to his watery grave. Seeing it again now, over thirty years later, was somehow disquieting, as if a ghost had risen from the depths of the Atlantic and come to haunt her.

"I don't understand. This is the lighter your father gave to you on the eve of his wedding. It must be."

"Yes it is, Aunt. And I gave it to Megan in April 1912."

There were still things one couldn't tell her, things one could never say to one's aunt: details of those spring days in London that he kept to himself; but it was a relief to finally confess, to have it in the open, to expunge the residue of guilt he felt at having deceived his grandparents and his school friend in order to seek adventure in the metropolis.

Letitia had not been entirely in the dark about that episode, he discovered. Megan had mentioned it in her letter of 1915, the letter he had never seen. But of course his aunt had no idea of the significance that meeting held for him — unless, of course, she could read it in his face as he spoke about it now. He wouldn't have put it past her. Not a lot escaped her; he had learned that over the years. But she tended to keep her own counsel: he knew that too.

"Surely, Hugh, if Megan has kept this lighter all these years, it tells you something?"

"But that's just it, Aunt. She didn't keep it. She gave it away — or had it stolen from her."

"Then how did you . . .?"

"I met a man — a soldier — in the war: the first war."

Hugh closed his eyes, trying to sort out his jumbled memories of that incident, trying to decide what was real and what his subconscious had invented later, tormenting him as he lay in hospital week after week, month after month, with his wounded leg. He had been in shock, lost in no-man's land, losing blood: it was no wonder it was all so hazy in his mind. Or had that come later? Had he blotted out what he didn't want to know — what he couldn't bear to know? It was impossible to get to the truth after so long.

"He was a petty thief, this soldier. He'd stolen that" — he pointed — "that lighter. That's how I came to have it again. I . . . I took it from him. But before I did, he as good as told me that he'd stolen it in London from a . . . a prostitute."

"And you believed him?"

"I don't know what to believe. I thought of asking Megan. I thought of showing her that." He pointed again to the lighter in her hands.

"What if you're wrong? It might destroy everything, asking such a question." She dropped the lighter onto the table, reached over to grasp Hugh's hand in both of hers. "Hugh. Ask yourself. Does it matter? If you love her, does it matter what she did in the past, what lengths she went to in order to survive? If she did sink so low — and I don't think she did: I don't for a minute — but even if she did, would it matter? Would it matter now, knowing her as you do?"

"Great-grandfather would have said so. The bishop would have said it mattered."

"I am not asking the bishop ..." Letitia's voice wavered, then grew firm again. "I am not asking *him*. I am asking you."

Me, thought Hugh: *she is asking me. It is my opinion that counts.*

The *only* opinion that counted.

Why had he not seen that before? It seemed obvious now. But he had been young, confused, grieving for his father. He had wanted answers. He had thought there had to be answers.

But what if there *were* no answers?

He remembered suddenly, at the beginning of the war, sitting here with Letitia in this very kitchen as the Luftwaffe rained bombs down on London. They had been talking about his father. The *Titanic*, she'd said, had not been an act of Divine vengeance or a symbol of

226

man's frailty: it had been a terrible accident. Simply an accident. No one had been to blame, she'd said. Why hadn't he listened to her? Why hadn't he seen it for himself? He wouldn't make that mistake again. His aunt was right about Megan. *Knowing her as you do* .... It was impossible that she could ever do anything he couldn't forgive. It wasn't in her nature. He knew he was right about that. He had to trust his own instincts. That, in effect, was what Aunt Letitia was telling him.

He took a deep breath and, as he did so, it was as if he could hear the last echoes of the bishop's polemics — the polemics he'd read so avidly in the library at Overton long ago — fading away, fading to nothing.

He pointed to the lighter one last time. "What about that?"

Letitia pushed it away from her across the table. "Get rid of it. Forget about it. All these years, I thought it was at the bottom of the Atlantic. Send it into deep water now. Throw it into the Thames."

In the Thames? And yet why not?

Hugh nodded. "I will. I'll do it."

He would throw all his doubts and suspicions away with it, too. It was the perfect solution. Aunt Letitia had come to his rescue once again.

Even after all these years, she never ceased to surprise him.

After lunch, when Hugh had gone back to bed to sleep off his fever, Letitia sat in the half-light of the kitchen thinking of Arnold whose life had come to an untimely end on a cold calm night in the mid-Atlantic thirty years before. Poor Arnold. Yet he had known love in the end with Daffodil, and he had been reconciled with Hugh, the son he had almost grown to fear.

She remembered sitting by the fire at The Firs in 1902, Arnold slowly coming to terms with the loss of his wife and child. *To be hated by one's son*, he had said, *as well as one's father, would be too much.*

Poor Arnold. And poor Jocelyn. Poor, poor Jocelyn.

Letitia used unsteady fingers to wipe away the tears from her parchment-like cheeks, knowing that she could never have told Arnold who his real father was.

CHAPTER
TEN

Hugh, having survived Mrs Mansell's cabbage soup, headed back to Buckinghamshire to resume his hush-hush work, while in Europe Paris was liberated and General de Gaulle entered the city a hero. The Germans were everywhere in rapid retreat. A day came when there was neither sight nor sound of a doodlebug, no alerts. Another followed. People hardly dared to think that that menace of the air raids might be over. They had been cheated of this hope before. But this time there was a real sense of optimism bubbling under the surface. One could sense it everywhere.

The war will soon be finished, thought Letitia. If only Hugh and Megan would get a move on, stop beating about the bush. At least then she would know Hugh was settled, would need her no more. It had happened once before. She had prepared the way to fade into the background of Hugh's life, thinking he had found happiness with Cynthia; but Cynthia had been a blind alley and Letitia had suddenly found herself centre stage again as his marriage dissolved. This time it would be different. Megan was different. Letitia was sure of Megan, whereas she had always had lingering doubts about Cynthia.

It was the fifth anniversary of the start of the war and Sunday had been designated a day of national prayer. As she put on her Sunday best — the habit of a lifetime — Letitia imagined grimly the sort of prayers her father would have declaimed on such an occasion, prayers not of reconciliation but of retribution. Thankfully the bishop had long ago mouldered away in his grave and the long reach of his authority was finally failing.

She dismissed the bishop, thinking instead of a previous day of national prayer, in May 1940, when things had looked so bleak: Europe conquered, the British Army shattered; it had seemed at the time like the end of everything. But now, looking back, those events had paled into insignificance, like one of the intense catastrophes of youth from which one believes one will never recover. May 1940 now seemed a time of sunshine and heroism when she had still been nimble on her feet, always dashing off, visiting or shopping or merely walking for the fun of it, perambulating round London as newspaper placards proclaimed the miracle of Dunkirk and the new prime minister roused the nation with his stirring speeches.

All the same, Letitia said to herself as she lowered herself onto the stool in front of the dressing-table, all the same, those catastrophes leave scars, and the scars never fade. She picked up her hairbrush, avoiding scars of her own and considering the scar of May 1940: the once mighty empire of the Victorians reduced to ferrying its defeated army across the Channel on pleasure boats. The world would not forget.

She looked at the face staring out at her from the mirror: the sunken eyes, the wrinkles. Was that really her? How had she got so old?

It seemed to her that she could hear gulls mewing, the sea crashing onto rocks; that she could smell damp; that a bewhiskered doctor in a frock coat was standing over her.

Pleurisy and pneumonia, Miss Benham. You might have died.

I wanted to die. I thought I had nothing to live for. But when you are young, you can't see ahead, you don't think about what might be waiting round the next corner.

She put her brush aside, straightened her pearls. There. She was ready.

Getting to her feet, she made her way slowly downstairs to help Mrs Mansell with the Sunday lunch.

Running for the bus, Megan tripped as she jumped up onto the platform.

"Whoopsie daisy!" The conductress put out an arm, saved Megan from falling flat on her face. Bottles chinked in her basket.

Smiling her thanks at the conductress — one professional woman to another — Megan mounted the stairs to take a seat on the top deck, lifting the cloth on her basket to check that no bottles had broken. As the bus patrolled the quiet Sunday streets, Megan looked out of the window, slowly sponging away the detritus of another busy week from her overtaxed mind, a week taken up with patients: patients queuing outside the consulting-room, patients waiting in their homes for a visit. Megan smiled her way through it, taking pulses, writing prescriptions, offering advice. Today, though, belonged to her. She regretted that her bicycle was out of service, but there had been no time to fix it, and taking the bus had its compensations. She relaxed into her seat, watching as London flitted past, recognizing all the familiar landmarks: not the great public buildings which everyone knew, but the landmarks of her life. In that street, she had broken windows in her days as a suffragette. And there, in that house, she had once lived for a few weeks in the 1920s. On that corner by the theatre, she had rowed with Julian Lambton in the early months of the first war.

I have never stayed put, I have always moved on, she reflected. Looking back at her nomadic existence, she wondered if, at her age, it was time to take root, to find a place that she could call home. She had never had a real home. Her mother's jobs had taken them from country house to country house until, taking the position with Lady Mereton, Bridget O'Connor had been compelled to palm Megan off on unsuspecting hosts such as Mrs Lambton.

After living in splendour as the guest of well-to-do families, Megan had found it difficult to get used to sleeping on Aunt Eileen's bare boards again, listening to rats scrabbling beneath her. But even that had been luxury compared to what came next: huddling in doorways and dark alleys, living from hand to mouth, begging on street corners, until she and Jack found work and a tiny room of their own. Things had looked up until Jack was arrested and sent to prison. Alone, Megan had taken rooms where she could, one near Victoria Station, another in Limehouse, waiting for the day that Jack was released; but he had not been a free man for long. Unable to kick his bad habits, he had found himself in court again. It had been then that Julian Lambton had unexpectedly reappeared in her life after a gap of more than ten years.

Julian had been posh, a man from a different class, brusque and interfering, like his mother. Megan had resented him, resented the names he called her, but even in the earliest days of their acquaintance, the attraction between them had been indisputable. There might have been a pang of regret for Hugh — more than a pang — but she had crushed it. Hugh, after all, had abandoned her without a word.

Julian had known nothing of Megan's meeting with Hugh in 1912. Megan had never mentioned it. All the same, Hugh had cropped up. It was Julian himself who had first spoken of him. Julian had accused her of being in love with Hugh. That was what the row had been about as they left the theatre that the bus had just passed.

"What you are saying is ridiculous!" she had shouted at him at the top of her voice, taking no notice of more refined theatregoers who had looked askance at this uncouth couple airing their dirty laundry in public. "I was seven years old! One knows nothing of love at that age!"

Julian had shouted back at her, waving the theatre programme in her face. "I knew about love at that age. I knew, because I was in love with you!"

"Balderdash! Poppycock! How can you stand there and say —"

"How can I? How dare you, in that tatty dress —"

"Tatty dress? You bought this frock!"

"You chose it. If you don't like it, you can —"

"I like it, but I don't want it. I don't want your money and I don't want you. This is madness. What we are doing is madness. I have had enough."

"I don't give a fig about money, you can have every last penny. I just want to know why you gave that doll to Hugh bloody Benham. Why didn't you give it to me?"

"Because I hated you. You were rude and arrogant and nasty to poor Hugh —"

"Poor Hugh! *Poor Hugh!*"

"I felt sorry for him."

"Aha! So you admit it! You did love him! You see, I was right! And now you must also admit — Hey, where are you going? Come back here this instant! Don't expect me to come running after you . . . That's it. This is as far as I'll follow you . . . Look at me, you bloody woman, when I'm talking to you . . ."

They had often argued in those early days. It had been wonderful, exhilarating, firing their passion for one another; but Megan had never been under any illusions about their relationship. Julian was married. She could never be anything other than his mistress. Nor could she entirely forget Hugh, however much she tried. He had been so different to Julian: quiet, sensitive, would never have dreamt of raising his voice to her. And so, unable to get him out of her head, she had written to The Firs in 1915 hoping for news of him. She had not admitted to wanting more than that. Just news. But all the same she had been bitterly disappointed when no reply came. She had taken that as his final answer. He didn't want her. And so the chapter of Hugh Benham was finally closed — or so she'd thought.

By then, her relationship with Julian had changed. War had altered him. In his letters and when on leave, he had talked of giving up Law, going off somewhere remote and rural, taking up pig farming — or sheep, he could never decide which. He made plans, what he was going to do after the war. It had still been possible, in 1915, to make plans. No one had imagined how the nightmare would all drag on, how the world would change. Julian had become dissatisfied with second best, had decided from then on that he would squeeze out of life everything that he possibly could. And what he had wanted more than anything was to take up farming and to marry Megan.

He had talked of divorce. Megan had counselled against it. They were happy as they were, why create a scandal and turn society against him?

"I don't give a damn about society. Why should I care a fig what those people think, the same people who have got us into this god awful mess? I love you, Megan, and I want to be with you. I do not love

Eleanor; Eleanor does not love me. A divorce would be best all round, best for little Jimmy, too."

Julian had made his moves, prepared the way for divorce, found a smallholding he wished to buy. He had made ready for life after the war, a life that would at last be of his own choosing.

Fate, however, had made other plans for him and snatched that life away early one sunny morning in July 1916. Megan, the secret mistress, had not received a telegram, had not known he was dead until she saw the notice in *The Times*. She had panicked, imagining that the family would somehow find out about her, come looking for her, seek revenge. She had fled Julian's London flat as quickly as she could.

Twenty-eight years later, Megan got to her feet, rang the bell, picked up her basket, edged down the stairs as the bus slowed and stopped. Stepping down onto the pavement, Megan heard the conductress call out, "Mind how you go!" Turning to wave, Megan watched the red bus pull out into the road and gather speed, its engine coughing and rattling.

As she started walking, she found herself, from force of habit, listening out for the menacing buzz-buzz of flying bombs. Relaxing again as she remembered that the days of the doodlebugs were over, she let her mind drift back to a notice in *The Times*: not Julian's death, but her own name in black and white in the first weeks of 1919. There had been a message, asking her to contact a certain solicitor who would tell her *something to her advantage*.

The solicitor had told her that Mrs Lambton wished to meet her. For a moment, Megan had thought he was referring to the meddlesome Connie and felt sure that the message in the newspaper had been an elaborate plan to trap her. The solicitor said no, it was Mrs *Eleanor* Lambton who wanted to speak to her. But that had seemed just as sinister. By then, however, she'd had nothing to lose, so she'd agreed to a meeting.

She had been crippled with nerves, going to lunch with her dead lover's wife in the winter of 1919. They had met in a restaurant on the Strand whose name now eluded her and which, later on, had been bombed flat in the early days of the Blitz. It had been neither too posh nor too common, as if Eleanor Lambton had chosen to meet on neutral ground; but Megan had been on her uppers by then, had been tattered and shabby. She remembered the grating condescension of the elderly waiter, the way he had let the word *madam* linger on his tongue as he saw her to the table. She remembered Eleanor Lambton pale and thin in black, wearing one of those tube-like dresses which had been the fashion back then, and a cloche hat.

The food had been delicious, her fish flaking off the bone, the sauce piquant and creamy, but she had barely touched it, her stomach clenched with nerves. She had been terribly conscious of the waste in those hungry days. She could not now remember what sort of fish it had been or what the sauce was called; she just knew that, when the waiter came to clear her plate, he had rolled his eyes at her, disdainful, before turning to fawn over Eleanor Lambton.

"Will you have coffee? I always have coffee. Where has that waiter gone?"

Megan agreed to coffee, her heart sinking, and watched as Eleanor Lambton summoned the waiter with an imperious, brusque little gesture. She wished the terrible meal was over. As a refined form of torture, it was particularly effective. Perhaps that was what Eleanor intended.

Eleanor, dabbing her mouth with her napkin, said, "I'm sorry if the food was not to your liking."

"I am afraid I have lost my appetite. I was rather terrified at the prospect of meeting you." Megan had learned that honesty was often disarming, but Eleanor's expression remained blank.

They sat in silence until the coffee came. Megan stirred in sugar, tapped her spoon on the side of the cup to get the drips off — and immediately wondered if that was a vulgar thing to do. She looked around to see if the elderly waiter had noticed, but he was not there. The lunchtime rush was over, the place emptying. Through the steamed-up windows she could see indistinct figures hurrying along the Strand, huddled against a whipping wind. She wondered if she had ever, during the course of her career as a suffragette, broken those particular windows. She felt an almost overwhelming urge to do so right then and there.

"You must understand," Eleanor Lambton began suddenly, biting off her words, "that I was not interested in Julian's will. I neither knew nor cared what was in it. I didn't even read it."

Megan stirred her coffee again, watching the brown liquid whirling in the cup. She was at a loss to explain this meeting. It seemed pointless. What did she care if Eleanor had read Julian's will or not?

"It was the Lambtons' family solicitor who suggested that Julian had not been of sound mind when he made the latest changes to it. It was his opinion, he said, that Julian had become unhinged by the war. He said we should destroy the last version of the will and replace it with an earlier copy. No one need ever know. My mother-in-law agreed. Indeed, I think it may have been her idea in the first place. I didn't think to question it. It never occurred to me that it might be against the law. You must think I was awfully naïve."

Eleanor's voice was clipped, precise; but it betrayed her every so often. It suddenly struck Megan that this was as hard for Eleanor as it was for her; perhaps harder. Why?

Eleanor had not even looked at her coffee yet.

"We knew of your existence, of course, even before Julian's death. At least, I knew. I thought I was the only one who did. I didn't realize until afterwards that his mother knew too. Nothing much gets past Mrs Lambton. When Julian was killed, she was quite determined that not a penny of his money would be handed over to a trollop." Eleanor looked at Megan, meeting her eyes for the first time. "That was her word, not mine."

"I wouldn't have blamed you if you'd used it."

Eleanor looked away. "I am afraid I have always been slow on the uptake. It is only now that I have come to realize the injustice of what they did, Mrs Lambton and the family solicitor: the injustice that I connived in."

Megan shifted in her seat. This absurd conversation — or monologue — had gone on long enough. "I'm sorry, I really don't have the faintest idea what you are talking about."

Eleanor reached for her bag. "Perhaps this will explain." She took out a piece of paper, unfolded it, flattened it against the tablecloth, then handed it across. "My solicitor prepared this document. You could, of course go to the police, but I don't think there will be any incriminating evidence. They would have been careful about that. So I have made my own arrangements, in lieu."

Megan read what was written on the paper. It was impossible to take it in all at once. She was aware of Eleanor, with a sudden jerky movement, spooning sugar into her coffee: one spoonful, two spoonfuls; a third remained poised above the cup. She was aware, too, of every single waiter in the background, clearing tables of napkins and cutlery and glasses and bottles, sweeping away tablecloths, placing chairs neatly. It was not just the waiter who'd served them who was elderly: none of the others was less than middle-aged. She wondered if perhaps there were no young waiters left. Maybe they had all been killed in the war.

Even as she was noticing all this — even as her thoughts jolted round in her head — the meaning of the note was slowly sinking in.

240

Abruptly, she put the paper aside. "I don't understand. I don't want his money. I never did. It belongs to you."

"It belonged to Julian. It was up to him whom he gave it to." Eleanor looked down, noticed as if for the first time the sugar poised above her coffee. With a slow, smooth motion she withdrew the spoon and tipped the sugar back into the bowl.

Megan picked up the paper and read it again. "It's so much."

"He obviously felt you were worth it." She spoke flatly, no hint of irony.

"But what does Mrs Lambton say — your mother-in-law, I mean?"

"It's nothing to do with her." Eleanor took a sip of coffee (it must be cold by now, thought Megan) and then wiped her lips. "She no longer takes an interest in such matters, in any case. They are all dead, you see. Her sons, I mean. They are all —" Eleanor broke off, pursed her lips, turned away, blinking.

Without expecting to, Megan felt a sudden compassion for the woman. Eleanor was not being remote and off-hand because of some snobbish sense of superiority, she realized. She was simply being herself. And there was nothing there. She was just a shell. There was grief — for Julian? for someone else? — but even that seemed little more than an echo. It was, Megan felt, a terrible waste.

"Mrs Lambton, I can't possibly take your money."

"Oh, but you must, I insist."

"But your boy . . ."

"Jimmy inherits the estate: the Manor, the land, everything. He doesn't need this money."

Megan smiled. It seemed little enough, but she wanted desperately to give Eleanor something and a smile was all she had. Eleanor blinked again, as if in acknowledgement. It was impossible to imagine that she would ever smile. "You needn't have done this, Mrs Lambton. I would never have known."

"I couldn't have lived with myself if I hadn't at least tried to put things right. It was wrong of me to let myself be pushed into a corner by Mrs Lambton over the will. It was wrong of me, for that matter, to let them push me into marrying Julian. I didn't love him. I loved somebody else. But . . . it was impossible . . ."

"Perhaps . . ."

"It's too late." Eleanor picked up her cup, put it down again. "It's too late now." Her lips snapped shut and the conversation was over.

As they parted, shivering in the bitter wind blowing along the Strand, Megan suddenly turned back.

"Mrs Lambton, I should like to write to you, if I may."

Eleanor pulled her stole closer. "Write to me? Why should you want to write to me?"

"To tell you how I spend the money. I don't intend to waste it, you see."

Eleanor digested this, nodded slowly. "If that is what you want, Miss O'Connor, I should look forward to hearing from you."

242

And then she was gone, walking rapidly along the Strand towards Charing Cross Station, a thin black figure rapidly swallowed by the crowds.

Walking through the balmy streets in September 1944, Megan had reason to be grateful for Julian's legacy. Without that money, she would never have been able to train as a doctor; but it had also come as a timely moment, when she was not only destitute but demoralized too, thinking that life had nothing left to offer. She had lost everyone she had ever cared about: her mother, Hugh, Julian and finally Jack — for Jack had been released from prison just as conscription was being introduced and had been swallowed up by the army. She had seen him only once after that, when he came on leave in the bitter cold of January 1917. She had done all she could to make him feel at home, to give him every comfort, pawning or selling what few relics she had left of her time with Julian, clothes and bits of jewellery. They had not spoken of the war. He had told her nothing of what life was like at the front. Nor had Julian for that matter, but he had always wanted to look forward, to life when peace came; Jack never looked beyond the next meal. Her only glimpse of what was going through his mind, how he was feeling, had come at the end, when she was seeing him off. He'd suddenly leant out of the train and caught her hand, staring into her eyes. She remembered the feel of his calloused fingers. He had knocked his cap against the window frame and it had fallen off, fallen back into the carriage. His hair — black, so different to hers — had stuck up in unruly tufts as it always did.

"I don't want to go, Meggie. I shan't come back. I know that I shan't come back."

"Yes you will. You must. You have to."

There had been a terrible crush on the platform, people dashing last minute to catch the train, steam hissing, smoke billowing, noise reverberating round the high roof. And at that moment the whistle had blown — when he was holding her hand as if they were children again. He was asking her to protect him as a big sister should — begging her.

She had reached into her pocket for something to give him, some token to represent everything she did not have time to say: money, anything — and her hand had closed round the cigarette lighter that Hugh had given her five years before, that she had kept as a memento, a reminder, clinging to the nostalgia of those brief few days. It was almost the only thing of any value that she had left.

She had given Jack the lighter as the train pulled away, passed it from her outstretched hand to his: an amulet, a lucky charm; had watched as he disappeared in clouds of steam, swept away from her into the cold and dark of the winter evening.

She had never seen him again. The lucky charm had failed. A telegram had come: *missing, believed killed*. And that had marked the end. She'd had nothing left.

As she walked towards the familiar square where Letitia lived, she wondered what had become of the cigarette lighter. Lost in the Flanders mud, she supposed; and Jack with it.

Her life after that had dwindled to a drab existence of ceaseless toil until even that had failed her and, two years later, she had gone to meet Eleanor Lambton on the Strand jobless, almost homeless, with nothing to wear but what she stood up in. Little had she known how things had been about to change.

Eleanor had never exactly become a friend, but had encouraged Megan in her new career — living vicariously, Megan had sensed: for whatever ambitions Eleanor might have cherished as a little girl had been crushed by her upbringing and education — or lack of it — and by what Megan called Eleanor's *secret sorrow*. The secret sorrow Megan could only guess at. In all the years they had known one another, Eleanor had never confided in her; probably thought Megan, had never confided in anyone. She remembered how, in that restaurant on the Strand, Eleanor had suddenly turned aside, blinking back tears that weren't there. She remembered thinking what a waste it was, Eleanor crushed and desiccated when, with her advantages, she ought to have had the world at her feet. She wished now that she'd had the courage to question Eleanor, to make her speak, break the icy hold of her misery; but she had felt at a disadvantage in her shabby clothes, with Eleanor so sure of herself, so at home, so elegant. That Megan — the Megan of 1919 — could never have got close to Eleanor Lambton.

And now it is too late, she thought, crossing the road, passing the place where the bombed house had been. *Our long acquaintance has taken a different path, fallen into a well-worn groove. I will never now discover Eleanor's secret. But what about my secret? Is it too late for me, too?*

Megan thrust her memories aside as, swinging her basket, she descended the area steps towards Letitia's basement, the smell of cooking rising to meet her. What would Mrs Mansell have for them this Sunday? Woolton Pie, was it?

The kitchen was a brighter place than of late. Clive had been persuaded to take the boards down from the windows now that the doodlebug menace appeared to be over. Everyone was gathered — all the inmates, as Letitia called them — plus someone else: a stranger, Megan thought at first, a young man sitting at the table. Only when he got up to greet her did Megan recognize him: Hugh's son Ian, whom she had not seen for three years. Most definitely Hugh's son, Megan thought, looking at his battle-hardened features. There was something familiar about the curve of his nose, the cut of his jaw. It was how Hugh must have looked in his twenties. Megan experienced a twinge of regret that she had not known Hugh in his twenties. All those wasted years. *And still we waste time,* she said to herself: *I waste time; I hesitate. I am being slowly smothered by my secret just as Eleanor was by hers.*

She pulled up a chair, joining the throng. As well as Letitia and Ian and Mrs Mansell, there was Mr Mansell sitting morose in a corner, never more than monosyllabic; Clive listening in awe to Ian's stories of

246

Italy and Normandy, and Susie helping her mother with the cooking.

"I've bought some orangeade and some beer." Megan unpacked her basket. "And a cake."

"That will do for tea." Mrs Mansell appropriated the cake with practised dispatch and shut it in the larder. "You will be staying for tea, I hope, Doctor Kramer?"

Megan said yes, laughing, and Letitia caught her eye and winked.

Ian set about the beer. He was telling them now about his journey home, how he'd been seasick crossing the Channel before squashing into a train that had crawled towards London like a snail. He had arrived only that morning. Mrs Mansell, Megan noted, was decidedly frosty towards him. The upset over the Immaculate Conception had obviously not been forgotten. Presumably the real test would come when Peggy's husband came home. That could not be far off now, the way the war was going.

Megan poured herself orangeade, offered the bottle to Clive.

"Clive'll have beer," said Ian, slapping Clive on the shoulder.

"Clive will not," said Mrs Mansell darkly.

Clive had orangeade, but eyed the bottles of beer with regret and Megan smiled, relaxing into her chair, easing her shoes off, thinking that all-in-all there was nowhere else she would rather spend her Sunday than in Letitia's basement kitchen — with the old lady herself sitting there, presiding over it all, frail but determined. There was a kind of ethereal beauty about her: shrunken, wizened, her hands knobbed and twisted and spotted with age, her skin translucent, like silk, blue veins showing. Her clothes hung off her as she was terribly thin; but there was a fierce, vital spirit within that seemed almost to shine out of her. A blue fire burned in her eyes. She was a marvel, all-in-all. Indomitable. And the best of friends. One could tell her anything.

Anything . . .

On Tuesday a rumour spread that the Germans had capitulated and the war was over.

"I was nearly run down by some American soldiers in a taxi," Mrs Mansell complained on returning from work. "Drunk as lords, they were, and telling everyone the war was won, the daft beggars."

"You don't think it's true, I presume?" said Letitia.

"Of course it's not true!" Mrs Mansell snorted. "Old Adolf won't give up that easily. Even his own people couldn't blow him up, though if you gave me a rolling pin and locked me in a room with him, I think I might have more luck." She sighed. "Well then. Let's see what I can get us for dinner."

After dinner, reading in her room, Letitia heard a furtive step on the stairs. She struggled to her feet and crossed to her door which was slightly ajar. Peering through the narrow gap, she saw Ian descending and behind him Clive. From the sound of it, they let themselves out of the little-used front door, thereby avoiding the kitchen where Mrs Mansell would be washing dishes and mopping the floor.

It was gone ten when Ian and Clive returned. Clive had not been missed. He often stayed in his room all evening after dinner. Everyone was in bed except for Letitia, who had ventured down to the kitchen to have a nightcap now that Mr Mansell was out of the way. She heard the front door open above her. There followed a lot of muffled noise, dragging footsteps and whispered curses. At length the noises receded.

A little later she heard footsteps again, coming down. It was Ian, permanently hungry, looking for something to eat. If he was surprised to see Letitia sitting at the kitchen table, he took it in his stride. He raided the larder then sat down opposite her. She could smell the beer on his breath.

"Oughtn't you to be tucked up in bed, Aunty?" he asked with his mouth full.

"I don't need much sleep at my age."

"We've been to the pub."

"We?"

"Clive and me. As I expect you already know. Nothing gets past you, Aunt. Clive is rat arsed. I had a devil of a job getting him to bed."

"Are you absolutely determined to make an enemy of Mrs Mansell?"

"Oh, come on, Aunt. She mollycoddles him, stifles him. The lad's sixteen years old. He needs taking out of himself. He wants to have a bit of fun."

"You call getting blind drunk 'having a bit of fun'?"

"It's a rite of passage."

"If you say so." Letitia pushed her glass towards him. "Pour me another, please. I will tell you where to find

249

it. You may help yourself, too, as long as you solemnly swear never to reveal the hiding place to Mr Mansell."

"Talking of hiding places," said Ian, as he fetched the whisky and poured, "you know, I suppose, that old Ma Mansell won't tell me where she's hidden Peggy."

"Peggy was evacuated when the flying bombs started."

"She has my kid with her, apparently."

"I'd leave well alone, if I was you. With any luck, the POW husband will take the child on as his own. But he will probably want to punch you, all the same."

Ian put the bottle back in its hiding place, straddled his chair. "Perhaps *I'll* be the one doing the punching. I might want to take *his* child on — and his wife, too."

"Oh, Ian . . ."

"I know, I know. I'm a bad boy and all that. Doctor Kramer said as much on Sunday. *Never mind what you want*, she said; *what about Peggy? Has anyone thought to consult her in all this?* From the way she was talking, you'd think I was going to grab Peggy by the hair and drag her back to my cave. All I want is to do what's right. If the kid is mine . . ."

"And what about Clive? What do you want with him?"

"I suppose you think I am leading him astray." Ian looked wistful — younger — for a moment in the glow of the electric light. "I suppose I . . . Well, I always wanted a little brother. Or a sister, I'm not fussy. And these Mansells: they seem to be our surrogate family now. You seem to have adopted them, Aunt. So I am just doing my brotherly duty."

250

"You used to disapprove of the Mansells."

"You have taught me to see things differently." He took a large gulp of whisky, downing it without flinching. "Why is it, Aunt, that we are so miserly when it comes to offspring in our family? I'm an only child, Dad is an only child, as was my drowned grandpa."

Letitia chose not to answer, said instead, "You, my boy, are not as tough as you make out."

"Oh yes I am, Aunt. I've had to be."

This time when he swallowed his whisky he grimaced and Letitia, watching him, felt a sudden intense desire to live — to go on living. Nothing was settled, there was still so much to do; and here was Ian, not ready to talk yet, but who might be ready one day — might need to let it all out, the fear, the pain, the madness and cruelty; the comradeship, too, and all the little moments of unexpected beauty. He had crammed a lifetime's experiences in five short years. Who would be there to listen to him when the time came?

"Another thing, Aunt." Ian had recovered his equilibrium, was never thrown off his stride for long. "What's going on with Dad and Doctor Kramer?"

"That," said Letitia, "is a very good question."

"She can be a bit waspish, Doctor Kramer, and she's getting on a bit, but I think she'd suit Dad right down to the ground."

"Let us hope your father realizes that before it is too late."

Ian yawned, got to his feet, having polished off his whisky and a piled plate of leftovers. "I'm about ready to turn in. Will you be all right getting up the stairs, Aunt?"

"Oh yes, don't worry about me."

"Then I'll say goodnight. And I promise not to get Clive drunk anymore."

"Just be careful around Mrs Mansell, is all I ask. Mothers are overprotective. It's their job to be."

"Not all mothers. Oh, I suppose you've not heard. Mine has upped sticks, moved to America. She says Britain is washed up, finished. America is the place to be now — just so long as the Jews are kept out of power. She tells me there are one or two very nice neighbourhoods over there where one need never see a Negro."

He went without further comment. She listened to him climbing the stairs a little unsteadily and felt again the sense of responsibility, the desire to go on living.

He needs taking out of himself . . . . Had Ian needed that too? What had it been like for him, growing up with Cynthia as a mother, pushed from pillar to post: from school to Cynthia's parents to Hugh? Ian had become a mess of contradictions, his personality in the balance: that was how it had always seemed to her, watching him grow up. She had never been sure of him.

Was it the army which had taken Ian out of himself? Life in the ranks had certainly given him a veneer of coarseness which promotion to sergeant had not erased — but it was not necessarily a bad thing. Indeed, he reminded her at times of someone else she'd known — a young man, rough-and-ready, plain-spoken — *ill-bred, churlish, a bumpkin, a peasant, an animal:*

252

those were the words they had used; they had never uttered his name — but also, like Ian, he had been somehow pure and honest-to-goodness — tender-hearted, too . . .

But that was long ago. Here and now, she knew one thing for certain: she could be sure of Ian at last.

As he'd said, there were so few of them in their family — just Hugh, really, and latterly Ian: so few, and they needed each other. She might have a part to play yet. But of course Ian didn't know about all the children who had died, Arnold's children: the one who had died with Cecily in childbirth, and the one Daffodil had been carrying when she drowned. If they had lived, things might have been very different. And the other child, the child that had been taken away —

She blinked, dismissing that thought, turning instead to her brother Jocelyn who had found it impossible to father even one child — and no wonder . . . no wonder . . .

She closed her eyes, hearing in her head the terrible angry voice of her father which, as an inquisitive child, she had heard as she crouched by the keyhole of the study door.

". . . and don't lie — don't lie to me, Jocelyn. You were seen. The maid saw you. You are a disgusting boy, a filthy boy, a wicked sinner. You will go blind, you will burn in hell . . ."

But Jocelyn had been locked in a cupboard first, before the advent of the hellfire — locked in a cupboard with no supper, alone in the dark, and she'd not been permitted to go near him.

It had been years before she understood what it was he'd done.

Jocelyn had never been quite the same afterwards. It was as if he'd been crippled inside — that was how she thought of it, years later, reading his journal.

She seemed to hear, echoing faintly as from a deep well, a voice: her voice. *Of course, one knew nothing of Freud in those days.* Some snippet of a forgotten conversation, lost in the shadows of the past.

She opened her eyes, smoothing away the memories, cleansing her mind, preparing herself for the climb up to her room.

Friday morning was bright and sunny, an optimistic morning. The newspapers were optimistic too. *Except possibly for a few last shots the Battle of London is over,* they quoted. The threat of the doodlebugs was officially ended. They were consigned to history, like Dunkirk and the blitz and bananas.

"Why should anyone want to make war on a morning like this?" Letitia leant on her stick as she looked out of the door at the patch of sky above the area.

The last to leave, Mrs Mansell was gulping back a final mug of tea. "I don't know about that. I reckon we should frizzle and frazzle 'em, those Germans. Sort 'em out good and proper. No good going soft now, just when victory is in sight. Look where that got us last time. My Ned done in, and hundreds others too, and all for nothing. We've had to fight the whole bleeding war over again. Well, I don't want to be here in twenty years time seeing my grandkids being bombed and gassed and lord knows what else. We should put paid to the Germans once and for all. That's what I say. Anyway, I'll be off now, Mrs Warner. I'll see you later."

Megan popped in after lunch as she sometimes did, on her way from one house call to another, staying sometimes just a minute or two, at other times lingering long enough for a quick cup of tea. Today she showed no signs of hurrying away, seemed troubled, pacing the kitchen, looking out into the area, letting her tea go cold. Letitia sat patiently, waiting.

At last Megan turned, faced her. "There is something I have to tell Hugh. There is something I have to tell him before we can go forward. I have to tell him — but it might mean the end for us, too."

"What is it, my dear? You can tell me."

Letitia's mind went back a few weeks to her conversation with Hugh: how he had been perturbed by long-held suspicions about Megan's past. Were those suspicions about to be confirmed?

But Letitia was unprepared for what Megan had to say.

"It's this. It's this. Thirty years ago I conceived Hugh's child. I conceived Hugh's child and I murdered it."

Megan let out her breath, closed her eyes, the words she had never thought she would say resonating in the basement kitchen.

She had found herself pregnant in the summer of 1912 and had not known what to do. Hugh had vanished, didn't seem to want to know her, certainly wouldn't now that this had happened. Jack had been in prison, beyond reach. She'd had no one to turn to. She'd had to make her own decisions.

There was no choice to be made, she'd thought. She couldn't have a baby. She couldn't possibly have a baby — not at her age, unmarried, living hand-to-mouth, teetering on the edge, always on the edge. She had to get rid of it.

Easier said than done. Hot baths had not worked, nor some revolting potion called hickery-pickery which the girls in the sweatshop swore by. She had tried drinking gin, gulping it down in her lodgings in Limehouse until the squalid little room span around her, until the tears were running down her cheeks, until she was sick over and over again into her chipped chamber pot, kneeling on the wooden boards and demanding, beseeching, begging for the unborn child to set her free, to go, go, go . . .

In the end, she had been given an address by one of her colleagues on the suffrage action committee. She had scraped together a few shillings, clutched them in her trembling hand as she made her way to the man who was her last hope. He had been discreet, reassuring, businesslike — and a complete charlatan. He had made a dreadful mess, nearly killed her. Afterwards, the baby had gone, there was no question about that: the baby had gone, and so also, she was told later when seeking proper medical advice during her time with Julian: so also was any chance of ever having another. She would never be a mother.

At the time she had felt a pang of regret which she had thought would slowly fade over the years but which, mingled with her long-delayed mourning for the child she had lost, had grown and grown, making her feel bereft, making her feel — as she stood in Letitia's kitchen in September 1944 — that there was a hole inside her, a gaping black hole which would always be there, which would never be filled.

This was the last piece of the puzzle, thought Letitia. Now she knew everything. Now she was aware of all the forces bringing Hugh and Megan together yet keeping them apart.

She summoned her reserves. This would be the hardest moment of all, but she could not afford to flinch, having come so far.

"You did what you thought was right, my dear. You did what was necessary."

"But you see that I must tell Hugh?"

"No, I don't. I don't see that at all."

"Then lie to him?"

"It is not a lie, to keep silent."

"But —"

"Listen, my dear. We have all done things we regret. We all have things we wish we could change. There is no point dwelling on them. There is no point dwelling on the past, as you yourself told me once. If you start digging up what time has buried, there is no knowing where it might end. One might discover other things, terrible things, things one would not be able to live with —" Letitia stopped, closed her eyes for a moment, gathering herself. When she opened her eyes again, she said, "Maybe you will tell Hugh about the child one day. Maybe you will never tell him. You do not have to decide now. You have your whole future together in which to decide."

"You make it sound . . . easy."

"No, my dear. Simple, but not easy. I know. I, too, had a child once. I had a child, but I lost him."

Megan looked up, startled. "I'm sorry. I didn't know." Her eyes searched Letitia's. "Do you . . . do you ever think of him?"

"All of the time."

And Letitia, to her surprise, found herself able to smile, as they looked at one another across the kitchen.

She accompanied Megan up the area steps to get a breath of air and a look at the square — to escape the kitchen where the odour of the past still lingered but was slowly melting away. Megan got on her bicycle, opened her mouth to say goodbye — but at that precise moment there came the unmistakable sound of a distant explosion away to the west. Seconds later, another, fainter detonation was heard.

Megan and Letitia looked at one another, old fears reawakening.

"I didn't hear a siren," said Megan.

"It may be nothing. The Battle of London is over, they said."

258

"Don't speak too soon is my motto. I expect it's the doodlebugs back again. I thought it was too good to be true to think we had heard the last of them."

As Megan pedalled away, Letitia looked up at the sky. The early brightness had gone, grey cloud now veiled the blue. The afternoon was close and suddenly tense.

Letitia shivered as she made her way back down the steps.

She telephoned Hugh in Buckinghamshire.

"This has gone on long enough."

"Aunt? Is that you?"

"Normally I wouldn't dream of interfering, but this time . . ."

"What was that? This is a frightfully bad line."

"You must stop dithering, Hugh. I have quite lost my patience with you. Can you not see what is right in front of you?"

"But, Aunt, she blows hot and cold, I am not even sure if she —"

"I am sure. You must stop doubting yourself, Hugh. You must seize the next opportunity. There is no time to waste. I am only saying this for your own — Oh, but there, our three minutes are up. Goodbye, Hugh, goodbye."

Putting the receiver down, Letitia felt elated, just as she'd done in years gone by when returning home to collapse into a chair after a lengthy ramble round London's streets. But as she climbed the stairs to her bedroom, she found herself thinking of the mysterious explosions. They seemed to her somehow ominous, a reminder that however close the end might be, the war was not over yet. No one could tell where the next twist might take them.

CHAPTER
ELEVEN

This war, even more than the last, was a succession of farewells. Now Ian was off again, back to the killing fields of Europe, promising to write as he always did.

"This time I mean it, Aunt. I'm to write to Clive, too."

"He has taken quite a shine to you."

"He is under the impression I am some sort of hero. It's only the golden sheen of war. It will soon wear off. All the same . . ."

"You want to be a brother to him, take care of him?"

"And Peggy too, if she wants me. And my kid. But what's the use of saying it? I might not come back. I've ridden my luck so far, but . . ."

"You will come back. Everything will be fine now. He can't do anything to us anymore."

"Who? Adolf?"

"No, the bishop. My father. His influence has withered away."

"Sometimes, Aunt, I think you might be going funny in the head."

"My dear boy, I went *funny in the head* — as you put it — years ago! Now come here and let me hug you, never mind if it's beneath your dignity."

And so Ian had gone. Hugh was still ensconced in Buckinghamshire. The war continued. The Americans had actually crossed the border in one place — crossed into Germany — but it seemed there was to be no sudden dénouement, no unexpected armistice, this time round. The bloodshed continued unabated. And the war with Japan was also far from over: people tended to forget that.

Closer to home, more mysterious explosions had been heard at intervals all over London. Not doodlebugs, people said. Exploding gas mains, some suggested. But Mrs Mansell was not convinced. Why should so many gas mains start exploding all at once? No, it wasn't that. What she had heard was — and here she lowered her voice and looked round for the wall with ears: what she had heard was that the Germans were sending over bombs by a new method. Rockets, they were called. They travelled so quickly you couldn't see them, and they came without warning. Should one land near you, the first you would know of it would be when you woke up in a pile of rubble — if you woke up at all.

Letitia took the story with a large pinch of salt. A new super-weapon quicker than the human eye? It sounded nothing more than a fairy-tale — like the story in the last war in which the entire Russian army had been said to have passed through England early one morning with snow on their boots. Connie Lambton, the silly old dear, might have believed such tales, but one knew better now. There had been nothing about rockets on the BBC. Megan would know the truth of the matter. Megan kept her ear to the ground. But Megan had been a stranger of late. Letitia wondered very much what was going on.

It was several days later, getting on for lunchtime, when Megan suddenly reappeared, bursting in on Letitia as she sat quietly reading the paper. Megan was glowing, her eyes sparkling, and her news so startling it put all thoughts of war in the shade.

"Hugh has asked me to marry him!"

"At last!" said Letitia. "Is he here, then: in London?"

"No. I went to him. I went to Buckinghamshire. I couldn't wait any longer."

Letitia laughed. It seemed so typical, Hugh hanging back, Megan taking the lead. But they were happy, however it had come about.

"My dear, this calls for a celebration! I've a bottle of champagne buried in the cellar that I was saving for the end of the war but this news, I think, is more important."

Megan went in search of the champagne whilst Letitia found a tablecloth, spread it out, loaded the table with cut glass flutes, a vase with dried flowers, biscuits, a ration of cheese and a sliver of precious butter. She felt almost spry in her pleasure. *All's well that ends well*, she said to herself: even if that end had been a long time coming.

Megan returned with the champagne.

"Well, my dear, don't stand on ceremony. Open it up!"

Megan wrestled with the cork, talking as she did so. "We had a terribly muddled conversation — this cork is stuck, it won't budge — I was on the verge of proposing myself and then — but here goes, get the glasses ready!"

The champagne cork popped. Champagne fizzed out, glinting in the daylight. But at the moment a strange atmosphere swept through the kitchen. The beads of liquid seemed to hang like diamonds in the air, as if they were frozen in time, motionless. There was a sound like a sigh, and then a sudden airless quiet.

And with that, the kitchen and everything in it dissolved into blackness. Letitia knew no more.

Letitia opened her eyes. She was lying on a bed with a yielding mattress, looking up at a beamed ceiling. She felt that she had been asleep for a very long time. The clock was ticking but all else was quiet. It was twilight.

Why had no one come to light the lamps?

She sat up, unable to shake off a feeling of unease. Everything was as it should be, yet she still felt that something was wrong — almost as if she had become somebody else whilst she was asleep. Which was preposterous. A silly notion.

"My name is Letitia Benham." She spoke out loud to banish any lingering doubts as she looked round the room. There was Grandma's rocking chair, and next to it her new crinoline draped over the mahogany fire screen. There was no fire, so it must be summer. It was odd that she could not remember the date.

"My name is Letitia Benham. I am nineteen years old."

All her treasures were set out, safe and sound on the dressing table: her gold brooch set with turquoise and the six row pearl necklace with the diamond clasp which had belonged to Mother. Mother herself was there, young and smiling in a daguerreotype framed in a mother of pearl case. A later version of Mother, still smiling but looking somehow sadder, was fixed in a folding leather frame which also contained three other photographs: her father, Jocelyn and herself.

And Angelica?

But of course, there were no pictures of Angelica. It was not allowed.

Someone should really have come by now, to close the curtains and light the lamps. It was getting quite dark and she did not like the dark. Perhaps if she lit one of the lamps herself, the one on the bedside table. It stood on the mat she had cross-stitched with her own hands in Berlin wool work.

She reached for the lamp — but recoiled in horror. The flowers were all dead! The flowers in the vase next to the lamp: they were all dead, more than dead: putrefied, the stalks drooping, the withered petals all stuck together. And there was a smell. She hadn't noticed it before. It seemed to be getting stronger. A terrible, foetid smell as if the water in the vase had not been changed for weeks on end.

She jumped up, backing away from the dead flowers; but she found it was difficult to move. She felt as if she was swimming through treacle. At last she felt the solid dressing-table behind her and she slowly turned, stretching out a hand, watching as it inched its way through the thick, gloomy air. Inside her papier-mâché box was a heart-shaped locket. There was no picture inside but it represented — everything: safety, love, life itself. She clasped it to her breast.

"Tom," she murmured. "Tom."

Even as she whispered the name, everything came back to her in a flood. She was rocked back on her heels, remembering. Of course, of course. The door was locked. She was a prisoner. Tom had gone. They had sent him away, he would never come again. And —

"The baby. They've taken my baby."

The locket dropped from her fingers, fell in slow motion, spinning round and round, the chain trailing behind it. As it bounced once on the Persian rug, the clasp flew open. It came to rest, the blank insides staring up at her.

Somehow she had to find a way to escape. She had to go now, before they came back. Her eyes slid towards the door, terrified lest she heard the key in the lock, saw the handle turn. What if her father came? But no, he wouldn't come. In all the days and weeks, he had never come.

The window was open. The window was the only way out. She fought her way through the treacle, kneeled on the window seat. She could climb down the ivy; she could slip away in the dusk, she could get right away, start looking for Tom, start looking for . . . for . . .

But the ivy had grown wild. The window was choked with it. Tendrils stretched into the room — and the tendrils were coming alive! They were wrapping around her, tugging her down, drawing her into the morass, enmeshing her. She was being suffocated, she could see nothing but green leaves, the ivy was tearing at her, pulling her apart, ripping her open . . .

"Letitia! Letitia!"

Someone was calling her. She struggled to free herself, frantic.

"Tom? Is that you? Tom?"

But it was no use, she couldn't get free. She was breaking into pieces, dissolving, fading into nothing . . .

"Letitia! Letitia! Can you hear me?"

The voice was not Tom's. It was not a male voice at all. But it was calling to her, insistent — and afraid. She moved towards it, climbing out of a deep void.

Letitia opened her eyes. Nothing. She must have gone blind. There was a terrible pain in her leg and her mouth was choked with dust. She tried to stand up, a feeling of claustrophobia assailing her; but she couldn't move, felt as if she was slowly being squashed.

"Letitia!"

That voice: she recognized it. It belonged to the woman called Megan.

Letitia opened her mouth to say, "I am here, Megan, I'm here!", but all that came out was a croak.

"Letitia? Is that you? Thank goodness!"

Letitia coughed, spat out dust and grit. It tasted of plaster and bricks.

"What . . . where . . .?" Her voice sounded terribly thin and feeble in her ears.

"I think it must have been a bomb. A UXB perhaps. The ceiling has come down on us."

A bomb? Letitia's mind struggled to make sense of it. One moment she had been in her room in Chanderton, the next . . . There had been bombs in the war. Hugh had written to her about them.

But this was a different war.

Her mind raced, leaping across the years towards the present moment.

"Are you hurt? Letitia, can you hear me? Are you hurt? I heard you shout out, but then it all went quiet."

"I can't move my leg. I can't see."

"Neither can I. It's too dark. Listen. Don't try to move. Do you understand? They will come and dig us out. But you must try to lie still."

A bomb. The house must have collapsed. But she had survived bombs before. One had fallen on her terrace in 1940. She had survived that. But whatever Megan might say, it was impossible not to make some attempt to move. Her body was all twisted, her leg was hurting. She struggled, but it was no good. Something heavy was lying across her calf, crushing it.

She gave up the struggle, breathing heavily. The effort had exhausted her.

Somewhere water was dripping, and there was an occasional ominous creaking sound as the unseen rubble shifted around her. There was no relief from the pitch dark and she felt weak and confused, her mind choked with dust as her throat was.

"I must have been asleep." The sound of her own voice made her feel a little less helpless. "I dreamt I was back in my room in Chanderton."

"That's it. Keep talking," said Megan. "I'm going to see if I can reach you. I need your voice to guide me."

Letitia could hear a scuffling sound. Somewhere in the dark, Megan was breathing heavily.

"Keep talking. Tell me about your room in Chanderton. Tell me about Tom. You called out his name. You called for Tom."

"Tom. Yes, Tom." Letitia stopped, bewildered. Why would she have called for Tom?

I must take a grip of myself, she said; *I have been in worse situations. I just need to hold on.*

"Who was Tom?" Megan's voice sounded closer. But then there was a rattling sound, like pebbles falling down a cliff. Megan caught her breath. After a pause, she said, "I daren't come any nearer. I can't see what I'm doing. I might dislodge something, move something."

Letitia started trembling. She felt as if the darkness was slowly consuming her. Perhaps it might be easier to give in to it . . .

"Talk to me, Letitia." Insistent, badgering, not leaving her alone. "Tell me about Tom."

"Tom was . . ." Tom was a long time ago, a long way away. But could she smell new-mown hay? Could she still smell it after all this time? "Tom worked on the farm. Home Farm. There was a meadow. I met him there at haymaking. We used to meet often after that."

"That's good, Letitia. Keep talking. Tell me more."

"We sat in the meadow. We were happy. But they said it was wrong. They said . . . Megan, are you there?"

"I'm here, my dear. I'm right here. Go on. You were happy with Tom . . ."

With a great effort, Letitia assembled the words in her head. "One evening, I left him as usual. I said goodbye. I went home. *They* were waiting. *They* said I had been a wicked, sinful girl. The housekeeper had spied on me. The servants always spied. They spied on us, they spied on each other. My father told them to. The housekeeper had seen me in the bath. I was getting fat, in those days. I thought I was getting fat. But it was a baby. I didn't know babies could happen like that. I thought one had to be married."

"Yes? What next?"

"I was locked in my room. I was locked up for a very long time. No one came except the housekeeper — the housekeeper and a doctor. He was not the usual doctor. He was not nice. He had cold hands. Afterwards, when they had taken the baby away, when they had washed me and put on my clothes, I was taken to a carriage with the blinds down. I left at night. I went on a long journey, to a place by the sea, a tall grey house with damp walls. There were moors, and gulls wailing. I was ill. Pleurisy, they said, and pneumonia. I might have died, they said."

"Go on, Letitia. Keep talking to me."

"I might have died, but I didn't. I got better. And then they said I had to get married."

Lying in the dark, Letitia found that shapes and colours were beginning to appear before her eyes. The pain in her leg was like a jagged, piercing red off to one side; but further away there was a pale grey ghost, fluid and indistinct, fading in and out. She strained her eyes, desperate to make it out, afraid that it might be William Warner — William Warner waiting for her as he had waited that day at the altar. As she had walked up the aisle in the cold empty church, he had looked over his shoulder at her: cold, calculating, without pity. She had known at that moment that he was her new master. She belonged to him now. She had passed from slavery into slavery.

But the grey shape exuded no menace: it was simply floated there, on the edge of sight. She wondered if she might be mistaken, if it was not her husband but somebody else . . .

"Jocelyn?" She stretched out her hand.

"Letitia? You must stay with me, Letitia." Megan's voice was hard and solid blue, blotting out the spectral shape. "Tell me about Jocelyn."

"He was my brother." Letitia stared at the blue, was drawn into the blue. "He got married too but, unlike me, he was happy — they were happy. But they had no children. Jocelyn, you see . . . they had locked him in a cupboard when he was a boy . . . he couldn't . . . he couldn't . . . But they didn't mind, they were happy. They were happy until . . . until . . ."

What had happened next? Trying to remember exhausted her. She didn't want to remember. Her eyelids were heavy. She wanted to sleep. Just to sleep.

"Letitia? Are you there, Letitia?"

Letitia's eyes fluttered open. "Annie? Is that you? But I thought you were on holiday."

"Not Annie. It's me, Megan."

Letitia roused herself. A last vestige of energy flickered somewhere deep within her. She grappled with the hazy thoughts taking flight from her mind.

She was drunk, that was the problem. All that champagne had gone to her head.

But wait. They had not touched the champagne. The cork had popped, and then . . . and then . . .

There was a sudden noise, a rending and squealing, the sound of bricks crashing down and timbers falling. The ground quivered. Flakes of plaster and brick rained onto her face. Then it stopped, and the water was dripping again and everything else was still.

"Hello! Help! Hello there!" Megan began shouting. "We're down here! We're trapped! Hello!" She paused, listening, and then said quietly, insistently, "Look, Letitia! Can you see the light?"

"No. There is no light."

"But I can see now. I can see you. Reach out your hand towards me, towards my voice. That's it. Just a little more. There! I've got you. I've got you."

Megan gripped Letitia's hand. In the dim, grey light she could see that Letitia was trapped, a beam having fallen across her ankle. Her body was twisted at an angle and her face covered with dust. The rubble beneath her leg was stained red. It was impossible to assess how much blood she had lost. She needed to examine the old lady as soon as possible, Letitia sounded weak, befuddled, Megan was anxious; but the rubble was unstable, she dared not move.

"Jocelyn?" Letitia's voice wavered.

"What is it, dearest? What's wrong?"

"Jocelyn is going away. He is leaving me. He has waited too long. I promised to follow him. I made a promise on his grave. He has grown tired of waiting."

"Don't worry. We are going to be all right. They will get us out. They are coming. They are nearly here. Can you hear their voices?"

Letitia seemed not to hear, lost in her own world. "Do you think he will be angry with me? I read his journal, you see. He left me his journal."

"I'm sure he won't be angry, Letitia. I'm sure he won't mind."

"They said it was an accident. It was dark when he fell out of the boat and he was not a strong swimmer. But it wasn't an accident. When I read the journal, I understood: I understood why his wife lost her reason so they had to put her in an asylum. And Jocelyn . . . Jocelyn drowned. He drowned himself. My father didn't care, you see. All that mattered was to carry on the family line. He had to make up for Jocelyn's shortcomings. He had to make up for them himself. That's why he did it. And Arnold never knew . . ." The voice trailed to a stop.

"Letitia? Letitia? What was it Arnold didn't know? You must tell me. You must talk to me. It's important."

"Important? Yes. Yes. It is important. It's important that Arnold should never know. Arnold must never be told that Jocelyn is not his father. Jocelyn, you see, is his brother."

There was a heavy thump, a grinding sound, and light suddenly poured into the pit. Megan, kneeling in the wreckage, hemmed in by fallen masonry, was half-blinded. She felt woozy, leaned against the fallen joist in front of her. On the other side of the joist, Letitia was pinned in a narrow, coffin-like space. Her sightless eyes were darting this way and that. Gradually she seemed to become aware of the light. She held up her free hand, pawing feebly at the air.

"Please, William. Let me alone. You're hurting me. Take the candle away now. Please, William. Oh, please . . ."

Megan squeezed Letitia's hand. "Letitia! It's all right. You're here with me, with Megan. There is no William."

At the sound of Megan's voice, Letitia grew calm. She lowered her hand. Her face, which had showed terror when she thought her dead husband was near, became blank and neutral.

"There is no William?" she echoed. Her eyes stopped moving, seemed to focus on some distant point. Suddenly lucid, she spoke in her ordinary voice, as if they were sitting gossiping in the kitchen. "How silly of me. He is gone. I had forgotten he had gone. I had forgotten that I killed him. I gave him poison. I put it in his porridge. I watched him die and then sent for the doctor. I expected they would take me away, but they never came. I waited but they never came. It was his heart, they said. It was his heart that killed him. We will

274

leave you to grieve, they said. We will leave you in peace. But I could not grieve — not for him. Not for him." She shuddered, then was still. "I was alone but I could not forget what I had done. I could not live with myself, with the memory of it. So I made a promise to Jocelyn — I promised on his grave. I told him that I would join him. So I sent Annie to the seaside and then I went up to the attic where the poison was hidden. I lay down and I went to sleep."

"But you didn't, Letitia! You didn't take the poison!" Megan spoke urgently. "You are still here, still alive! You're with me, and we are going to be rescued!"

"I didn't go to sleep?" For a moment Letitia looked confused, eyes fluttering; but then unexpectedly she smiled. Her whole face lit up. She seemed relaxed — at peace, if that was possible. "Of course! I remember now! It was all arranged. Annie was packing, I had written my letter, everything was in order. And then the doorbell rang. I was not expecting anyone. I didn't know who it could be. But that was the day Hugh arrived."

"What have we got here?" asked the policeman, arriving at the emergency scene.

"Another of Adolf's bleeding rockets." A short, wiry man was looking down at him from a pile of rubble. His face was dour and grimy. "It flattened that house over there, made a crater here, demolished those others."

"Any survivors?"

The man shook his head. "None so far."

A faint voice carried across the bomb site. "Here, Bill! There's someone here! She's alive, and all."

The policeman scrambled up onto the rubble, followed Bill across the ruins, slipping and sliding. He could see a woman with red hair being lifted clear. Her head was lolling, but she was conscious, groaning.

The policeman knelt beside her. "Hold on, love. Soon have you safe." Her lips moved. He leant close, put his ear to her mouth.

"What's she saying?" asked Bill.

The policeman looked up. "She says there's someone else. Someone else was buried with her."

Bill scrambled down into the pit, agile as a monkey. The policeman shone his torch.

"I can see her!" Bill called. "An old lady."

"Want any help, mate?"

"No need." Bill's voice came floating up, grim, matter of fact. "It's too late for her. She's had it. Pegged out."

The policeman switched off his torch.